I Wish I Could Moonwalk

D1636034

Sandra Lee

Royalty Publications
www.RoyaltyPublications.com

Royalty Publications titles are published by:

Royalty Publications
P.O. Box 3645
Phenix City, AL 36868
Email: *info@RoyaltyPublications.com*

Royalty Publications is a Christian Book Publisher dedicated to expanding works that uplift Jesus Christ through the written word. The Royalty Publications logo is a registered trademark.

ISBN: 978-0-9840882-9-4

First Printing: April 2016

Printed in the United States of America

ISND Cover designed by:
Alex Johnson III
AJ3 Photography & Designs
Email: *ajiii3@aol.com*

Dedication

To Martin, Sr.

Chapter 1

"I'm having a cookout this evening," said Cheryl. "I hope that you can make it."

Michelle looked at her neighbor as they stood on the front porch of her house. "I don't know. David is out of town, and Sasha is staying at my mother's house."

Cheryl smiled before she spoke. "Yeah; that's exactly why I'm inviting you, so you won't be alone." She paused and studied Michelle's face before sitting down and continuing. "Plus my cousin is in town; he'll be staying with me for a while."

Michelle was really looking forward to a quiet weekend alone. Her husband, David, was away at a business conference, and their daughter, Sasha, was spending the weekend with her grandmother. Michelle took a seat on the porch next to her neighbor. "I guess I can come by for a little while; get a plate and meet your cousin."

Cheryl put an arm around Michelle and squeezed her shoulders a little bit before rising from the porch. "Come back in, say about an hour, or so. My fiancé and my cousin will be there striking up the grill."

Michelle smiled before standing from the porch she'd been sitting on and walked to her house. It was a short trip; only two homes separated hers and Cheryl's. The house was especially quiet when Sasha was away. A six-year-old could really keep a house jumping. Michelle trotted up the stairs in her house and entered her bedroom. She lay on the bed and closed her eyes to relax for a while.

Twenty minutes later, she opened her eyes and glanced at the clock-radio on her nightstand. She sat up on the bed and prepared to get ready for the cookout. When she arrived at Cheryl's place she inhaled the pleasant smell of the roasting spare-ribs. She and her neighbor walked side by side through her house and onto the back patio where the cooking was taking place.

When they reached the patio, Cheryl whispered to Michelle, "Come on. I want you to meet my cousin. He'll only be staying here a week, thank God." When Michelle gave her a hard stare and a raised eyebrow, Cheryl added, "I know, I know. I shouldn't have said that, but my cousin

1

is a handful."

Once she had a full view of the backyard deck, Michelle saw the two men working the grill. Initially, their backs were all that could be seen, but they turned around when they heard the two women's footsteps. Michelle readily recognized Cheryl's fiancé, Paul, but even the other man looked sort of familiar. They walked closer.

"Michelle, this is my cousin, Freddie," said Cheryl while the two of them shook hands.

Cheryl's fiancé waved, and Michelle returned his friendly gesture as well. Michelle looked at Freddie again and caught him staring at her. She knew this man from somewhere, and looking at him made her extremely nervous. She had a strange urge to get away from Freddie before she got sick to her stomach.

Michelle raised her hand and gave a small wave to all of them and walked back to the kitchen to take a seat. A minute later Freddie strolled into the quiet area. He stood in front of her, staring briefly before finally speaking.

"Michelle. I'd never forget that face and that body," he said while leering at her.

It was *him*. It was that monster she had known from the club. Michelle lost her appetite and narrowed her eyes at the man, then bounced out of her seat and escaped to the patio to join her friend on the deck.

"Girl, where did you go all of a sudden?" asked Cheryl. "The food is ready; let's fix us a plate."

Michelle could barely walk, let alone eat. But she followed her friend through the buffet, spooning food onto her plate. Michelle and Cheryl sat on nearby lawn chairs and ate their food. At least Cheryl did.

Michelle looked up and saw Freddie stepping back onto the backyard deck. "Cheryl, I don't mean to be rude, but I gotta go. I've got a splitting headache; I need to lay down."

Cheryl looked up at her neighbor and she did look sick. "I'll wrap up your food for you and you can eat it later."

Michelle quickly vacated her chair and dashed into the kitchen.

2

Cheryl followed behind her to prepare the food for her journey home. From the front porch, Cheryl watched her friend and neighbor until she made her way safely home.

The next day, on Saturday morning, Michelle awoke to knocking on her door. She looked at the clock-radio on the nightstand and noticed the time was 8:02. *Who could that be?* she thought. She jumped out of bed, reached for her robe, and stuck her feet into her bedroom slippers before walking down the stairs.

"Who is it?" she asked standing at the front door.

The answer that came back was, "A friend of yours, sweetheart. Your friend, Freddie."

Michelle stiffened and a scowl covered her face. She didn't want anyone to see him standing on her porch, so she opened the door. As soon as he was inside, that queasy feeling returned. She quickly closed the door behind him and stared into his awful face.

"You still look good," he said. "That body is sure keeping up." The smile on his face was as filthy as he.

"What do you want?" said Michelle "I'm a married woman with a family now."

Freddie looked her directly in the eyes before speaking. "I wonder if your husband knows I know you the way he knows you," he said before taking visual note of the neatness of her home.

"Get out of my house. Get out of my house, Freddie, before I call the police," threatened Michelle.

He didn't even blink; he knew she had no intention of calling the police and putting her business out there like that. "I won't be long," he said, "but I do need some money; a loan."

Michelle looked at the man. She wanted to slap him across the face. Was he really trying to blackmail her for something that took place in her past?

He continued. "I need five hundred dollars from you, and then I'll be on my way; I promise."

What does a promise mean from somebody like him? The thought

3

filtered through Michelle's head. But then she reconsidered. The possibility that he would actually keep his word was a long shot, but she really didn't have much of a choice. Maybe if she gave him the money, she would be through with him once and for all. Her husband and daughter would be home on Monday morning. She decided she would pay him the money to be rid of him.

"I'll give you the money, if you go away and never come back."

Freddie nodded his head. "I'll be back to get it. Two o'clock sharp," he stressed.

She knew it was a longshot, but Michelle hoped beyond hope that Freddie's blackmail act had been just that; *an act*. But like clockwork, the monster returned to her house not one minute late. Although she felt as though her life was sinking into a dark hole, she searched for a bright side. He'd kept his promise to return for the money; maybe he'd keep his word to leave her alone too.

Michelle immediately handed him the money so that he could get out of her house and out of her sight. He tried to hug her after receiving the cash, but she quickly sidestepped and opened the front door for him to leave. The sight of the man made her skin itch like insects were crawling on her. Michelle slammed the door behind his exit and slid to the floor. She stayed in that position for a while, inhaling and exhaling to try to calm her unraveled nerves.

The next morning, she and Cheryl walked to church together in preparation for Sunday worship. It was a ten-minute walk from the house to Peace Baptist Church.

"I sure feel like praising God and shouting for joy this morning," said Michelle.

Cheryl nodded in agreement as the two of them waited on the curb for the light to change.

Upon entering the church they were met by the man that everybody knew simply as Brother Earl, one of the best loved greeters at the ministry. "Good morning and God bless you, Sister Michelle and Sister Cheryl."

They smiled and returned his greeting before walking through the door and into the sanctuary. They walked down the front aisle on the red carpet until they reached the pew, four rows from the front, and took a seat. Michelle looked around the church. For some reason her eyes always stopped on the stain glass windows. She thought they were so beautiful and spiritual. As she gazed at the lovely glass, she felt someone tap her on the shoulder. She looked up and saw her best friend, Katrina, smiling down at her. She and Katrina had been friends for fifteen years; ever since they were twenty years old.

When they were younger they went to the nightclubs together, and now they were saved together. Michelle was the first to give her life to Christ. Katrina got saved a year later, and they never looked back. Michelle rose from her pew and gave her friend a firm, warm hug. Cheryl looked up from the pew and gave Katrina a little wave before the woman sat down on the other side of Michelle.

They all sat together, exchanging lighthearted chatter while waiting for morning service to begin. When worship got underway a few moments later, Michelle forgot all about her troubles from the day before. Between the praise songs, the sermon, and the prayer that was offered, she felt refreshed. But it was a feeling that would quickly dissolve.

"Pastor Jenkins sure knows how to breathe life and spirituality into a sermon," said Michelle as they descended the steps of the church after the service was over.

"You got that right," returned Cheryl. "I feel so good and so free, thanks to Pastor Jenkins and my cousin."

Michelle's earlier smile was replaced by a frown. She wondered what her neighbor meant by the last part. What had Freddie done to Cheryl? She knew what he had done to her. The women said their goodbyes to Katrina, and then continued to talk as they walked the short distance to their neighborhood.

"I came home from work and the house smelled like reefer," Cheryl said. "Freddie had been smoking weed in my house."

Michelle stopped walking and turned to look at her. "You mean Freddie is into drugs?" It shouldn't have surprised her. She wanted to chastise herself for asking such a dumb question. She knew he was capable of almost anything. Freddie was not a good person. Cheryl began walking again, and Michelle rushed to catch up with her.

"Freddie has been involved with drugs for a long time," said Cheryl "I care for my cousin, but I told him he'd have to leave if he didn't stop smoking that burnt smelling stuff."

They walked the remainder of the way home in silence. Michelle was delighted to hear that Freddie was history.

"Are you going to Bible study on Wednesday?" asked Cheryl when they reached the front steps of her house.

"I wouldn't miss it," Michelle replied with a raised voice before walking two doors up to her house. She entered her house revived and spiritually satisfied. She even did a little dance across the floor. Her husband and daughter would be returning home tomorrow, on sweet Monday morning.

Sasha was spending the weekend with her grandparents, and David was away on a business trip. When her baby was born, Michelle left her job and had never returned to the working world. She was getting sort of restless staying home all the time, but she and her husband had agreed that she would stay home with their daughter for the time being.

David's mother didn't work outside the house when he was growing up, and he wanted the same for their daughter. Michelle and her husband had a joint bank account and separate personal bank accounts. The money she paid Freddie was from her personal account and it nearly wiped out her entire balance. She'd have to build it back up again, but her husband didn't have to know that.

When Monday morning rolled around, Michelle was as happy as a clown in the circus. She woke up early to prepare a family breakfast consisting of pancakes with maple syrup, scrambled eggs, and sausage. A glass of freshly squeezed orange juice completed the meal.

David arrived home first. Michelle was sitting near the front door waiting for him to walk in. When he caught sight of his wife, he dropped his luggage in the hallway and embraced her. They stayed wrapped in each other arms for a few seconds before breaking apart.

"How was your trip?" she asked "Did you take care of business?"

He smiled, and then sniffed the air when he caught a whiff of the pancakes. He closed his eyes in delight for a brief moment. "I'm going to clean up," he said. "I'll be down for breakfast in a few minutes." He picked up the luggage and headed for the stairs.

Sasha arrived a little while later, accompanied by her grandmother. After giving her daughter a quick kiss on the cheek, Michelle's mother said, "I've got to go. I just wanted to deliver my beautiful granddaughter home before I went to my appointment."

Michelle hugged her. "Thanks, Mama. I really appreciate you keeping Sasha for the weekend."

Her mother smiled and gave a small wave before walking out the door. Sasha had to go to school this morning, so she quickly washed her hands and sat down to eat breakfast. Michelle and David sat at the kitchen table watching their daughter as she ate. Michelle thought it couldn't get any better than this. She and David walked Sasha to school, hand in hand, with their daughter in the middle.

After dropping off Sasha at school, Michelle and David strolled through a nearby park holding hands. The weather was still warm in early September in Washington, D.C.

"Coming to the park was a wonderful idea," David remarked. "It reminds me of when we first started dating."

Michelle smiled and looked into his eyes. Words weren't needed as they sat on a bench in the park. Michelle reached for David's hand and held it. She didn't want to let it go; so for the next hour, she didn't.

Chapter 2

By Wednesday morning, life had returned to normal. David was back at work, and Sasha was in school. Michelle was home all alone making plans for evening Bible study with Cheryl. David attended church on Sundays, but rarely made it to mid-week services. That evening, the two women walked to Bible study, chatting all the way there.

"I got a call from my cousin last night," said Cheryl as they walked down the bricked sidewalk. "He said he might pay me another visit soon, but not to stay over or anything."

Michelle gave thought to what her friend had just said. Inwardly, she prayed and hoped that Freddie wouldn't follow through. "I thought he'd left town for good." As she spoke the words, Michelle mindlessly stepped into the street. When a driver blew his horn at her, she quickly stepped back on the curb.

"Are you trying to get yourself killed?" asked Cheryl. Then she gave Michelle a sideways glance. "You don't like my cousin very much, do you?" Without waiting for an answer, she continued. "I can't say I blame you. I'm not fond of Freddie either."

Michelle smiled slightly, but said nothing while they continued walking to the church. She didn't want to see the man again in her entire lifetime; that was for sure. Michelle felt a sense of serenity engulf her when she walked through the door of Peace Baptist Church. *Bible study, here I come,* she thought to herself and a hint of a smile crossed her lips.

* * * * * * *

The rest of the week passed with no further mention of Freddie. Michelle was almost able to forget about him, but when the weekend rolled around, the pastor's message seemed to be aimed right at her. Sunday morning church service had Pastor Jenkins speaking on the topic of the past; mainly on guilt from the past. Michelle sat up rod straight in her seat on the pew, and her ears perked up. Was this a message for her?

"I know you might be saying that you'd love to change," said Pastor Jenkins. "Change something from your past."

Michelle could hear people in the church saying, "Yes, yes Lord."

"I'm here to tell you, you can't," her pastor continued. "But you can change the future. That's something that you still have time to take control of. I'm sure some of you wish you could moonwalk, moving backward and retracing your steps; changing things from your past, changing regrets and the guilt."

When the pastor began to moonwalk, the church broke out in a roar of laughter and clapping. The sound was deafening as the pastor continued moon walking on the platform. When the church finally quieted down, Pastor Johnnie Jenkins eventually brought his sermon to an end.

Upon dismissal, he sent them home with a huge smile, saying, "And don't forget to hug at least three people before you leave today."

David rose and hugged his wife. Michelle then turned and hugged Katrina. Releasing her, she said, "David, Sasha, and I are going out for dinner. Do you and Frank want to join us?"

"Thank you, but Frank and I are going to his mother's house for dinner," Katrina replied. "I'll give you a call during the week. Okay?"

Michelle nodded her head and went to collect her daughter to join her and her husband. They were ready to eat. The family of three walked up the red carpet toward the exit door with Michelle holding her daughter's hand. She saw a missionary in a white uniform near the door and hugged her before exiting the church with her family. When they reached the sidewalk, they crossed the street and walked past the church-owned diner which was always closed on Sundays.

They kept walking, enjoying the fresh air and the scenery. Convenience was what Michelle loved about Washington, D.C. A person could walk to wherever they wanted to go, and if they couldn't because of distance, the public transportation system was excellent. Cars weren't a necessity in the nation's capital.

"Pastor Jenkins was sure in his element today," said David. "Who wouldn't want to moonwalk back to their past and change something?"

Michelle couldn't speak; she just nodded her head as she clutched her daughter's hand. She had thought the pastor was speaking just to her. She certainly wished she could moonwalk back to the time when she met Freddie at the nightclub. She'd go back to that time and never leave the club with him. She and Katrina should never have left the club with Freddie and Leo.

"Earth to Michelle," said David. "We're here. You don't need to walk any farther."

Michelle blinked her eyes and a weak smile crossed her face before they all entered the restaurant.

* * * * * * *

Monday morning, Michelle was alone again. She and David had talked once more about her working outside the house, and they both determined that she should continue to stay at home with Sasha until she got a little older. But this time, they'd also agreed that working a few hours a day might be doable. The phone rang, and Michelle extended her hand toward the nightstand in her bedroom where the telephone rested. "Hello?"

"Hey, girl. Do you have any plans today?" It was her friend, Katrina. "I got today off and thought we could hang out or something."

"Hang out or something?" Michelle said with a laugh. "You sound like a teenager."

Katrina was silent for a few seconds before giggling through her reply. "I'm only thirty-five, but I feel like a girl sometimes."

They agreed to meet for breakfast at the church-owned diner. Michelle was the first to arrive at Peace Diner, and she sat at their favorite booth and waited. Katrina arrived, walking fast and sporting a smile on her face.

"Sorry I'm late, but when you got a hurricane named after you people don't expect much from you." Ever since that terrible storm in New Orleans that killed so many people and devastated the city, Katrina had become very sensitive about her name. She took a seat across from Michelle and they immediately began to talk.

"Do you sometimes think about when we used to hang out at the club?" Michelle leaned across the table and continued. "I hadn't for a long time, but when Pastor Jenkins talked about wishing you could moonwalk back to the past and change something, I thought about us at the club." She was glad she had someone to talk to about it. Before

Katrina could say anything, Michelle spoke again. "Guess who I ran into a couple of weeks ago?" She didn't wait for Katrina to put in a guess. She knew that could take forever. "I ran into Freddie from the club."

Katrina opened her mouth to speak, but nothing came out before they were interrupted.

"Good morning, Michelle and Katrina," said the waitress. "What can I get for the two of you?" She was also a member at Peace Baptist Church. After exchanging pleasantries, the ladies placed their orders and tried to smile at her before she left the table.

After clearing her throat, Katrina asked the question, "Where did you see him at, and was he with Leo?"

Michelle shook her head. "No, he was alone. Turns out that Freddie is Cheryl's cousin." Michelle wanted to tell her friend that she gave Freddie five hundred dollars not to tell her husband what happened between them, but she couldn't find words. Must she and Katrina pay forever for that night they left the club with Freddie and Leo? "When I talked to him, he gave me the creeps," she confessed. "I hope I never see him again, *ever*."

Katrina nodded in agreement. "That happened before we were saved. We confessed our sins, asked God's forgiveness, and repented; so we are okay, aren't we?"

Michelle knew that God had forgiven them because they had come with a sincere heart and confessed their sins. But would her husband forgive her if he found out? Would Katrina's husband forgive her? The incident happened when they were just twenty years old and now they both were thirty-five with a husband and a child.

It was as if Katrina had read her mind. "God has forgiven us, but will our husbands forgive us?"

The waitress returned and set their food on the placemats in front of them and left the table. They ate their meals in a silence that was only drowned out by the words of their deepest thoughts.

* * * * * * *

Katrina had a hard time sleeping that night. She kept tossing and turning in bed, and at one point she let out a loud scream. Her husband shook her and woke her from her nightmare.

"Honey. Honey, are you all right?" he asked.

Katrina sat up in bed inwardly recounting her bad dream. She told him she was okay before excusing herself and walking into the bathroom where she shivered and closed her eyes. She remembered speaking with Michelle earlier that day and it made her think about things she dearly wanted to forget. Her nightmare had taken her back to that night when she and Michelle left the club with Freddie and Leo and all that had happened afterward. She wondered if Michelle ever had those awful flashbacks. She would ask her in the morning, but right now she was too afraid to go back to sleep; too afraid to revisit that horrible dream.

* * * * * * *

At Michelle's house peaceful sleep was also a distant dream. Cheryl had called to say that Freddie was coming back in town. She explained that he was a drummer and was convinced that Washington, D.C. was an excellent place to find employment in his trade. It worried Michelle that of all the cities that Freddie could have picked, he had chosen her beloved hometown to try to make a name for himself.

"He said he'll be in the city in the morning to holler at me," Cheryl had informed her. "I don't know why though, because I'm not interested in hollering at him."

It was obvious that Cheryl was still upset about the weed-smoking incident. She told Michelle that Freddie believed that smoking dope made him a better musician. Michelle had heard people say that before. She thought it was strange then, and she thought it was strange now.

At about six in the morning and still unable to sleep, Michelle slipped gingerly out of bed, as not wake a sleeping David. She carefully slid her feet into her bedroom slippers, eased into her robe, and headed for the bathroom to shower and brush her teeth. After getting cleaned and dressed, she walked down the stairs and into the kitchen where she began to prepare breakfast for her family and herself. She needed to keep busy.

During the breakfast preparation, Freddie stayed on Michelle's mind. She shook her head in an attempt to expel him from her thoughts. It worked for a few minutes but returned like a raging fire. A half hour later, she turned and somehow managed a smile when she saw David enter the kitchen. Her thoughts had drifted so far away that she hadn't heard him approaching.

David returned her smile before taking a seat at the kitchen table with a newspaper in his hand. He quickly began to scan the paper. Michelle was glad for this. It gave her the time she needed to get herself together so he couldn't tell how strange she was really feeling on the inside.

David looked up from the paper and said, "Do you want me to wake Sasha up?"

Michelle shook her head no and gave a small smile before turning to face the stove. She looked into the pot of grits and stirred longer than necessary. She removed the spoon and placed the lid back on the pot before walking to the refrigerator and pulling out a pitcher of orange juice and placing it on the table. "The food is almost done," she announced.

David stood and walked to the cupboard to pull out three drinking glasses while Michelle set the table. Just in time, Sasha joined her parents at the breakfast table, and they all linked hands and blessed their family meal. They were on a schedule, so chatter was held to a minimum while they quickly finished their meal.

After breakfast, David and Michelle walked Sasha to school. David planned to catch the subway to work in downtown Washington, D.C. afterward. It was a hassle driving and parking downtown, so he always took the subway to work. Sasha had been deposited at her school and Michelle and David were saying their goodbyes. David released Michelle from an embrace before heading for work and her for home.

When she reached the house a familiar figure was standing on her doorsteps. Michelle opened her eyes wide and stared. "What are you doing here?" she asked. "I thought you were at work."

Katrina walked toward her with her arms extended. "I had the worst dream last night," said her friend as she gave her a hug.

Michelle's head bobbed up and down. Words weren't needed in this case. She knew what had upset Katrina so. It was the same thing that had kept her awake for most of the night.

Chapter 3

David entered his workplace and took the elevator up to his office at the Housing Department. He entered the room and smiled at his secretary before walking into his office. He was expecting a phone call; she said she would call today at ten o'clock. It was not a call he was looking forward to, but when it came through, he had to take it.

Walking to his desk, David pulled out his chair and took a seat. He knew he had to take care of his responsibilities. He always had and wasn't about to stop now. He lowered his face into his open hands and shook his head. How had he gotten himself into this mess, and how was he going to resolve this problem? He knew he would have to man-up and confess what he knew to his wife.

What would happen then, he didn't know. But it wasn't something he was looking forward to. He glanced at the clock on the wall. She would be calling soon. No doubt, they wouldn't talk long, but he had no choice but to do the right thing. The clock was ticking away.

* * * * * * *

Michelle and Katrina hadn't made it into her house yet. In fact, they'd decided to do their talking at the church's diner. As they finally walked from Michelle's front yard, out the gate, and down the street, they had talked a little and then walked the rest of the distance in silence. When they reached the diner, the women slid into their favorite booth, facing one another. Katrina spoke first.

"Did Leo come to town with Freddie?"

Michelle looked helplessly at her friend because she didn't know the answer.

"We were dumb as two rocks back then," Katrina added.

Michelle smiled and then began laughing in spite of herself. Katrina could always make her laugh even when she was stressed out.

* * * * * * *

Cheryl pulled back her curtains from the window and saw Freddie walking toward her house. She hoped this would be a short and uneventful visit. She walked to the door and opened it before he knocked and stepped aside so that he could enter the house.

"Hi, cuz," he said, as he tried to hug her. When she backed away from his opened arms, he stuck his bottom lip out theatrically and asked, "Did I do anything to you?"

Cheryl put her hands on her hips and stared at Freddie. She knew he hadn't forgotten that she'd caught him smoking. She stared him dead in his eyes that were clearly filled with reefer and finally spoke. "No smoking in my house."

He blinked a few times and smiled at his cousin. "Are you and Michelle good friends?" he asked before walking toward the couch and taking a seat.

Cheryl followed quickly behind him. "Michelle and I are sisters in Christ."

Freddie chuckled under his breath. He thought about when he first encountered Michelle at the club all those years ago, and he chuckled again. "Are you sure she's a Christian?"

Cheryl nodded her head in the affirmative. Michelle was a Christian woman and she resented her cousin for questioning the fact. She thought he should become one himself and stop doubting those who already were.

* * * * * * *

Michelle rose from her seat at Peace Diner, followed by Katrina, and they walked to the front door to exit. Michelle was feeling refreshed after talking with her best friend. They walked down the street smiling and chatting before stopping at the crosswalk light.

When they reached Michelle's, the two women looked down the street in the direction of Cheryl's house. Freddie was standing on the front porch and began descending the steps as soon as he caught glimpse of them. As he got closer, Michelle gasped. Katrina shook her head and her eyes widened. When he waved at them, the women moved swiftly for the house, but Freddie had gotten too much of a head start. He caught up with them before they could make it inside.

"I hear you women are Christians now," he remarked with a

mischievous grin on his face.

Michelle and Katrina looked at him for a second and then turned to go into the house.

"Have you seen my man, Leo, lately?" added Freddie looking directly at Katrina.

Katrina averted her eyes to the ground and a tear rolled down her cheek into her mouth. Michelle came to her friend's aid and returned his gaze before narrowing her eyes, "What do you want?" she nearly shouted.

He smiled before speaking. "I need a loan again like you gave me last time."

Katrina stiffened like she was a statue in the park. She looked at Michelle with inquisitive eyes, but said nothing.

"I'll be waiting outside my cousin's house in two hours for the money," Freddie added. And with those words, he turned and walked down the street.

"You gave him money?" Katrina whispered harshly.

Michelle had to almost drag Katrina into the house. Once inside, she slammed the door, and then locked it. They stood near the front door, unwilling or unable to walk away. But they weren't too frozen in place to do what they knew had to be done. Two hours later, they sat together in Michelle's living room counting the money they had withdrawn from the bank to give to Freddie. Michelle had only a hundred dollars to contribute this time, so Katrina gave four hundred dollars to reach the sum of his blackmail demand.

Now Michelle had only enough money remaining in her personal saving account to keep it open. She gathered the money together and rose from the couch, and together they walked out to the front porch. When they looked toward Cheryl's home, just as promised, Freddie was standing on the front porch. But he wasn't there alone.

"Who is that?" Katrina asked the question, but her tone said that she kind of already knew the answer. And there was a good reason for that. The man standing with him was all too familiar. She couldn't have forgotten Leo's face no matter how badly she wanted to.

The two men walked up the street to where the women were standing and stopped. Leo looked from Katrina to Michelle, and then back at Katrina again. She stiffened.

Freddie stepped closer and extended his hand. "Do you have that loan we talked about?"

Michelle placed the envelope in his palm and said, "Get this straight, okay?" And then with a glare, she continued. "There's not going to be no more money, understand?"

Freddie gave her a crooked smile. "I understand. I don't need another loan." He looked at Leo and grinned wider, and then he gave the women a little wave before walking down the street with Leo following behind.

Michelle and Katrina scurried back inside Michelle's home and slammed the front door behind them. Once inside, they sat at opposite ends of the couch with their mouths shut.

* * * * * * *

The following day, Katrina returned to Michelle's house again, but this time with her four-year-old daughter. To get their minds refocused, they had decided to take their little girls and go sightseeing on the National Mall. The Freddie and Leo mess was behind them, and that's exactly where they wanted to keep it. The only things on Michelle and Katrina's minds today were their beautiful daughters.

Michelle used her hands to press down her black shoulder length hair and stood from the couch. Katrina's dark brown hair was in a ponytail, and she stood as well, reaching for her daughter's hand in the process. They had packed snacks for today's mall outing. Michelle adjusted the tote bag that housed the food on her shoulders and led the way as they all headed out the front door.

Katrina held her daughter's hand as she followed behind carrying a camera. They didn't get to go to the National Mall very often, so even though Washington, D.C. was their hometown, today they were going to blend in with the tourists.

* * * * * * *

David stayed home alone, sitting at the kitchen table talking on the telephone as he watched through the window blinds as his wife and her best friend strolled out of sight. "Yes, she's gone," he said into the receiver. "I can talk."

He remain quiet for a while listening to what his caller had to say. The timing had been perfect. The telephone rang just moments after the women and girls walked out. "No, I can't give you any more money," he blurted, trying to control his rising anger.

David clutched the phone tightly to his ear and listened intently. "What?" he snapped. "I need to make Michelle get a job? That's none of your business!" he shouted, and then almost immediately calmed down.

He began to listen again, tapping his fingers on the kitchen table as a means to help him keep his cool.

* * * * * * *

Michelle, Katrina, and their daughters had finally reached the National Mall, and they were enjoying the scenery as they took in their surroundings. Their entire tour was already planned, and they would start with a visit to The Air and Space Museum on 7th street in downtown D.C. They held their daughters' hands as they entered the building and looked forward to what the rest of the day would bring.

It was a long day, but they were still excited when they arrived at the final stop on their sightseeing tour: the Washington Monument. They rode the elevator to the top of the white, pencil-shaped structure. Michelle remembered her mother telling her that when she was young, she and her friends had walked the many steps to the top of the monument.

Now that Michelle and her party had reached the top, they exited the elevator, walked to the window, and looked out and down at the scenic view. The group smiled and took pictures once they were on the monument grounds again. They were acting like genuine out of town sightseers and having a ball. Both mothers and their daughters walked to a nearby bench and everyone took a seat. Young Kayla rested her head on Katrina's lap.

Meanwhile, Sasha was looking tired as well. She yawned as she tapped Michelle's shoulder. "I'm hungry, Mommy."

Michelle reached into her tote bag and pulled out sandwiches for everyone.

"I wanted to eat there," said Kayla, pointing to a spot on the monument ground.

Katrina stood and pulled a blanket from her tote. She walked the short distance to the spot where her daughter had pointed and spread it on the grass. They had a picnic right there.

Chapter 4

David had just returned from his errand. He had gotten the money out of his personal savings account and had delivered it as instructed. He was glad that was over; now maybe he could relax. Walking into the dining room, he sat in a chair that faced the television. He would watch a game and wait for his family to return home. David loved and missed his wife and daughter; he really did.

* * * * * * *

Katrina beamed as they walked home from the National Mall. "We've got to do this more often."

Michelle nodded her head in agreement as she tenderly held Sasha's hand. When they were a few blocks away from Michelle's house, Katrina again broke the silence that rested between them.

"Let's put these photos in the shop before I forget," she said. "I know me."

As they entered the drugstore, Katrina walked to the photo department while Michelle and the two little girls looked around the store.

"Mommy, don't forget your newspaper," announced Sasha.

Michelle smiled and walked with the girls to the newspaper rack. She grabbed a newspaper and headed toward a check-out line to pay for it. She could feel someone behind her, so she paused momentarily. Without looking around, Michelle knew this wasn't good. The hairs on her arms were at full attention, and her heart began to race. The person was so close behind her that when he finally spoke, he did so directly into her ear.

"Thank you for reminding me. I almost forgot my newspaper."

Michelle spun around and saw Freddie there, smiling at her. She took a step back and returned an angry glare. As if amused, he smiled again before taking backward steps to get a paper of his own. Michelle stared dauntingly at him as he turned, walked down another aisle, and disappeared from her sight. She quickly paid for the paper and walked outside with the two girls to wait for Katrina.

Katrina emerged from the drugstore like she was being chased by a lion. Looking behind her instead of where she was going, she bumped right into Michelle. Her breaths were coming in pants, and her voice cracked when she spoke. "Leo came up behind me at the photo counter," she told Michelle; still looking around like she thought she was being followed.

Neither woman knew what the two men wanted. They were clearly unnerved by the unexpected run-ins. Were Leo and Freddie following them? Would they ever leave them alone?

"We need to talk," said Katrina. Michelle nodded in agreement before they began walking briskly down the street; periodically looking over their shoulders as they made their way to safety.

After dropping their daughters off at Michelle's house with David, Michelle and Katrina headed for Peace Diner, a place where they could talk without being overheard.

"I'm not giving them no more money," said Katrina once they were seated.

"They didn't ask for money this time," replied Michelle, trying to sound hopeful.

It was hard to discern the motives of men like Freddie and Leo. Maybe they were just trying to frighten them. Freddie was dealing drugs, or at least using them. He was capable of almost anything, and the same went for Leo. One thing the two women agreed on was that they would not fall prey to any more blackmail demands.

Katrina raised a finger in the air, as if she had a bright idea. "Precious's husband!"

Michelle nodded her head in understanding. Precious's husband was a detective on the D.C. police force and a member of Peace Baptist. Could Ed really help them get rid of those guys? Could he get them off their backs for good? Tomorrow was Sunday, and they could approach Precious after church services and ask for her husband's help.

Michelle smiled as she thought about the possibilities. Katrina liked her own idea as well. She didn't say another word, but when she gazed at Michelle, she, too, smiled.

* * * * * * *

On Sunday, after Pastor Jenkins brought the Word of the Lord to the congregation in his usual animated fashion and after the benediction had been given, Michelle and Katrina approached the woman who they both prayed was the link to the man who could help them.

"Hello, ladies," said Precious as she watched them come near her.

Michelle took a deep breath, and then said, "Sister, we need a word with your husband."

Precious jokingly looked them up and down and said, "Girl, those are fighting words. You know my husband is off limits."

Michelle and Katrina started to giggle.

"Precious, you're crazy," said Katrina. "We need your husband, the *detective*, not the deacon. We have a few questions but we thought we'd run it by you first. We didn't want to just go to him without your knowledge."

Precious laughed and pointed toward Ed who was standing near the front of the church. The women thanked her, and then turned to walk where the detective was standing.

Ed saw them walking toward him, and a welcoming smile appeared on his face. Once they were beside him, he spoke. "Good afternoon, ladies."

"Good afternoon," they replied in unison.

"Pastor Jenkins, sure hit another home run for the Lord today," Ed continued.

Michelle nodded her head in agreement. "Pastor brings living water to those thirsting for the Word of God," she said, all the while allowing her eyes to scan their surroundings. Their conversation with the detective needed to be private.

Michelle and Katrina took turns explaining to Ed that they needed his professional help with a problem they were having. He listened intently and once they were done talking, Ed agreed to help them in any way he could.

Before walking outside with the women, he looked at his wife who was sitting patiently in a pew, and she smile and waved to him, giving him the silent consent that he'd non-verbally asked. He waved back and motioned for the two women to follow him outside. There, after a short chat, they agreed to meet in an hour at the restaurant down the street

* * * * * * *

"Do you know his full name?" asked Ed as soon as they were all comfortably seated at the table.

Michelle knew Freddie's first and last names and shared that information with Ed. Katrina also gave the detective the first and last names of Leo. When he asked the women for more pertinent information about the two men, they opened up and told him everything they knew. They felt they could trust him.

Michelle folded her hands on the table and studied the detective's face. "You see, Brother Ed, we have a past."

Ed looked at Michelle for a second, and then turned and looked at Katrina before speaking. "Most people have a past that they're not all that proud of." He paused for a moment. "I know I have one, and mine would uncurl your hair. But that was the past and this is the present. I'm a Christian now."

Michelle and Katrina listened to the detective in silence. Before getting up from his seat, Ed agreed to find out information about Freddie and Leo, and he promised to stay in contact with them. After shaking the detective's hand in gratitude, the ladies watched in continued silence as he exited the restaurant. Once they were alone, Michelle reached for her root beer and took a sip, while Katrina stared at nothing in particular.

When Michelle arrived home, there was a note on her refrigerator. David had taken Sasha to the park for a while, and Katrina's husband had picked up Kayla. Michelle stuck the note in her pocket and dashed upstairs to her bedroom. She took off her church clothes and slid into a pair of jeans and a sweatshirt. She sat on the edge of the bed, thinking about the discussion she and Katrina had had with the detective.

She thought they had made the right decision to get him involved in their situation. What had the detective said about his own past was enough to uncurl a person's hair? Michelle had been surprised when he said that. Now she wondered why. As he had so eloquently reminded them, most people had a past. While that was true, Michelle was really afraid that David might not understand about hers. She didn't want to jeopardize her marriage and her family. Maybe her husband would understand, and maybe he wouldn't. Right now, she wasn't mentally strong enough take a chance on finding out.

Chapter 5

The summer had come and gone so fast it was a blur. Fall made its entrance without much drama. The turning of the leaves made for a beautiful picture against the season's skies. As October rolled in and out, things continued to look up for Michelle and Katrina. Halloween had gone and they hadn't heard anything at all from Freddie and Leo, which made the holiday less scary.

November brought in an unwelcomed change though. Thanksgiving was two weeks away. Michelle and Katrina planned to go grocery shopping together like they did every year. Little did they know that they were going to have to dig deep to try to find reasons to be thankful this year.

* * * * * * *

"Freddie, when are we going to get married?" The question came from his girlfriend as soon as she joined him in the living room where he sat.

Freddie rose from the sofa and walk to her. She was eight months pregnant and this wasn't her first time asking the question. Freddie reached for her hand and softly rubbed it. "Baby, we don't need a piece of paper to prove we love each other. You're my woman, and it's always gonna be like that."

The expression on Dana's face softened somewhat, and he continued. "Girl, I love you more than anything in this world." A faint smile appeared on her face. Freddie returned her smile and hers grew wider. "Go get the kids," he added. "I'm taking my family out for dinner."

As Dana turned and wobbled down the hall, and then disappeared into a bedroom, Freddie's smile turned into a smirk. *She sure is an ignoramus*, he thought to himself. She was still buying the same tired game he'd been playing for years.

The bedroom door opened, and out ran three kids, ages two, three, and four, all shouting, "Daddy" like some pitiful children's choir. Freddie bent down to pick up the two-year-old and cuddled him in his arms. He was nothing more than a bum. The game he'd been playing had resulted in three children with his girlfriend and another baby on the way.

Dana wobbled into the living room to join them. They gathered the children and walked out of the apartment. Freddie was keeping his word for a change. He was taking his family out to dinner.

* * * * * * *

"Have you heard from Freddie lately?" asked Katrina as she and Michelle talked on the telephone.

"Not a word," answered Michelle. She rested on the edge of her bed and stared down at her freshly polished toenails. "Brother Ed said that Freddie has an arrest record, but he wouldn't go into details."

"I know," Katrina said sarcastically. "I was there when he said it; remember?"

Of course Michelle knew that she was there. She had more or less been thinking out loud. She reached for the pillow by her side and ran her hand over it. They thought Ed was hard at work on the case. It was obvious that he had more information about Freddie than he cared to share, and that was fine with them.

"I think I saw Leo the other day," blurted Katrina, "but he was a distance away from me."

Michelle punched her pillow in frustration. She didn't want to believe it, but Katrina was probably correct. But regardless of whether she'd seen him or not, they were not giving Freddie or Leo any more money. "At least Detective Ed didn't find anything wrong about Leo," said Michelle after she'd taken a calming breath. "He promised to investigate him further."

Katrina let out a loud sigh. "I'm sorry, Michelle. But I'll pay him whatever amount he asks for. I want to save my marriage and family."

Michelle was disappointed with her friend. They had agreed to pay the men no more money. Ed had chastised them for succumbing to blackmail in the first place. Michelle sort of understood how Katrina felt, because she'd felt that way earlier. But not anymore. Freddie wouldn't get another penny out of her. "It'll work out all right, Katrina." Michelle hoped and prayed with all her heart that she was telling the truth.

They soon ended their conversation. Talking about their situation on their home phones wasn't the means of communication that either of them preferred. Anything could happen. They usually met at the church-owned diner to hash things out or plan their next move on this particular matter. Talking face to face was far more comfortable.

The next day, Katrina caught the elevator down from her place of employment. It made a stop on the second floor, and a man walked inside and glanced at her. Katrina returned the glance and stepped out the elevator at the next stop; the first floor. She made quick steps in an effort to get away from the man on the elevator.

"Katrina, you don't have a minute for an old friend?" said Leo.

She was about to walk out of the building when Leo tapped her on the shoulder. She turned around and stared in his eyes before walking out of her place of employment. How did he know where she worked? Was he following her? He had to be. She'd certainly never told him about her job. Katrina slowed down, turned, and saw Leo close on her heels. She decided to stop and talk to the man because she didn't want to make a scene in public.

"What do you want from me?" The tone of her voice was low and stern.

A smile appeared on Leo's face. "Can't I just chat with an old friend? I could use a little money, if you care."

Katrina narrowed her eyes to a slit, and then she opened them as wide as she could. "How much do you want?"

She listened while Leo informed her he wanted five hundred dollars. He was leaving town, he said; going back to Philadelphia for good, and he promised never to see her. Katrina heard him out but didn't believe him for one minute. He sounded sincere and truthful, but he had proven over and over again to be a dishonest man.

Just listening to him speak gave Katrina the creeps. She wanted to end the conversation and get away from him as soon as possible, so she nodded her head in agreement to his terms.

"You can bring the money to that church diner tomorrow evening," said Leo. "Does your husband still work for that bank on K Street?" he asked as he slowly walked away.

Katrina dashed to the side of the nearby building and pulled out her cell phone and dialed Michelle. In the brief, yet emotional exchange that followed, the two women agreed to an emergency meeting at Peace Diner. The forty-five minute time frame that they'd agreed upon couldn't come quickly enough for Katrina.

* * * * * * *

Freddie and Dana sat together on the sofa in their living room. "Baby, I'm going to get you an engagement ring," said Freddie. "I just want to make you happy."

His girlfriend smiled and leaned over to give him a kiss on the cheek. "We're getting engaged, and then we're getting married." Dana's face beamed as she spoke.

He looked at her and grimaced. "I didn't say nothing about getting married. We can get engaged, and I'll be your fiancé for now; not your husband."

The woman crinkled her forehead and seemed to ponder over what Freddie had just said. "My mother asked me when we're getting married."

Freddie had been through this before with her, and had always managed to use double-talk to soothe and control her. "I thought we agreed that we don't care nothing about marriage. That's your mother's thing and not ours."

Nodding her head in slow agreement, Dana said, "Freddie, I'm happy being your fiancée." I just want to buy the ring before our baby is born."

Freddie looked at her, and a smile grew deep inside of him. He owned this woman and he knew it. He was her all ruling master. Freddie's mind easily shifted from his girlfriend who was annoying him, to his good buddy who was in Washington, D.C. hitting Katrina up for money. Michelle and Katrina were gold mines, and Freddie smiled to himself at the thought of it. He planned to join Leo in D.C. soon. In fact, he wanted to bring his family to the nation's capital, and live there permanently.

Freddie figured that he could easily move his small drug business there without stepping on the locals' toes. He planned to stop selling once he earned enough money to buy a house, car, and put some money in the bank. That shouldn't take too long, and then he planned to leave the drug game. He wanted to be a retired drug dealer and a respectable citizen who had a woman and children, but he wasn't trying to be anybody's husband. He smiled at his plans, and leaned back on the sofa to wait for Leo's call.

Chapter 6

Michelle and Katrina sat at their favorite booth at the church-owned diner and spoke in hushed tones as they discussed their ongoing situation.

"Should we call Brother Ed?" asked Michelle.

Katrina shook her head from side to side, and her voice trembled as she spoke. "No. I'm afraid after hearing this, he might go to my husband and spill the beans."

Michelle looked at Katrina and sighed. She didn't know what to do. Leo was probably capable of everything imaginable and unimaginable. She understood why Katrina didn't want to cross him, but Freddie and Leo's threats had to end. Ed had instructed them not to give the men any more money. She knew the detective was right, but knowing and doing were two different birds.

"Can you go to the bank with me?" Katrina's tone was pleading.

Michelle looked across the booth at her and blurted out in a harsh whisper, "Don't give that man any more money!"

Then she watched in silence as her best friend slid out of the booth, scrambled to her feet, and briskly exited the diner. Michelle remained seated in the booth thinking. Katrina had replayed the entire encounter with Leo to her. They definitely needed to do something, but Michelle didn't know what. Should she call Detective Ed and risk alienating Katrina? They needed to put an end to this blackmail. To be able to relax and just chill out was what Michelle wanted to do, but instead, she sprang from her seat and walked out of the diner; each step faster than the one before.

Once outside, her swift pace continued. She knew where she was going and wanted to get there in a hurry. Twenty minutes later, Michelle opened the front gate and mounted the steps to the house. She knocked on the door, and after making known her identity to the voice that called out from inside the home, the front door opened and a woman stepped out and hugged her right there on the porch.

"Come on in," said the woman. "We haven't talked in a while."

Michelle followed her into the house. "Mama, I hope you have some free time. I just needed to see you."

Once inside, Michelle's mother put her arms around her daughter, and they stayed embraced for an extended length of time. Bethany always seemed to know what her daughter needed most.

Michelle felt the tension drain from her body. "Mama, can I be a ten-year-old again for about ten minutes?"

Her mother smiled and held her daughter even tighter. Even as they slowly made their way to the sofa, they remained in a tight embrace. They sat down together, and Michelle placed her head on her mother's shoulder. She sat with her eyes closed, thinking about what a good mom she had. Bethany had never ever turned her away, even when she and Katrina were hitting the nightclubs, doing their thing. Bethany warned her on many occasions that the club scene was no good and that she would never find a decent man there.

Michelle didn't listen though. She was twenty years old, and she and Katrina wanted to go clubbing. As legal adults they needed no permission or supervision, so that's exactly what they did. She got tired of her mother reprimanding her for coming home at two in the morning, so she and Katrina had gotten an apartment together. Michelle looked back now and all she could think was how stupid she and Katrina had been. They had wasted a lot of precious time going after no-good men. Even back then, her mother would show her love whenever she came to visit.

"I want to get my granddaughter this weekend." Bethany's words broke through Michelle's thoughts. Her mother stroked her hair as they sat on the sofa.

Michelle thought to herself, not only was Bethany a good mother, she also a good . . . no, an *excellent* grandmother. She always made a big fuss over her Sasha. Plus she didn't mind being called Grandma like many women did in this day and time. So many grandmothers preferred to simply be called Mama or a creative combination of some other words; anything other than Grandma. Michelle's mother wasn't like that, and that made her more than happy.

Bethany was in her late fifties, but she had always been well-kept. She was 5'5", and her weight fit nicely on that frame. She went to the beautician every two weeks, and she dressed age appropriately. But as good as Bethany looked, she didn't wince at being called Grandma. But as wonderful and understanding as she could be, Michelle still wondered if she should tell Bethany of her dilemma.

"I made dessert," said her mother. "We could talk over cake in the kitchen."

Michelle opened her eyes and lifted her head from her mother's shoulders. "Okay, Ma," she said as she got up from the couch. Michelle wasn't about to turn down her mom's cake, but she still didn't know whether she wanted to burden her mother with her troubles.

An hour later, Michelle was leaving her mother's house with her secret still intact. She'd taken so much time deliberating whether she'd share what was truly on her heart, that she ran out of time. Now she needed to pick up Sasha from school.

Bethany was no fool though. She knew that something was wrong, but she didn't press her daughter to tell her what she obviously wasn't ready to share. Instead, as she walked Michelle to the door, she told her that she could call her day or night, whenever she was ready to talk.

Her words had given Michelle relief. She had to get in touch with Katrina and find out how everything had gone with her. Michelle glanced at her watch as she walked to the elementary school. The sudden sounds of her ringtone alerted her that someone was calling. One look at the screen revealed that it was Katrina.

"Hello." Michelle tried not to sound anxious.

"Can you meet me at the diner in about an hour?" asked Katrina.

They both knew the answer was yes. Michelle immediately made plans to meet Katrina after picking up her daughter and giving her an afternoon snack. An hour later, David was watching Sasha while Michelle and Katrina sat in their favorite booth.

"Girl, I'm disappointed in you." Michelle shook her head slowly as she spoke. "Ed told us not to give them any more money, and you go—"

Katrina put up her hand to stop Michelle's rant. "Tell me you wouldn't have done the same thing," she challenged, staring Michelle directly in the eyes.

Michelle stopped, and with her mouth half opened, she thought about what Katrina had just said. "I don't know," she had to finally admit. "I may have."

Katrina reached into her pocket, pulled out a small device, and placed it on the table.

Michelle eyed it carefully. "What's that?"

Without verbally responding, Katrina reached forward and pushed a button on the device. The volume was low, but voices could be heard coming from speakers. Katrina's voice was one of them. She pushed the stop button and looked at Michelle with a smile on her face. "I recorded the conversation I had with Leo," she confessed. "I have him blackmailing us on tape."

Michelle looked at her friend and her face brightened. "Katrina, you are a genius; a bona fide genius."

Katrina's smile grew bigger. "I don't know if I'm a genius, but I sure am a woman who can take care of herself."

Michelle nodded in agreement, but at that moment, she did feel her friend was a genius. As far as Michelle was concerned, Katrina was doing more detective work than the detective who'd promised them both he'd help in their situation. Michelle glanced at her watch. She wished she had more time to get all the details from Katrina, but she had to get home. She slid out of the booth and stood, looking at her friend. "I've gotta get going," she said.

Katrina nodded in agreement, grabbed her recording device, and stood. The women walked out of the diner together.

* * * * * * *

On Sunday after church, Michelle and Katrina managed to corner Ed. He noticed their excitement and said, "Sisters, you act like you have urgent news for me."

Katrina could barely hold her tongue. "Brother Ed, while we tried to wait patiently for you to catch Freddie and Leo, we got a little antsy and decided to help you on this case."

Ed looked at Katrina for a few seconds, and then turned to look at Michelle. Katrina reached into her pocket and pulled out the miniature

33

tape recorder and handed it to him. "This is a tape of us being blackmailed by Leo."

Ed took the tape from her and started walking toward the church doors. He stopped when he realized the women were not following him, and he motioned with his hand for them to come along. When they were all outside and in a location where no others stood close by, he spoke. "I told you not to make contact with either of the men."

Katrina and Michelle exchanged glances, and then turned their eyes back on him. Michelle thought to herself, *you should be thanking us and the detective work Katrina did that you didn't do.* She was pretty sure that Katrina thought the same thing, but something entirely different was said.

"We thought this was an opportunity to get them. We're sorry if we made a mistake," said Katrina in a voice masked with regret.

Ed looked from one to the other again. Then he reached into his suit coat pocket and pulled out a white envelope and handed it to Katrina. She looked puzzled as she took the envelope from his hand and opened the flap. There were picture inside that she slowly slid out. Glancing at the photos, her jaw dropped. She handed one photo to Michelle.

"I told you, I was handling this case." Ed's tone was sharp. "Katrina, I took that photo of you and Leo during your little meeting." He was clearly unhappy that she'd gone against his wishes. "Trust me. I got this; I really do."

After once being so sure of themselves, Michelle and Katrina were now embarrassed and at a loss for words. They remained silent during the rest of their meeting. In spite of Ed's disappointment, he did manage to thank them for the taped recording before he walked away. The women parted ways too; both still silent. It would be that evening before they would talk to each other again.

"Brother Ed's got this," said Katrina as they talked on the phone.

"I know," returned Michelle. "I almost choked when he pulled out those pictures."

They laughed together at the thought of how Ed had reduced them to silence. But it was really no laughing matter. What Katrina and Michelle didn't know was that they weren't the only ones talking on the phone at that hour.

****

"Man, I got the money," bragged Leo into the mouthpiece of his phone.

"Great!" The pleasure could be heard in Freddie's reply. "I gotta get back to Washington, D.C., and shake that Michelle down for some more cash," he added with a chuckle.

Leo sounded doubtful. "I don't know, man. It's getting harder and harder to blackmail them."

Freddie mulled over Leo's words. He couldn't deny that his blackmail buddy was right. But he wasn't going out without one last thrill. "Let's ask for one last large amount of money, and then we'll be done with them."

As if Freddie could see him over the phone, Leo nodded in agreement to the proposal. They would extort money from the two women one more time. That was their plan.

Freddie knew when he left Philadelphia this time, it would be for good. He liked living in D.C. The only thing he wasn't sure about was if he would move his girlfriend and kids, with him or leave them behind and just move to the city by himself. He could move around more freely if he didn't have the extra baggage. Leo, on the other hand, had already informed Freddie that his plan was to soon settle down in Philadelphia with his woman and children.

****

On Monday, Michelle and Katrina were back at the place that seemed to have become a second home for them in recent weeks. It only took them a few seconds to get comfortable in their booth. The dropping outside temperatures had them sipping on warm drinks this morning.

"I don't work outside the house," said Michelle, "and you're off as much as me."

"I just have a good government job with flex-hours. Don't hate on a sister," said Katrina before tasting her coffee

"I love Christmas," said Michelle out of the blue. She, David, and

35

Sasha were going to do a little gift buying when he got off work that evening.

Katrina knew her husband would never, ever go Christmas shopping with her; he didn't have the patience.

Michelle looked around the diner. There was a fully decorated Christmas tree in a corner near the entrance. The tables donned red tablecloths, there was a holiday wreath on the front door, and the waitresses wore red Santa caps. Gospel Christmas music played softly in the background. The women sat in the booth taking in the sights and sounds of the holiday spirit a little longer before heading home.

* * * * * * *

David Davidson sat at his desk in his office listening to soft holiday music. He and his family would be going shopping for the holiday today. It wasn't really his thing, but it made Michelle and Sasha happy. There was a tap on his door, and he gave his secretary permission to enter.

"Mr. Davidson, I have ten messages from Nicola, asking you to call her," she said once in his office.

David looked away from the woman for a moment, and the without looking back at her, said, "Thank you, Ms. Smalls." The secretary gave him a crooked smile and placed the written messages on his desk. Then with a little wave, she left his office.

David waited until Ms. Smalls was on the other side of his closed door before picking up the phone and dialing. He knew his secretary was aware that another woman was involved in his life.

Nicola picked up on the fourth ring. "So, David; are you going to give me some money so that I can take our daughter Christmas shopping?"

David remained silent for a few seconds before speaking. Not many people knew he was the child's father, and he wanted to keep it that way. "I thought I gave her the amount I'm required to give," he said kicking the tiny trash can with his foot.

"Yeah you gave the *required* amount," snapped the woman," but I thought you wanted to be human for the holidays and all."

David thought about what she said for a brief moment, then while tapping his pen on the desk said, "Okay, be at my office in an hour; before I go home."

Nicola promised that she would make it there in time. "I'll even bring you a school picture of our daughter," she added before hanging up the phone.

The conversation left David feeling perplexed, as usual. He really did want to tell Michelle about the daughter he had with Nicola, but each time he tried, his mouth couldn't form the words. How would Michelle react to the news? Would she want to end their marriage? He didn't know and was too chicken to find out.

It didn't take long for Nicola to arrive. She didn't stay long; just picked up what she'd come for and left. She slid a photo of Davita on his desk just before walking out the door. David stared at it awhile before reaching forward and picking it up. He studied the face of the child. There was no doubt about it; she certainly was his daughter.

Davita was the spitting image of him. She was a miniature David in a dress. David thought she looked a lot like Sasha. Michelle would surely hate knowing that he'd had a child with another woman that looked like the little girl he'd had with her.

David put the picture of Davita in his desk drawer and gathered his things to leave for home. Two hours later, he was holiday shopping with Michelle and Sasha at Union Station like all was right with the world. Their first stop was at the food court for a meal before hitting the shops. David had a smile plastered on his face, Sasha was giggling, and Michelle was in la-la land, filled to the brim with happiness.

Christmas would be special this year, thought Michelle to herself, and there's no way they would leave Christ out of Christmas. Jesus was always the reason for the season, and this year, they planned to limit spending. As the family walked toward the fountain where the coins were tossed, David looked up and saw a woman and girl entering the station.

His entire face dropped, and he made an excuse so he and his family could depart the building. "I'm starting not to feel well. Let me find a restroom before we go into any stores." It wasn't true. David felt fine . . . physically. But at the moment, he felt like he might turn into an emotional wreck if he didn't get out of there.

That was Nicola and Davita entering Union Station. He shook his head at the thought of what could happen. *What kind of sick game is she playing?*

Michelle turned and looked at him through concerned eyes. He plastered a phony smile on his face, hoping it would hide the truth. David knew that he needed to tell Michelle about his other daughter. He needed to man-up and lay everything on the table, and that's exactly what he would do.

Sasha grabbed his hand, and he looked down at her with a genuine smile. She was so special to him. Sasha trusted him, and to her he always wanted to be the model of what a good husband and a good father looked like. A good husband and father included being an honest man. David made his decision then and there to tell Michelle about his other daughter. But right now wasn't the time. He'd wait until after Christmas; in the beginning of next year. Coming clean about his dirty secret would be his New Year's resolution.

Chapter 7

Every Christmas Eve, Michelle and her family threw a party for their friends and loved ones. The plan was to continue the tradition this year. With less than two weeks before Christmas, Michelle walked down the street to give a personal invitation to her neighbor. Michelle knocked on the front door, and Cheryl must have looked through the peephole because she called out Michelle's name before opening the door.

"Hey! What do I owe this visit to?" she asked, fully opening the door and moving to the side to let Michelle enter the house.

Once inside, Michelle positioned herself near the front door. "I want to invite you to our annual Christmas Eve party," she said. "I hope you can make it."

Cheryl nodded her head. "Girl, I wouldn't miss it for all the chocolate cake in the world." She pointed toward the kitchen. "I'm baking some cookies; come on in and have some."

Michelle smiled and followed Cheryl's lead and could smell the oatmeal raisin treats even before she entered the kitchen. She inhaled the aroma and exhaled through parted lips. While Cheryl slipped on an oven mitt and removed the hot cookie sheet from the oven, Michelle sat at the kitchen table observing her neighbor as she worked.

"Do you want milk with the cookies?" asked Cheryl.

Michelle nodded her head yes. When Cheryl sat across the table from her and let out a long sigh, Michelle reached for one of the warm cookies and asked, "What's wrong?"

Cheryl looked up to the ceiling and rolled her eyes. "It's Freddie's girlfriend. She's eight months pregnant and my cousin's not treating her right."

Just that quickly, Michelle lost her appetite and placed the cookie down on a napkin in front of her.

Cheryl looked at her. "You remember my cousin, Freddie, don't you?"

Michelle didn't say a word. Of course, she remembered him. She only wished the image of him would be permanently removed from her mind. So he had an eight months pregnant girlfriend and he was dogging her. Yep. That sounded just like the Freddie she knew.

Cheryl further informed Michelle that Freddie's girlfriend was constantly calling her, asking her to make Freddie behave. When her friend informed her that Freddie was moving back to Washington, D.C.; this time for good, all Michelle could do was just listen and pray. She had nothing to add to the conversation. She only hoped and prayed within herself that the move would never happen.

"I wouldn't be surprised to see him on my doorstep any day now," said Cheryl before sucking her teeth.

Michelle felt like her head was a spinning top spiraling out of control. She breathed in and out slowly to try and calm her nerves.

"Are you okay?" asked Cheryl, staring into her face and noting her demeanor.

Michelle rose from her seat and walked toward the kitchen door. "I'm not feeling well. I'll talk to you soon." With that said, she walked out of the kitchen, down the hall, and out of the front door.

On the outside, she could breathe again, and with calculated steps, Michelle walked two houses up the street to where she lived. She needed to talk to Katrina, so she headed straight to her bedroom and flopped on her mattress before reaching for the telephone. The phone only rang twice.

"Cheryl says Freddie has a girlfriend who's eight months pregnant," blurted out Michelle as soon as Katrina answered her phone.

Katrina gave a sigh through the phone line. "I didn't know that, but I'm not surprised."

Michelle had to admit, she wasn't that surprised either. The man wasn't a good person, but she had to vent, and she knew Katrina would help ease her anxiety.

"Let's evict Freddie and Leo from our minds during the holiday season, okay?" said Katrina.

Michelle smiled. She knew her friend was dispensing wisdom, and she would be wise to apply her words. After they'd talked a little longer,

Michelle bid her best friend goodbye, sprung up from her bed, and galloped down the stairs to get a glass of eggnog. "Merry Christmas," she said aloud to herself.

* * * * * * *

Christmas music played at a medium volume at the Christmas Eve party. Michelle was wearing a red velvet dress and so was her daughter, Sasha. Red wasn't her favorite color, but she'd gotten caught up in the holiday spirit when she went shopping. The food was setup buffet style and everyone was busy serving themselves. David wore a red tie to be consistent with the family's color scheme.

Katrina was acting as co-hostess, lending a hand, whenever one was needed. Sasha was playing with Katrina's daughter, Kayla. So far, there were only about eight guests at the holiday function.

Michelle gazed at the fully decorated Christmas tree in the living room by the window. The doorbell rang, and Katrina volunteered to answer the door. She was being a great co-hostess. After inquiring who was there, she opened the door and allowed Cheryl and her future husband, Paul, to enter. She wore an eye-catching Christmas green dress, and Paul looked just as sharp.

A second man scrambled through the door and Michelle squinted at the sight of him. It was Freddie. What was Cheryl thinking, bringing that man to her party? Michelle looked at Katrina who was still standing by the front door. Their eyes met and Katrina shook her head in disbelief.

Approaching Michelle, Cheryl said, "My cousin showed up on my doorstep. I hope it's okay that I brought him to your party."

Michelle was at a loss for words. It seemed to take every ounce of strength she could muster just to nod her head. It really wasn't okay, but she felt backed against the wall. She couldn't even be mad at Cheryl; after all, she had no clue of what was really going on.

Smiling in relief, Cheryl gave her a sideways hug, and then headed to the buffet table to get something to eat. Once again, Michelle caught her friend's eye, and Katrina walked over to her and stood by her side. Together they looked on helplessly as Cheryl handed a plate of food to Freddie. Cheryl then motioned to Michelle's husband as she walked by.

Michelle held her breath. What was she doing? Was she introducing

41

David to Freddie? Michelle cringed as she watched her husband shake hands with her blackmailer. She felt a little light-headed and walked to the table to take a seat. Katrina followed close behind her. Michelle looked back out into the house again and Freddie was smiling at her and Katrina. The two women could only sit and observe; unable to speak. Freddie stared at them for a long while, but they averted their eyes. When he walked toward David to start a conversation, Michelle stared hard, trying to read his lips. She wondered what he was saying to her husband and prayed a silent prayer that their conversation would come to an abrupt end.

The doorbell rang, and Michelle rose slowly to answer with Katrina following behind once more. When the person on the other side identified himself, Michelle opened the door with a huge smile on her face. Katrina's wide grin matched hers.

Ed stepped inside the room. He returned the smiles of the two women and patted them both on the shoulders before walking deeper into the house and directly to the area where Freddie stood, now alone having finished his brief exchange with David. The ladies saw Ed reach into his pocket and pull out his official badge before flashing it in Freddie's face. This unfolding show had Michelle and Katrina nodding their heads in sheer satisfaction.

Freddie looked the detective in the eyes and the two men talked briefly before Freddie slowly walked away and out the front door. Ed looked across the room at the two women and gave them the thumbs-up sign, with them smiling hard in return. Then Ed walked to the table to fix himself a cup of punch. He took the time to drink the beverage before waving and leaving the party.

"Brother Ed is on the case," said Michelle as she stood next to Katrina.

"You got that right," replied her friend.

The ladies swiftly walked to the Christmas tree where their daughters were sitting together. "What a nice party," said Michelle as she began singing with the Christmas music that was being played.

Katrina swayed to the music with her hands on her daughter's shoulder.

Freddie was so completely out of their thoughts. Christmas was now bright and beautiful and righteousness reigned in the house of David and Michelle Davidson. From the moment Freddie was excommunicated until the last guest said goodnight, the evening was beautiful.

That evening, after a successful holiday party, Michelle sat on the edge of her bed with a head full of thoughts. David had told her that growing up, he hated his name. David Davidson was like some kind of mini tongue twister, and the children in his class made all kinds of games with it. His parents had told him they thought the name was cute and clever when they settled on it. Now that he was a grown man, he told Michelle he loved the uniqueness of his name. He said it was one that wasn't easily forgettable, and he felt that was a quality that was an asset in his business.

Michelle loved her husband's name and the man himself. She loved him too much to let someone like Freddie make her lose him, but if she were to keep her secret from him, she had to cover some of the tracks that her dealings with Freddie had made. One of the first things she needed to do was build her savings account back up before David noticed it had been depleted. In the last few days, she'd been tossing a few ideas around in her head.

Katrina needed someone to stay with Kayla until she got home from work, and she had told Michelle she would pay her for doing that. Michelle thought if she could get maybe a couple more children to keep, she could open up an aftercare program for a few hours a day. That way, she would still be there for her own daughter when she got out of school.

She decided to run the business venture by her husband and see what he thought about it. The idea of running an aftercare program became increasingly appealing to her. David had wanted Michelle to be there for Sasha when she came home from school like his mother had been for him as a child. If Michelle started her own in-home childcare program, it would allow for her to be there for their daughter and earn a little money at the same time. It was a win-win situation.

The phone rang and Michelle reached to answer it. "Hello?"

"You want to go to Peace Diner soon?" asked Katrina from the other end of the line. "I need to talk, and you know you're my talking partner."

Chapter 8

A few days later, the two women talked over warm beverages at the table where they'd been seated. It was lunchtime for many of the residents who worked nearby. This time of the day, the church's popular restaurant tended to draw its largest crowd.

Michelle gently blew into her hot chocolate before chuckling and saying, "You must have the best job in the world. You're off more than I am, and I don't work."

Katrina smiled. She'd lost count of the number of times she had gotten that from Michelle. "I told you I have flexible hours."

* * * * * * *

David Davidson sat at the desk in his office, staring at a picture of his wife and daughter. He thought to himself that they sure made him happy and his life complete. He placed the picture on his desk and reached into his desk drawer, pulling out the photo of Davita. His daughters shared a strong resemblance to each other, and both of them looked like him. Would they ever meet? In spite of the situation, he hoped that they one day would.

His secretary had left for an early lunch. David had sent her away early because he was expecting a call from Nicola. She was always so upset and jealous of Michelle and Sasha. He had never missed a child support payments, but there just seemed to be no way to make that woman happy. As sticky of a situation that he knew it could potentially become, he planned to keep the promise he'd made to himself to tell Michelle about his other daughter after the New Year.

The phone on David's desk rang twice before he reached to answer. It was Nicola, and the tone of her voice wasn't pleasant. He kept quiet and listened to her rant and rave, as usual.

* * * * * * *

"So you really want to take care of Kayla?" asked Katrina just as their meals were being delivered to the table.

"Yeah. I was thinking that maybe I could get a few other children and start an aftercare business." Michelle thought about it as she spoke. She could help her friend and others and put a jingle in her pocket as well.

They'd ordered a tuna fish sandwich on toast, oven fries, and a soda. As soon as they had graced their food, the conversation continued.

"I want some eggnog ice cream," said Katrina as she chewed on her first bite. "Are you supposed to eat fish with ice cream?"

Michelle had heard from somewhere that the two shouldn't be eaten together. She dismissed the thought with a wave of her hand and decided to join Katrina in ordering ice cream. "I'm told their eggnog ice cream is the best in the city."

By the time they finished off their lunch, their desserts were being delivered to the table. The ice cream lived up to its reputation. Michelle stuck her spoon into hers and quickly brought it to her mouth, closing her eyes in delight. "This is so good" she manage to say.

Katrina nodded in agreement having savored her first dose too.

"I think Freddie and Leo are history," said Michelle. "Did you see how fast Freddie left the party after talking to Brother Ed?"

Katrina began laughing; first softly, and then her laughter grew to being almost uncontrollable. Michelle joined in. Tears formed in her eyes and soon rolled down her cheeks. It had been quite a while since she'd laughed this long or hard. Katrina always had this effect on her. That was a big part of the reason why she was her best friend.

* * * * * * *

David's phone call with Nicola had just entered its second half hour, and she had finally finished ranting. It was his turn to talk now.

"I'm going to tell Michelle about our daughter," he revealed. "I plan to do it right after the first of the year." He didn't get an immediate response from Nicola, but he knew she'd heard him. He had already paid his child support for the month. Nicola was trying to get some additional money from him, and he didn't have it this time.

When David told Nicola about his strained cash flow, she responded with, "What? Make Michelle get a job; she's not disable." Nicola had used that same snide remark in the past when she wanted extra money. She always seemed envious of Michelle and even Sasha, for that matter.

Nicola wanted Michelle to get a job so the extra income could be given to her for Davita. As far as she was concerned, Sasha already had everything she needed; she never wanted for anything. It was time for David's other daughter to cash in. But did Nicola really have Davita's best interest in mind, or was she just being a greedy, jealous, and vindictive woman?

When his workday ended and he arrived home, Michelle met him at the door like she did most evenings. Somehow she always managed to hear his key in the lock. David smiled when he entered the house and placed his coat and briefcase on the table in the hall.

"I'm glad to see you too," he said placing his arms around his wife.

They stayed that way for a few seconds before Michelle pulled away and reached for his hand. She held it tight and led him to the couch in the living room. "I'm thinking about working a few hours a day," she told him. "I'll be working from home, so Sasha won't get neglected."

David's smile widened. "I think it's a great idea," he said. "Of course, I need to hear a little more."

Michelle threw her arms around her husband and didn't want to ever let go. He was truly a prince. All he wanted was for her to be happy. God could not have blessed her with a better husband.

With David's full support, Michelle hit the ground running. The days that followed had her shopping for small, but important items that would make her home more appealing to parents and children. Michelle wasted no time organizing her aftercare program, and with the help of Katrina, she had registered three children with Sasha making four.

As a part of her aftercare services, Michelle would pick her charges up from school and keep them at her house for a few hours until their parents came to get them. She was thrilled that her plan was coming to fruition. The new entrepreneur quickly got into the flow of her home based business. At the rate things were going, it wouldn't be long before she could replenish her savings. And having a job she enjoyed doing made the process even more rewarding.

One evening while caring for her group of children, there was a knock on the door. "Who is it?" Michelle called.

"My name is Ms. Brooks," said the voice on the other side, "and I'm interested in you caring for my daughter."

Michelle slowly opened the door and talked to the woman for a few minutes. Then she said, "Let me go get a form for you to complete. I'll be right back." Michelle locked the door once more before walking to the den where she kept her business paperwork and getting a registration form from the table drawer. It didn't take long before she was back at the door and handing the woman the form and her business card. Michelle smiled at the little girl after she'd said goodbye to Ms. Brooks, and the child smiled back. Michelle and the woman agreed to talk by telephone that night to further discuss the potential childcare arrangements.

Michelle watched Ms. Brooks and her daughter until they walked out of the gate. She then returned to her charges who were sitting on the rug coloring in their coloring books. Michelle smiled at the thought that she might have another child to add to her group. That would make five, including her daughter. A fifth name would fill her roster; she didn't want any more than that.

That night, Michelle took the cordless phone in a quiet area of the house and talked to Ms. Brooks some more. She asked numerous questions about her and her daughter, Davita. Ms. Brooks had a few questions of her own, and by the end of the conversation, they agreed she could bring the girl the next morning before going to work.

"How's business going?" asked Katrina as she dropped Kayla off at Michelle's house the following day.

Michelle responded with a smile. "It's going pretty good. I got another child just yesterday. She'll be starting today."

Katrina grinned and gave her friend a hug before turning to leave for work.

"Watch night service is at 10 PM. tomorrow," Michelle reminded just before Katrina exited the house.

Her childcare business seemed to breathe new life in her. It almost felt like a form of ministry. Each day, Michelle prayed with the children, and they prayed by themselves sometimes too. Her sitting service was a faith based one, and Michelle had explained to each parent upfront that they would be praying and reading Bible stories. It was written into the contract that every guardian had to sign too. To her delight, not one parent had complained.

There was a knock on the door and Michelle immediately knew that it was Ms. Brooks and Davita. They were right on time. "Come on in," said Michelle as she opened the door wide enough for them to enter.

"Thank you," said Ms. Brooks as she walked in holding her daughter's hand.

"I baked some fresh banana-nut muffins this morning, Ms. Brooks," Michelle said. "Would you like one?"

"Yes, I'd love a muffin, and please call me Nicola."

Michelle walked into the kitchen, picked up a napkin from the table, and wrapped a warm muffin inside. She walked back into the front room and handed it to Nicola Brooks. The woman smiled as she accepted it, and then she kissed her daughter on the forehead and waved goodbye before leaving.

What a pleasant woman, thought Michelle as she watched her leave. And Davita was just as sweet as her mom. The seven-year-old had a flawless first day, getting along great with the other children. She fitted in like a hand in a glove, adding the fifth finger to the hand.

Chapter 9

New Year's Day had come and gone, and the children would be back in school soon. David was devising a plan. Michelle wouldn't be a full-time caregiver to the children she kept anymore. She would just be doing her aftercare program. David sat in his office thinking of his first move. He planned to keep his New Year's resolution to tell Michelle about his other daughter. For days, he had been thinking about how he would break the news to her.

This weekend would be the best time; maybe after church services, he reasoned. David promised himself that he wouldn't get cold feet this time like he had done all the other times. Maybe his two daughters could have a relationship together, and Davita could come visit them sometimes. Michelle might even grow fond of the child.

He knew Nicola was a jealous woman, but maybe even she would bury the hatchet for her daughter's sake and allow visits to his house. Was this going to turn into something ugly? Would Michelle be able to forgive him? Would Nicola stop playing the victim? David had all sorts of questions swirling around in his head, but he knew that all them would be answered this weekend when he had that talk with his wife.

* * * * * * *

On Wednesday evening, right after Bible study, Michelle received a call from the mother of one of the children she cared for. It was Nicola Brooks on the line, and as she spoke all Michelle could do was listen helplessly to what the woman had to say. The telephone call concerned Nicola's daughter in a roundabout way. When the conversation ended and her telephone was resting back on the nightstand beside her bed, Michelle felt like she was hyperventilating. She tried to calm herself, and to a small degree, she succeeded. But her legs felt weak prompting her to remain on her bed in a seated position for fear she'd fall if she tried to stand.

At least an hour passed before Michelle heard David entering the house. She could hear his footsteps as he trotted up the stairs that led to the bedroom where she still sat in a daze. He entered the room, rounded the mattress, and kissed her on the forehead just like he'd done so many times before. But the response he got in return was anything but normal.

Michelle held out her hand and balled it up into a fist. He stood next to her and looked into her eyes, and what he saw made him take several long steps backward.

"What is it?" he asked in an almost panicked voice.

Michelle responded by attacking the mattress with her fists. She hit it hard, then harder. And in a few seconds she was in full attack mode, pounding against the mattress as if it had committed an unforgivable crime.

David backed up even farther; he had never seen his wife like that before. "What is it?" he called out again.

Slowly looking upward to face him, Michelle's teeth were clinched and her words were slow when she asked, "Is Davita Brooks your daughter?"

David looked up as if he were in a deep thought for a few seconds, and then his eyes slowly met his wife's. "Yes, she is," he admitted. "But please let me explain a few things."

Without hesitation, Michelle shouted, "Get out of here, David! Get out of this house . . . *now!*"

He looked at her and wanted to demand a chance to explain himself, but David knew she probably needed some time alone to calm down, so he swallowed back his words and walked toward the door without a protest. But before he left the room he turned to her and spoke in a quiet tone. "We need to talk as soon as possible." With that said, he was out of the bedroom, down the stairs, and out the front door.

Michelle hadn't left her seated position on their bed. She heard the front door close behind David's exit, and then she heard his car leave the yard. Still half numbed by what Nicola had told her, Michelle didn't even know how to feel. It was like a nightmare. Only there was no way to snap out of it because she was already awake. It was hard to fathom that a day that had started out so well, had ended so badly. David had a child he'd never told her about. It was almost too much for her mind to comprehend.

To make matters worse, she had unknowingly taken care of his child. Nicola must be some kind of sick puppy. What kind of mother comes to a woman's house and employs her to take care of an outside child that she doesn't even know her husband has? Yes, this woman was twisted and scheming. She was vindictive and rotten as an apple with a worm inside.

But the funny thing was that even after the woman's disclosure, and as angry as her words had made Michelle; she couldn't bring herself to throw things at David. She could attack the mattress, but she had never lifted a hand to harm her husband, and she didn't think she could. Maybe she would have felt better now if she had thrown a shoe at his head or something, but somehow the thought to physically attack him hadn't even entered her mind.

* * * * * * *

Nicola Brooks sat in her car outside of Michelle's house. She'd parked just far enough away so that her vehicle wouldn't be spotted, but close enough so that she had a clear view of the front door. She had seen David go into the house, and not much later, she had seen he had left in a huff. The big smile on her face was evidence of the satisfaction the visual discord had brought to her heart.

Raising Davita alone had been difficult for Nicola. Did David even care about her feelings? Did he ever even give her a thought when he was at home with his perfectly little family? Her smile broadened as she cranked up the engine of her car. *I bet he's thinking about me now*, she thought as she drove away from the house and down the street.

* * * * * * *

The phone rang in Michelle's bedroom and had been ringing for a while. It rang six or seven times before she finally picked it up, but even then, she didn't say anything.

"Michelle, is that you?" asked Katrina from the other end of the line.

Michelle made some mumbling sounds, but her words weren't intelligible.

Katrina spoke again. "Michelle, are you all right? Are you sick or something?" When there was no immediate response, she added, "Girl, speak to me."

Michelle made more sounds, but she couldn't speak. She had heard Katrina ask her if she was sick, but for some reason she couldn't answer her. Was she really ill, she wondered to herself?

"I'll be over in twenty minutes," shouted Katrina before returning the phone to its base. Before preparing to leave her home, Katrina first called Cheryl and asked her to go over and check on their friend. Cheryl could get to Michelle much more quickly than she could. Katrina told her Michelle sounded like she might be sick and that she was on her way to the house to check on her as well. Ending the call with Cheryl, Katrina grabbed the spare keys to Michelle's house before leaving her home. They both had keys to one another house in case of an emergency.

* * * * * * *

Cheryl stood at Michelle's front door knocking and repeatedly calling out her name. Michelle heard the knocking, but remained sitting on the bed in what felt like a trance.

Sasha ran into her parents' bedroom and grabbed her mother's hand. "We got to get the door, Mommy," she said. "Somebody's knocking at the door hard. It might be Daddy."

It better not be Daddy, thought Michelle. She took a moment to gather herself before getting up. She had to not only gather her wits and good senses, but she also had to make sure her legs would be steady enough to hold her up. Once she was sure that her muscles were intact, Michelle cautiously followed her daughter down the stairs and to the front door.

Cheryl walked in as soon as the door opened. "Did you hear me knocking on the door all that time? Are you all right? Katrina told me to check on you."

Michelle managed to nod her head. Seeing her daughter standing next to her gave her a little strength. She had to swallow a few times before finding her words. "I'm okay; I'm just tired, that's all," she said.

Cheryl patted Michelle's hand as they stood near the front door. "I'll stay with you until Katrina gets here; okay?"

Michelle nodded again, and then reached for her daughter's hand and held it. Michelle led her daughter to the couch in the living room and Cheryl followed behind. Not long after they all had taken their seats, they heard a key in the lock, and then the door opened.

"Is that Daddy?" asked Sasha.

Katrina soon turned the corner and walked into the living room. She stared at the three of them sitting on the couch.

Cheryl rose and walked to meet Katrina midway to the living room floor. "Y'all call me if you need me." She gave Michelle and Sasha a small wave before exiting the house.

Katrina walked to the couch and took a seat on the other side of Michelle. "Are you all right? You almost scared me to death."

Michelle looked at her daughter. "Sasha, would you go get Mommy a glass of water?" She waited until the child was out of the room before she spoke again. "David is cheating on me," she whispered to Katrina. "He has a daughter with another woman."

Katrina gasped. "What? Are you for real?'"

Sasha returned with a glass of water in her hand before any more could be said. Michelle accepted the glass and took in a couple of sips before placing the glass on the coffee table. She looked at her daughter. "You look tired, Sasha. Let's get you ready for bed."

"I'm gonna make a quick phone call," Katrina said as Michelle and Sasha walked out of the room and upstairs to the master bedroom,

Sasha was fast asleep in a matter of minutes in the empty space on David's side of the bed. Michelle wanted her daughter near her for comfort tonight. Confident that she was sound asleep, Michelle crept quietly out of the room and made her way back downstairs where Katrina was waiting for her in the kitchen. She had made a snack of microwave popcorn that she'd poured into a bowl. The two women sat at the table.

"My husband said it's okay if I spend the night here," said Katrina.

Michelle smiled at her friend. "Thank Frank for me. I really appreciate you staying."

Katrina returned the smile and patted her hand. For the next few moments, they snacked on the popcorn in silence.

Michelle wondered what would become of her and David, but the thought almost paralyzed her, so she dropped it from her mind. She wanted to talk more about it, but not now. They could talk in the morning; this wound was too new and painful to examine now. "Katrina, you need to get some rest for work tomorrow," commented Michelle.

Katrina looked at her like she was out of her mind. "Girl, I'm not going to work tomorrow. I'm going to be shadowing you all day."

Michelle didn't say a word to try and discourage her. Right now, she welcomed being shadowed. At that moment, that flexible schedule that she'd kidded Katrina about so many times before felt like more of a blessing for her than it was for her friend.

Katrina was not telling a lie. The following day, she went everywhere that Michelle went. They had taken Sasha to school and were approaching the gate to Michelle's house, when they caught a glimpse of Cheryl, standing at the edge of the sidewalk in front of her house two door down, waving them over. Michelle walked over to Cheryl house with Katrina on her heels.

When they were at her front steps, Cheryl offered them a seat on the porch. "Hey, I baked some cookies. Do you all want any?"

Katrina smiled and Michelle nodded her head up and down.

"Okay, wait here; I'll be right back," said Cheryl. It was kind of early in the morning for cookies, but Cheryl was a master baker, and her friends weren't about to turn down one of her signature tasty desserts. Minutes later, Cheryl returned to the front porch carrying a plastic food container. She sat down between Michelle and Katrina and popped off the lid. "Help yourselves, ladies," she offered.

They reached into the container one at a time and pulled out an oatmeal-raisin cookie. Michelle brought her cookie to her mouth and took a bite. She closed her eyes as the warm, chewy cookie seemed to melt on her tongue. Katrina was taking small bites and savoring the sweet treat with each chew.

Cheryl looked at the two women and smiled. "I'm thinking about selling cookies," she informed them. "I'm taking a two-week vacation from my job to get my cookie business started."

Michelle reached for a second cookie. The smell was almost as good as the cookie itself.

Cheryl spoke again. "I need y'all to rate the cookie for me; on a scale of one to ten."

Michelle finished the cookie she was working on before answering.

"These taste better than store-bought cookies to me. I'll give them a nine."

Cheryl turned to face Katrina for her answer.

Katrina gave her the thumbs-up sign and said, "I agree with Michelle. I'll give them a nine too."

Cheryl giggled and rose from her seat. "Thanks, ladies. And thank you, Jesus. I'm going into the cookie business."

Cheryl's front door suddenly opened and out walked Freddie. He eyed his cousin and did not acknowledge the other two women.

"Freddie, it wouldn't hurt you to speak to people," said Cheryl.

Freddie was almost out of the yard when he finally stopped, turned around, and waved before swiftly walking out the gate. Michelle and Katrina exchanged looks. Cheryl apologized to them for her cousin's behavior. She also informed them that she'd told Freddie he must go to church if he wanted to stay at her house. Michelle wanted to get to the safety of her own house, and she could tell that Katrina wanted to get there as well.

Michelle stood up. "Cheryl, the cookies were great, but we've got to go now."

Cheryl nodded and handed Michelle the plastic container that held the remaining cookies.

Katrina stood as well, and she and Michelle walked out of the yard and up the street to Michelle's house. They almost raced to the door once inside the yard. When the front door closed behind them, Michelle was the first to speak.

"My husband has a child with another woman, and a man I made a mistake with won't go away." She let out a long sigh, and then continued as they entered the kitchen. "How much more can I take?"

Katrina placed her hand on Michelle's shoulder and left it there for a few seconds. That seemed to calm her some.

"I'll get through this with the help of God and you, Katrina," said Michelle while displaying a weary smile. She walked away long enough to get some tea to go with the leftover cookies, and then joined Katrina at the table.

* * * * * * *

That Sunday, Michelle walked to church with Cheryl and Sasha. They opened the door to enter the sanctuary and were greeted by Brother Earl and the first lady, Mary Jenkins. Over the years, the pastor's wife had gotten lots of ribbing for her name being Mary, like the mother of Jesus.

"Good morning, ladies," she said looking at each of them. Her eyes stopped on Michelle. "Why are you wearing such a sour face coming into the Lord's house?" she asked

Michelle felt guilty for looking so sad, and a small smile appeared on her face.

"That's a lot better. How's your aftercare business going?" inquired the first lady.

Michelle told her that it had been going well, but she also requested that Mary make time to talk to her privately real soon. The first lady agreed, and Michelle, Cheryl, and Sasha walked down the red carpet aisle until they reached the fourth pew from the front and took their seats.

Katrina was already seated there and smiled at them as they shared her pew. Michelle wondered if the first lady noticed that David was not with her today. It wouldn't surprise her if she had; Mary Jenkins didn't miss much.

* * * * * * *

Two weeks came and went, and Michelle hadn't heard from David. She went to church on Sundays, and he went to Bible study on Wednesdays. They didn't plan it that way because there hadn't been any communication between them, but that's how it was unfolding. Katrina had been a huge help to her. She helped Michelle keep her aftercare business afloat. There was no way Michelle could have done it without God and her best friend.

Michelle didn't know how this adultery thing worked. Did the husband call and explain himself and the wife just wait for that call? David's and her relationship had been so good over the years; she would bet her last nickel that he felt the same way. Had she been living in a fake, fairytale world and had awaken to the truth?

"Looks like it now," she said aloud while shaking her head.

Michelle sat on her bed clearing out her nightstand. Since her troubles with David and that awful person, Freddie, she had picked up the habit of cleaning to release stress. The phone rang, interrupting her chore. "Hello?" She propped the phone between her ear and her shoulder so that she could continue to work.

"Hello, Michelle; I could come by if you need anything," said a familiar voice from the other end of the line.

Michelle smiled at her best friend's consideration. "I'm fine, Katrina. You're the best, but I order you to spend some time with your husband and daughter."

* * * * * * *

A full month would pass before Michelle would hear from David. It felt more like a year.

"Don't worry about the bills or any of that. I've taken care of all of it," he said almost as soon as she answered the phone.

Michelle kept quiet and listened as David continued to speak. "I miss you," he said after a weary sigh, "and I miss Sasha. Do you think it's possible I can see her soon?"

Michelle didn't want to keep him from his daughter. "Sure. When would you like to see her?"

"I'd like to see Sasha *and* Sasha's mother. How about today?" David's tone was warm.

He may have wanted to see Michelle, but she wasn't ready to see him yet. She informed him that he could see their daughter tomorrow after school. He reluctantly accepted her offer to grant half his wish, but before they ended the call he told Michelle that they needed to talk soon

Michelle gently hung up the phone and rose from her seat on the bed. She looked around for something to clean. Cleaning was her way to relax, and right now, she wanted that so badly; like a teenager wanting to drive their parent's car.

The following day, Sasha was away visiting with her father, and it gave her mom the opportunity she needed. Michelle had worked her magic on the entire house, and it was white glove clean. As she stood back and admired her own work, she thought about something that made her smile. As disappointed as she was in David, she still liked the idea of Sasha spending time with her father. No matter how mad she got at him, she would never ever deny his request to see his daughter. But he didn't have to know that, and she would never tell him.

A thought suddenly popped into Michelle's mind. What if David took Sasha around Davita and was told that they were biological sisters? She shook her head to try and banish the thought. Nah, he'd probably given the girl's mother a verbal beat down by now. David hadn't been happy at all that Nicola had purposefully foiled his plans to confess.

Michelle tried to shift her thoughts elsewhere. There was no use thinking about things that would never happen. Besides, it wasn't like the two children hadn't already met. Sasha had played with Davita in her aftercare program. The girls knew each other, but Sasha didn't know the child was her half-sister.

* * * * * * *

David and Sasha sat side by side on a bench at the park. They were taking picture with a disposable camera.

"Smile, honey," said David, and then he laughed as Sasha struck a pose.

She gave a huge smile that showed off her missing front tooth, and her dad captured the picture. David could never have too many pictures of his darling daughter. Mentally, he made plans to have professional pictures taken of her in the near future.

"Can I take some of you, Daddy?" Sasha asked, reaching for the Polaroid.

Without hesitation, David handed her the camera and showed her how to use it. She seemed proud of her newly learned skills as she snapped a few pictures of him.

Unbeknownst to the father and daughter, someone was watching their every move from a park bench not too far away. It wasn't planned; Nicola and Davita just happened to be at the same park and at the same time. It was one heck of a coincidence.

"Isn't that Sasha from your aftercare program?" Nicola pointed as she spoke to her daughter.

"That looks like her," said the girl.

At Nicola's urging, Davita jumped up and ran to where Sasha and David were sitting. David almost slid off the bench when the girl approached them, but soon a huge smile appeared on his face. He reached for Davita, but she went to sit next to Sasha instead. In spite of the circumstances, David was overjoyed to have his two daughters together, and an unmovable smile lit up his face.

Then the ugly reality hit him. If Davita was there it could only mean *that woman* couldn't be too far away. The thought of it removed his unmovable smile in an instant. And as soon as his smile left, Nicola appeared. David was still upset at her for breaking the news of Davita's paternity to Michelle.

"Hi, David I hope you're not mad at me," said the woman as soon as she came to a stop in front of him. "I bring our daughter to the park almost every day. I didn't know I'd see you here."

David was furious with the woman; he thought she was a horrible human being. But sitting there watching his two daughters interact; he melted like a snowman in one hundred degree heat.

Nicola observed how he looked at their daughter, and she planned to play it for all that is was worth. "This is such a beautiful scene," she said. "A father and his two daughters. It doesn't get much better than this."

David smiled proudly as he sat on the bench staring fondly at his daughters. Nicola pulled an instant camera out of her tote bag and positioned it so that she could take a picture of herself and David.

"Nicola, maybe you shouldn't have done that," said David in a low stern voice.

"The scene was so beautiful and loving," said the woman, "and I just couldn't help myself." She immediately motioned for Davita to move closer to her father and the girl obeyed. She instructed Sasha to do the same. Once they were in position, she snapped the picture. "Davita," she called to her daughter, "take a picture of me before I run out of film."

Davita rose from her seat on the bench and walked to where her mother was sitting and snapped a few photos. Nicola purposely tried to sit as close to David as possible.

"David, take your daughters to the toys and sit on the bench and watch them,"

Like some kind of robot, David rose from the bench and did as Nicola had instructed him. She saw Sasha's backpack that was lying on the bench near her and reached to unzip the side compartment. She placed some photos in it and quickly zipped it back up. Nicola smiled as she looked at David playing with his daughters on the sliding board. She felt like she was at a family outing with David and their daughter; she thought that Sasha was a treat as well. Minutes later, David and his girls returned to the bench.

"I'm glad Davita got to spend time with her father," said Nicola once everyone was seated on the bench. "It's good for her as well as you, David."

David gave her a slight smile. He was not done with her for telling Michelle about their daughter before he could, but at the moment, he felt joy for the opportunity for his daughters to be together and to be with him.

Nicola decided to leave. She didn't want to wear out her welcome, but she didn't want to go far and definitely not for long. "David, I had a great time this evening," she said glancing at her watch, "but I think I need to get Davita, home."

David smiled and gave Davita a warm huge before Nicola and the girl walked away. He watched them until they vanished from his view. Soon David and Sasha exited the park too, and he drove her home and delivered her back to her front porch.

Michelle stood in the entrance of the front door and watched as David waved to her, and then walked away. She stood motionless as he walked out of the gate and back to his vehicle.

Sasha was smiling and waving at him. "Bye, Daddy. I'll see you tomorrow."

Michelle didn't know Sasha would be going with him again tomorrow. Nobody had asked her permission for that to happen. She took Sasha by the hand and led her into the house. It was at that time that

Sasha told her mother about all the fun she'd had at the park with her daddy . . . and Davita . . . and Ms. Brooks.

Michelle questioned her several times to make sure the child wasn't dreaming up some kind of make believe story about spending time with Davita and Ms. Brooks at the park. Her gut feeling told her that what Sasha had said was true; her daughter wasn't prone to making things up. But did this mean David was pursuing a relationship with Nicola? That was certainly what it sounded like, but Michelle knew firsthand how cunning Nicola could be.

Michelle and Sasha walked into the kitchen to eat the meal Michelle had prepared. After dinner, they sat and chatted awhile, mostly about school work. Michelle didn't want to get her daughter involved in her personal problems.

"When is your spelling test?" asked Michelle as they sat at the kitchen table they'd just cleared.

"Wednesday," Sasha answered. "I know most of the words already."

Michelle smiled and then gave her daughter a hug. "Let's study for a little while so you can get a fantastic grade on your test."

Sasha nodded and stood up from the chair and walked out of the kitchen to get her school work. Minutes later, she returned carrying her backpack and reclaimed her seat at the table.

"You study for a while, and then I'll quiz you," said Michelle as she watched her pull her list of spelling words from her bag.

Sasha nodded and immediately began studying the sheet of paper.

Meanwhile, Michelle lifted up the backpack and unzipped the compartment searching for something to write with. "No pencil," she mumbled while unzipping the other side. She didn't find a pencil there either, so she turned the backpack around to inspect the compartment on the front. "What is this?" she asked as she lifted the photos from their hiding place.

Michelle took a look at the pictures, and then she took a longer look "What?" Her voice had reached a screaming pitch, and she dropped the pictures on the kitchen floor.

"What's wrong, Mommy?" asked Sasha. Michelle's sudden outburst had startled her. She followed the direction of where her mom's eyes were locked and looked at the pictures that rested near her feet. "That's Ms. Brooks, and Davita, Daddy, and me," she explained as though Michelle wasn't aware of their identity. "I told you we had fun at the park, didn't I?"

Michelle bent down to pick up the pictures from the floor and held them in her hand, before straightening her back and standing to her full height. She tried to look and sound as calm as possible. "You study for the test, and Mommy will be back in a little while to quiz you."

Michelle walked out of the kitchen with the photos in her hand. Once out of her daughter's view, she stared at the photo of David and Nicola sitting near each other on the park bench. Sasha was also in the picture, but wasn't sitting very close to them. They looked like a family in that snapshot. Anyone walking by would have thought they were a couple with their daughter at the park.

Michelle wanted to turn away, but she couldn't stop staring at the image before her. David looked genuinely happy in the photo, and Nicola looked like she was having the time of her life. Had that tricky Nicola planned the whole thing with her conniving self, or was it David who desired a relationship with that woman?

"Mommy, I'm ready," called Sasha. "I'm ready for you to quiz me."

Tucking the photos in the pocket of her robe, Michelle walked back into the kitchen. The picture was now out of her sight, but she would never be able to get that image out of her mind; not even if she lived to be a thousand years old. Michelle sent Sasha to her room to study further, after they'd done a brief quiz together. Michelle wanted to find that woman's phone number. She opened a cabinet drawer and located the book where she kept the contact information of all the children she serviced.

"Hello," said Nicola, answering after only the second ring.

"Don't you hello me," returned Michelle. "Why did you put those pictures in my daughter's backpack?" She didn't wait for an answer. "Look; I don't want to jack you up with my fist because that's not my style."

"I . . . Uh . . . I . . ."

62

Michelle heard the woman fumbling for words, but she wasn't about to give her a chance to find them. Besides, she wasn't done talking. "Knocking you out isn't my style, but I will if you force me and if you keep messing with me and my family!" Having said that, Michelle slammed the phone back on its base and took a seat at the table, slowly shutting her eyes. But even with her eyes closed, she could still see those photos of her husband and Nicola together.

David phoned that night and asked if he could get Sasha again the following day. Michelle told him that he could and ended the conversation as quickly as possible.

* * * * * * *

Nicola Brooks laid in her bed that night thinking about her outing with David and the children earlier in the day. The memory of how close she had felt to him made her smile. Especially when she thought of how it seemed like he felt the same. He didn't even seem mad at her for telling Michelle about him being Davita's father.

The thought of Michelle's call that blasted her out didn't even faze her. As far as Nicola was concerned, that call just proved that Michelle not only knew she was coming after David, but would eventually land him.

Chapter 10

It was a phone call that Michelle hadn't looked forward to making and a conversation she hadn't looked forward to having. She couldn't get herself to do it last night, but the next morning, it was at the top of her "to do" list. "Could you meet me at the diner?" she said into the phone. "You wouldn't believe what I experienced yesterday."

An hour later, she and Katrina were sitting at a booth at Peace Diner, and Michelle was showing her friend the photos she'd discovered in her daughter's backpack.

One by one, Katrina accepted them from Michelle's hand. "Oh no," she said. Then it was, "Ah-uh." And that was followed by another, "Oh no." Katrina slowly placed each photo on the table.

Michelle eyes grew large as she spoke. "Can you believe that?"

Katrina couldn't, and she shook her head at the thought of it all. "You know Nicola is as sly as they come. This probably is all her doing, and things are not as happy as they look in these pictures."

Michelle knew that her friend was probably correct, but still—

"That woman has more tricks up her sleeve than a magician." Katrina's words broke into Michelle's thoughts. "I'll bet you any amount of money she staged the whole thing."

Michelle knew that Katrina was explaining things as they actually were, but Nicola had gotten under her skin and given her the itchy, creepy creeps. Michelle informed Katrina of the heated phone call she had made to Nicola. Katrina smiled at that and gave her best friend the thumbs-up sign.

Katrina began gathering her purse. "I'm sorry, Michelle, but I have to leave for work soon. You did good."

A smile crossed Michelle's face. Katrina had a job, but she rarely mentioned work, and it seemed to Michelle that she rarely went. Katrina had always made time for her, regardless of her job.

Katrina scooted out of the booth and stood by the table. "I got to make up some time before the pay period ends. Stay strong; I'll see you at Bible study tonight."

She reached forward and gave Michelle a hug before leaving the diner. Michelle spotted the waitress and waved her over. She needed some reward food for finally putting Nicola in her place.

* * * * * * *

Katrina looked at her watch at the end of the workday and smiled. She didn't have many more hours to make up. Another day of work, another skipped lunch, and she would have enough hours for the current pay period. She walked out of the office and strolled to the elevator. Once outside, she hopped on the bus for home so that she could get ready for Bible study. Upon arriving home, she put her key in the door, and walked into her house.

"Hey, baby," greeted Frank as she entered. "I gave Kayla a snack, and now she's upstairs taking a nap."

Katrina kicked off her shoes near the front door and placed her bag on the hall table. Now that her hands were empty, she walked over to her husband and gave him a tight hug. She closed her eyes and immediately felt soothed. He had taken part of the day off to care for their daughter.

Katrina slowly pulled away from the embrace and reached for her husband's hand and led him to the kitchen. She quickly prepared an easy meal of left-over chicken, mashed potatoes, and green beans, and Frank sat at the kitchen table and chatted with her the entire time. Even after they finished eating, they sat discussing their day. Then the conversation turned in a different direction.

"How is Michelle doing?" asked Frank. "Are she and David trying to get back together?"

Katrina reached for a glass of water and took a sip before answering. "Michelle is okay, but there are no plans to get back together as far as I know."

Frank looked at her and shook his head. "David really loves her. I hope she knows that."

Katrina nodded her head in agreement with him. "I think she knows he loves her, but. . ." Her words trailed off as she thought. Katrina knew that Nicola was trying to score points with David, and if Michelle didn't nip it in the bud there would be even more major trouble in her marriage. Trouble that couldn't be repaired, stitched, or mended in any fashion.

Katrina thought for a moment. She and Michelle told each other almost everything that went on in their personal lives; stuff they didn't share with other people. Men must be the same. They must share their secrets with their buddies as well. She proceeded with caution. "Frank, does . . . does David ever discuss his marriage with you?"

Frank didn't speak for a moment, but then his head started a slow nod. "Yeah, sometimes he discusses his marriage with me."

Katrina waited for him to continue. He had to know that he couldn't stop there. He had to know that she wanted to hear all the details.

He took a breath before saying, "I'll just say this. David wants to save his marriage, but when a woman banishes a man outside, sometimes she gives outside forces the opportunity to get in the way."

Katrina sat and thought about his words. She knew what he meant about *outside forces*. That would be Nicola. The woman didn't want Michelle and David's marriage to continue. She had a lot of tricks up her sleeve, and by pushing him away, Michelle had placed David right where Nicola wanted him . . . outside. Michelle needed to watch this woman carefully because her marriage depended on it.

Katrina rose from her seat stood behind her husband's chair. She lowered her hands and began massaging his shoulder blades, and he sighed and relaxed in comfort. Katrina didn't want anything coming between her and her husband. She appreciated him and valued him above everyone but God. No doubt about it, God was numero uno; number one. Frank was definitely second in line, and she wanted to keep it that way.

Lowering her face to his neck, Katrina kissed him once, and then twice. He was her very special number two man. After the third kiss, Frank took Katrina's hand and pulled her around the chair and onto his lap. They stayed that way for a long while holding one another. Katrina loved being married to Frank, and being able to be wrapped in his arms made her heart go out to Michelle. She prayed a silent prayer that Michelle and David would find their way back together.

* * * * * * *

The mail had come early today. Michelle rose from her bed and

66

slipped on her robe to retrieve it. Before bouncing down the stairs, she first slid her feet into her bedroom slippers. She sometimes went back to bed after taking her daughter to school, and today had been one of those days.

Michelle opened her front door wide enough to reach for the mailbox that hung next to her door frame. She pulled out the two letters that were there before heading back upstairs and into her room where she plopped on the bed. The first letter was from a charity organization asking for a donation, and she pushed it aside on the bed. The second letter had no return address. She studied it before opening the envelope.

"Oh no! What?" She threw the letter down on the bed. "The nerve of him!" she screamed. "The nerve of him!"

The letter was from Freddie. Michelle thought he had gone back to Philadelphia for a while. Would this man torment her for the rest of her life? Can a mistake made in the past ever be fixed? She had to get in contact with her best friend . . . and fast. She picked up the phone and dialed. Thankfully, Katrina answered her cell quickly.

"Michelle, what's up with you, girl?" As soon as Michelle informed her of the letter, she'd just received from Freddie, Katrina knew the drill. "I'll meet you at the diner in an hour," she said.

They arrived at Peace Diner not a minute late. In fact, Michelle had gotten there ten minutes early and was already at a booth when her friend arrived. Once Katrina was seated, Michelle handed her the letter from Freddie. Katrina looked at the paper and began reading the letter in silence. She made a few grunting sounds as she read.

Hey, Michelle; it's Freddie, and I'm not doing too good. See, I'm a drummer and I'm having a hard time getting a gig. I need some money to help support myself. My money is funny, and I need $500.00 on Thursday at noon. Have it in my cousin's mailbox by that time. I know I can count on you. Does your husband still work at The Department of Housing?

Katrina gave a final grunt after reading the letter and tossed it on the table. Both women sat in silence for a few moments to absorb all the dirt in the blackmail letter.

"He reminds me of a snake," Michelle finally said.

Katrina nodded her head in agreement and released a heavy sigh.

"Yeah, a rattlesnake."

Michelle had thought about little else since reading the letter. She had to come up with a way to keep Freddie from constantly yanking her chain.

"We'll find a way to deal with him once and for all," Katrina said with a scowl.

Michelle looked at her friend and managed a small smile. She sure hoped Katrina was correct, and she would wake up with this nightmare over and done with.

"I need to go to the grocery store and pick up a few things," Katrina announced. "Do you want to join me?"

Michelle nodded, but first she wanted to eat something from the diner. All they had done so far was chat, and Michelle felt guilty for occupying a table and not making a purchase. She pointed at the menus that still lay on their table. "Let's order a little something before we go."

Katrina motioned for a waitress, and thirty minutes later, they'd finished their soup and sandwiches and were outside talking as they walked to Safeway grocery store. Freddie was still very much on both of their minds.

Michelle and Katrina had known each other for fifteen years, and often had long, detailed conversations. Michelle felt comfortable telling Katrina nearly all the intricacies of her life; her life had almost been an open book to Katrina and to her mother. Of course, a woman had to have a few secrets she didn't tell to anyone, but for Michelle, those secrets were very few.

"Are you going to stop by the bank?" asked Katrina when they stopped at the intersection.

Michelle looked over at her. "No, I don't need to."

At the permission of the pedestrian light, they walked across the street. Michelle didn't know if she would give Freddie money again. She'd had a gut feeling that he would ask her for more blackmail money; that's why she kept a small stash of money at home, just in case. She had built her personal savings account back up to where it was before Freddie re-entered the picture.

"Do you think we should contact Detective Ed?" asked Katrina as they walked side by side down the street.

"I don't know," responded Michelle. "I don't think so."

Katrina glanced at her friend but then looked away, and they walked in silence until they were only a block from the Safeway grocery store. That's when Katrina spoke again. "Are you going to get something?"

"Probably so," replied Michelle. She thought about Freddie, and then her absent husband. A sigh released itself from her lips, and her steps quickened as they approached the automated doors of Safeway.

Inside, both women picked up baskets and proceeded to shop. The friends separated with Michelle heading to the produce section to get oranges and whatever other fruit caught her fancy. She tore a plastic bag from the roll to insert her oranges in.

"They're good this time of year," said a voice behind her.

Michelle turned around to see Mary Jenkins smiling at her. "First Lady, it's so good to see you." Michelle gave her pastor's wife a side hug.

"How are things going with you?" asked the first lady.

Michelle thought for a second about the question and crinkled her nose. She relaxed her facial muscles soon after, but not before Mary noticed.

"If you ever need to talk, know that I'm just a phone call away," she offered.

Michelle hugged Mary Jenkins again and said, "Thank you; I might take you up on that."

They smiled at one another, and then departed with a wave of their hands. After choosing her fruit, Michelle wandered into the meats section to get a log of ground turkey and finally to the deli to get fresh coleslaw. It would make a great side dish for the turkey burgers she'd prepare for dinner. All while Michelle shopped, she kept an eye out for Katrina. The oranges would make a great late night snack, she thought as she walked to Aisle 6 to get toilet tissue. It was then that she saw her friend reaching for a pack of Charmin.

"Katrina," Michelle called, "are you about ready to go?"

Katrina put the tissue in her basket and nodded her head. "Yes; I'm ready."

Michelle grabbed a pack of toilet tissue and set it in her red basket, placing it on the top. The women walked together to the checkout line.

"Did you see the first lady?" asked Michelle. "I talked to her in the produce section."

"I chatted with her too," Katrina said. "Just briefly though. We passed each other on the juice aisle."

Michelle eyes diverted to the entrance of the store as they stood in line, and she did a double take before nudging Katrina to look in the same direction. When Katrina looked, her mouth fell opened. Nicola Brooks was walking through the doors of Safeway.

Michelle turned her head to the side so she wouldn't be recognized by the woman, and Katrina redirected her eyes to the floor. Michelle's food was now riding down the conveyer belt.

"How are you doing today?" asked the polite cashier.

Michelle smiled at her and said, "Okay." A few minutes later, Michelle had her groceries all packed in a bag. While she waited for Katrina, her attention returned to the entrance of the store, and the person who walked in this time made her weak in the knees; literally. She held onto the counter for support. Her strange behavior caught Katrina's attention, and one glance toward the front entrance explained everything.

Katrina stood still, holding on to her grocery bag until David was out of sight. As soon as it was clear, she grabbed Michelle's arm with her free hand, and they made a mad dash for the exit door.

Outside the store, they walked for quite a while before either of them spoke.

"Michelle, it may not be as bad, as you think," said Katrina." You know how cunning that woman can be."

Michelle nodded and kept on walking. She knew Nicola could be very cunning, so she agreed with Katrina on that, but still he had no right to be shopping with that woman.

Katrina looked at Michelle and it was apparent that she wanted to ease her friend's mental pain. "Let's drop by the church this evening after all the children in your after school program are gone home."

Michelle managed to nod her head again, but she didn't want to talk anymore. Not right now. She felt as though a million thoughts were running through her mind at 100 miles per hour, and she trying to sort them out. The light turned yellow and they waited on the curb for it to change. Michelle knew why Katrina wanted to go to the church this evening. The benevolence ministry had ask for volunteers to deliver food baskets to the sick and shut-in. Michelle and Katrina had signed up to help, but with all the drama going on in her life, Michelle had almost forgotten about it. She was kind of glad that Katrina had reminded her. Maybe helping would take her mind off of her numerous problems.

At the next corner, the ladies headed in different directions toward their respective homes. Upon arriving at hers, Michelle stuck her key in the lock and opened her front door. She walked into the kitchen and took a seat at the table. She wanted to relax before preparing for her charges to arrive. She liked keeping busy so she wouldn't have time to think awful thoughts.

The rest of the evening passed quickly. After the last parent had picked up their child at the end of the day, Michelle let out a long sigh. The phone rang, and she rose from her chair at the kitchen table to answer it. "Hello?"

"Hi, Michelle." It was her estranged husband, and she really didn't want to talk to him right now. When she said nothing in reply, he continued. "I'd like to get Sasha tomorrow if that's okay with you."

Michelle had never kept Sasha from her father, no matter how angry she got with him. She was now *furious*, and she was going to make it known. "What on God's green earth were you doing shopping with your mistress?"

There was silence on the other end of the phone for a few seconds before he spoke. "I'm sorry." David sighed like he was tired. "I didn't know . . . I didn't know you were there. I'm sorry," he repeated.

The apology sounded genuine, and it touched her somewhat. Michelle took a moment to gather her thoughts. She was still mad with him; just a little less mad than before.

David's voice ended the silence. "I saw the first lady at Safeway, and she told me it was inappropriate to be shopping with a woman who isn't my wife."

Michelle smiled. She always did think that the first lady of Peace Baptist Church was the best. "You know she was right," Michelle said. She wanted to say more, but she restrained herself. "I've gotta go, David. And as for you getting Sasha tomorrow; that's fine. Goodbye."

"Wait a minute," he implored. "We told Davita that I was her father and not her uncle as she'd always been told before. We were at Safeway to get her favorite treats before we told her; that's all that was about."

Michelle curled the telephone cord around her finger as she sat on the kitchen stool. David's explanation had actually made her relax and release some of the tension she had felt throughout her body. She hoped David wouldn't take Sasha on any more outings in the park with Nicola though. "May I ask where you'll be taking Sasha tomorrow?"

There were a few seconds of silence before he answered. "Uh . . . probably to the park and to the diner for something to eat."

"Will Nicola and Davita be a part of this outing tomorrow?"

David bit his tongue before speaking. "Davita will be there for sure, but no; I won't include Nicola. I promise."

Michelle smiled; satisfied with his answer. "Okay, David; Sasha will be ready when you get here.

An hour later, they were all at the church; Michelle and Sasha along with Katrina and Kayla. They were preparing to deliver baskets of food to those in need. Katrina had her husband's car, and they would be driving today. Sasha and Kayla sat in the backseat of the car with their seat belts fastened. Michelle sat upfront in the passenger's seat with Katrina at the wheel.

"I like helping people," said Sasha from the backseat.

"Me too," Kayla chimed in.

"That's good," said Katrina. "Always stay that way."

Michelle glanced in Katrina's direction. "Where are we going first?"

"We're going right across the district line to Temple Hills,

Maryland."

They drove for most of the way with only the girls' backseat chatter to keep the vehicle from being completely silent. Michelle was in a pretty good mood and had almost forgotten about Freddie's blackmail letter. She had the money at her house and still hadn't decided whether she should give it to him.

What if she just went to David and told him about that night her and Freddie spent together? He couldn't get upset; after all, he had made a baby with another woman. She still didn't know if she wanted her estranged husband to learn that information though. There was no real rush; she had until tomorrow to decide.

They were now riding across the Washington, D.C. line to Temple Hills, Maryland. "We're almost there," said Katrina as she stopped at the stop sign and looked in the backseat. Both Sasha and Kayla were asleep. Katrina drove past a familiar building, and she and Michelle exchanged glances.

Michelle looked back at the building until it was out of her view. That was the nightclub where she and Katrina had met Freddie and Leo years ago. The memories of that particular evening came flooding back. In her mind's eye, Michelle could see the four of them sitting together at a table in the club. She could see them all leaving the club together, and going to breakfast together; all four of them.

She could see her and Freddie at his house cuddling on the couch. Katrina and Leo were in the other room with the door closed. She remembered Freddie handing her a drink and her initial refusal to take it. She'd finally given in to his pestering and took the glass, drinking half of its contents. She and Katrina hadn't planned on staying the entire night at the house, but that's exactly what had happened.

The conversation they were having at the club had been so interesting, and when the club closed, they continued the conversation at the restaurant over breakfast. Freddie and Leo suggested they go back to Freddie's house to keep the discussion going. Michelle and Katrina knew in the backs of their minds that it wasn't a good idea, but they went with the flow and had regretted it ever since.

"We're here," announced Katrina. Michelle stayed in the car with the two girls, and Katrina got out and walked to the back and opened the trunk. She pulled out a food basket and carried it up the steps to the first house on her list. A teenage girl answered the door and called to an elderly woman that they had company. Katrina stayed at the house for about ten minutes before rejoining them in the car. After delivering the next four food baskets, they were done for the day.

"It does make you feel good to help others, doesn't it?" asked Michelle as she leaned back on the headrest on the drive home.

Katrina nodded her answer, and then turned on the radio. They listened to gospel music all the way home; sometimes they all sang along.

When they arrived at Michelle's home, she and Katrina hugged before Michelle and Sasha exited the car. Michelle's life was far from perfect, but she had a song in her heart, and she felt pretty good as she held her daughter's hand. Tomorrow's problems would take care of themselves.

A short while later, a bit of her reality came rushing back as Michelle sat in her bedroom counting carefully before placing her hard earned money in an envelope. She slipped the envelope into the pocket of her sweater and patted it a few times as she sat on the edge of her mattress. She didn't like herself for giving in to Freddie's blackmail yet again. Michelle rose from the bed, picked up the terrible letter from Freddie, and read it for the last time. Walking into the master bathroom, she took the letter and tore it into many pieces before depositing it into the stool and flushing.

A little smile crossed her lips and she trotted down the stairs and out the front door. She looked down the street toward the house where Freddie was staying. The walk to Cheryl's felt longer than normal, but when Michelle arrived, she opened the mailbox and deposited the envelope. She scouted out her surroundings before returning to her own porch.

Once inside her house, Michelle blew a long stream of air from her mouth. She walked into the kitchen and plopped down in a chair at the table. Her eyes wandered to the calendar on the wall, and it hit her like a ton of bricks that Valentine Day was just days away. Last year this time, things were drastically different.

The phone rang and Michelle rose to answer it. "Hello?"

"Michelle?" said Katrina in a puzzled tone. "Are you all right?"

Michelle could only release a soft sigh in response.

"Well, I hope you're okay," said Katrina. "I just called to tell you that I don't need you to pick up Kayla from school today. Frank and I will be getting her."

Michelle wondered what was going on with Katrina. "You are? Why?"

"You won't believe this, but Frank is taking me to Hawaii for Valentine's Day,"

Michelle narrowed her eyes and a puzzle look appeared on her face, but she didn't readily reply.

"He surprised me last night." Katrina sounded happy. "We'll be gone for a week."

Michelle was really glad for her best friend, but she couldn't help but be sad too; sad for her own life. She tried to withhold the sadness from her voice though. "Have a good time, Katrina. Call me when you get back. I'll talk to you later." And with those words she was off the phone.

Katrina was at work, so if she asked Michelle about her shortness later on, that was a good reason to give her for cutting the conversation so short. Michelle walked out of the kitchen and into the living room to look out of the window. She wondered if her money was still in Cheryl's mailbox.

What a despicable person Freddie was, she thought to herself as she walked back upstairs to her bedroom and lay across the bed.

Chapter 11

That evening, Sasha sat on the front porch waiting for her father's arrival. It was still cold outside, but she'd bundled herself in her warm coat and said it was what she wanted to do. Michelle stood at the window watching her daughter and waiting for her estranged husband to come. Five minutes later David entered the front yard and took Sasha by the hand. He saw Michelle in the window and waved to her. Michelle waved back and watched their every movement until they got into the car. When the car was no longer in sight, she felt abandoned and alone. Her feet felt heavy as she mounted the stairs to her bedroom and crawled under the covers.

On Sunday morning, Michelle and Cheryl walked together to church.

"I told Freddie if he wants to stay with me he would have to go to church," said Cheryl.

Michelle shook her head in silence. She hated the thought of now having to see Freddie in church with her, but if there was one thing her blackmailer needed, it was to get some religion in him and soon.

Peace Baptist was a modest size church with a membership of about a hundred worshipers. Michelle loved the cozy, intimate feel of the church. A mega church wasn't her style, but she understood that everyone didn't share her views.

"You don't like my cousin, huh?" asked Cheryl. She must have noticed Michelle's change of demeanor.

Michelle shrugged her shoulders. She didn't want to tell Cheryl what kind of man he was, and how she knew it.

Cheryl spoke again. "You won't hurt my feelings if you say you don't like him. I told you before; he's not my favorite person either. If he weren't blood, I would barely look at him let alone talk to him."

Michelle smiled at the comments, but she didn't have the chance to respond. They had arrived at the church and entered through the gate

They both returned the greeting of Brother Earl who met them at the door before picking up a program and walking into the sanctuary. The musicians were adjusting their instruments on stage. Michelle looked up and saw Freddie on the drums, and her heart sank. She stepped back, then turned and walked back into the lobby to chat with the deacon and catch her breath. Michelle had hugged Cheryl before she left, and her neighbor had looked at her with a raised brow.

"I wish I could moonwalk. That sermon touched a lot of people," said Brother Earl to Michelle as they stood in the lobby chatting and greeting other arriving members. "We could go to the diner, and I could tell you all the mistakes I've made in my life."

Michelle nodded in agreement.

He continued. "I'd like to retrace my steps and change some things in the past."

Michelle smiled; she couldn't agree more. "We all would," she voiced, "but we can't."

A rueful look appeared on his face, but he knew he couldn't go back. Michelle chatted with the greeter for a few more minutes before excusing herself and walking back into the sanctuary, down the red carpeted aisle, and sitting next to Cheryl on the pew. She looked toward the stage and Freddie was still sitting there with the drum sticks in his hands. Michelle taped Cheryl on the shoulder to let her know that she was going to the restroom. She looked at Freddie one last time before walking out again.

The church only used the drum set on rare occasions, so if the drums were what attracted Freddie to Peace Baptist, he shouldn't be a regular. Michelle felt badly for feeling that way. Freddie needed to be in the house of the Lord, for sure. She only wished that he'd choose one of the other hundreds of churches in the nation's capital. She looked in the mirror above the sink when she entered the restroom, and what she saw put a frown on her face. Gosh, she sure looked tired, and her vision seemed a bit out of focus. Michelle forced a smile on her face, which greatly improved her reflection in the mirror. She needed to get back in the sanctuary before morning service started.

A child almost ran into Michelle as she exited the restroom, but her arm was grabbed just before they would have collided. Michelle looked down at the little girl, and then she stared up at the person who had interrupted the accident. The woman returned her look and gave her a brief smile before walking away to take a seat. Michelle stood still with her eyes growing larger by the second.

She wished her eyes were deceiving her, but she knew better. That was definitely Nicola and Davita walking up the aisle on her church. How much more was she required to take? Michelle let out a long sigh before walking back to her seat. En route, her eyes caught the sight of the illuminated cross at the front of the church, and a slight smile curved her lips. She settled in her seat next to Cheryl and looked to the front. Pastor Jenkins was standing at the podium with a Bible in his hand.

"Good morning, saints. Would you please turn to Psalm 32 and follow along in your Bible?" He paused to give the people a chance to find the scripture, and then he began reading the first verse of the chapter. *"Blessed is he whose transgression is forgiven, whose sin is covered."*

After the verse was read and discussed, a praise song was offered up to the Almighty God. The pastor bowed his head and took a step back and out of the way of the singer and the musicians. Freddie positioned himself on the drums, and the lead singer took a step forward donned in a red robe and belted out the song, "I'm Sold Out." She stomped across the stage as the choir joined in. Freddie was playing the drums with spirit, and the sound was vibrating throughout the sanctuary.

People were clapping and responding to the music with great glee. The soloist continued singing, "I'm all sold out, I'm all sold out," and more people began coming to their feet, clapping, stomping their feet, and keeping beat with the music. At the end of service, Michelle and Cheryl hugged several church members before making their way out.

Michelle was holding Sasha's hand as they walked down the front steps of the church and out the gate. David had brought her to church with him.

"Mommy, I saw Davita. Daddy said she's my sister."

Michelle had to stop to catch her breath. When she looked at Cheryl, the woman raised an eyebrow. Michelle started walking again. Because of her brief pause, both Cheryl and Sasha were a little bit ahead of her, and as far as Michelle was concerned, that was a good thing. Why had David told Sasha that Davita was her sister without running it by her first? And another thing . . . why was Nicola and Davita at church today?

Everything had been blindsiding her lately. Was she supposed to pretend like everything was okay in spite of the tailspin her life was in?

Michelle looked up the street and saw Cheryl now holding Sasha's hand. She must have been able to tell that Michelle needed some time to herself and she wanted to keep Sasha out of the mix. No need in messing up a perfectly good Sunday for everybody. Michelle sighed. She'd take care of her business tomorrow for sure.

Monday evening, Michelle sat on the front porch of her house, awaiting a visit from her estranged husband. Michelle saw his car enter the block and watched as he stopped in front of the house they once shared.

He got out of the car and walked toward her with his nose crinkled. The first words out of his mouth were, "Where is Sasha? Is she still inside getting ready?"

Michelle looked David in the eyes and patted the spot next to her. When he was seated, she said, "We need to talk before you leave with Sasha."

He raised his hand in the air as if in surrender and waited for her to proceed.

"Why did you tell Sasha that Davita was her sister without consulting with me first?"

David ran his hand over his face and shook his head. When he removed his hands, he said, "First of all let me say that I had no idea Nicola and Davita were going to come to church; honest." He turned away and rubbed his chin with his hand. "And it was a mistake to tell Sasha that Davita was her sister without making sure you were okay with it first. I'm really sorry about that."

Michelle looked at David and felt very close to him at that moment. She felt like he was telling the truth, but still he had to consider her feelings more.

He continued. "I'm glad we're talking, Michelle. I begged you to let me explain my side. Don't you get it?" he said. "Davita was born before you and I got married. She's seven and a half years old, and we been married only seven years."

"Huh? Say what?" was Michelle response to the new information. She still wasn't happy with him. "Why didn't you tell me about her before we got married?"

David gave a small smile and reached for Michelle's hand. She pulled back. She wasn't trying to hold hands with him, right now. He returned his hand to his lap, but the smile remained on his face." I never told you about Davita because I always got cold feet. I was chicken, I guess," he said, searching her face as he spoke.

"I do feel better knowing you didn't cheat on me." A smile appeared on Michelle's face. She didn't know where that had come from, but there was still something that she couldn't understand. "How could you keep your daughter a secret from me for seven years, David?"

He placed his hand on her shoulder, and this time she didn't move away. He slid his arm around her shoulders, and she still stayed put.

Michelle didn't know what to think, but she knew she was too vulnerable to continue the conversation with him. She needed to be alone and sort things out in her mind. She rose from the stoop they'd been sharing. "I'll go get Sasha; she's taking a nap." Michelle turned and walked into the house to retrieve their daughter. Minutes later, Sasha walked out of the house slowly, and when she spotted her father she became animated.

David lifted his daughter off the ground and into his arms, and Michelle smiled as she watched David and Sasha get cozy and comfortable together. He placed Sasha back down on her feet a minute later and steadied her. "Go wait in the car; I'll be there in a minute."

Sasha smiled and did what she was told. When they were alone on the porch, David made a request. "Please, can we talk some more tonight on the phone?"

Michelle agreed, but the nighttime seemed to roll around quicker than she could prepare herself. Not only did she need to mentally prepare herself for the conversation, but had a few chores to get done. When David called, she needed to give her full attention to what was going to be said about where they were heading.

That night with Sasha tucked safely in her own bed, the phone rang, and she picked up and immediately said, "David, how could you keep Davita a secret from me for seven years?" Michelle was lying in her bed, and she reached for the box of tissue on her nightstand. She didn't need them now, and she wasn't one to easily cry, but she could think of a thousand reasons she might need them before this conversation was over.

They talked for almost four hours. Virtually nothing was left unsaid, and afterward, Michelle fell into peaceful sleep.

Chapter 12

"I don't need any help," said David to his wife as she made a move to help him bring his boxes back into their house on Saturday morning.

Michelle felt good about the decision to work on their marriage together instead of apart, and Sasha was literally dancing around the house.

"It's good to be home," said David before dropping the boxes near the bottom of the staircase.

Sasha ran to him and grabbed his hand. "Can my sister come over?"

David looked at Michelle who was seated on the bottom stair. "Sure, she can," he said. He and Michelle had already discussed this, and it was all right with her as long as Nicola wasn't with her.

Michelle knew David's wish was that his daughters would grow up together as sisters, and she wouldn't deny him that. She rose from the stair and walked swiftly into the kitchen to make snacks for her family; it was almost as if David never left.

* * * * * * *

Katrina sat on the beach in Hawaii with her husband. Frank had his arm around her as they sat on a blanket in the sand, and her mind traveled back to Washington, D.C. and to her best friend. She wondered how Michelle was holding up, or if in fact, she was holding up at all. Katrina had her eyes closed and she now felt Frank rubbing her back. No doubt about it, he was the best husband in the world. In her life, he was only second to God.

He whispered in her ear, "Do you want to take a walk, baby?"

Katrina opened her eyes and smiled before rising to her feet. She smoothed down the back of her bathing suit before strolling down the beach hand in hand with her amazing husband.

* * * * * * *

Valentine's Day was here and Michelle wondered if the timing played a role in David's return home. She didn't think it did, but heck . . . she was too happy about his being home and too afraid to closely examine the underlying reasons why. They made their Valentine's Day plans as a family, with Sasha included.

In the morning, they all went to Peace Diner for breakfast and planned to have lunch and dinner there as well. David came home at lunchtime, and they walked to Sasha's school to take her to lunch with them. That morning, they had all stopped at the Rite-Aid Pharmacy for bags of candy to take to Sasha's class. The teacher was visibly grateful when Michelle handed her the treats for the children.

They waved at their daughter's classmates as Sasha headed to lunch with her parents. Michelle had to look down. She was so happy that she wondered if her feet were actually touching the ground, or if she were simply floating.

They reached the diner and took a seat in a booth. Michelle and David sat side by side, and Sasha sat across from them. When Michelle looked at David, he was smiling, and that made her smile too. Sasha giggled at the sight of them. It hadn't been this way in a long time, and Michelle sent up a silent prayer of thanks to God.

When their food arrived, they all held hands while David blessed the food. When the meals had been consumed, they had to get Sasha back to school and David back to work. They scooted out of the booth and walked out of the diner. Michelle had to tend to her childcare business; that would kill some time until her family got back together. She loved this thing about David not wanting her to cook on the holiday. Michelle was almost afraid to see the day near its close.

Valentine's night was movie night for the Davidson family. They watched several family oriented movies and munched on popcorn in three varieties while drinking homemade punch. Michelle had enjoyed sharing Valentine's Day as a family. She looked at the coffee table and at all the postcards Katrina had sent her from Hawaii. The island looked beautiful; maybe one day she and David might take that trip.

On Sunday morning, the Davidson family walked through the doors of Peace Baptist Church, and Brother Earl greeted them. "Good morning and God bless."

Michelle and her family entered the sanctuary. Sister Precious stood near the back of the church and grinned at the sight of them. She hadn't seen them together as a family in awhile. Precious's father, Elder

Peterson greeted each of them, too, before walking away. Elder Peterson was a widower in his mid-seventies, and had been a founding member of the church. Since his wife's passing a year ago, he had been living with Precious and her detective husband, Ed. Michelle remembered Precious once telling her that even at his advanced age, she wanted her father to find someone special and maybe remarry.

Cheryl looked up and smiled when her neighbors reached the pew. She'd informed Michelle during a telephone conversation they'd had last night that Freddie had just left for Pennsylvania. Michelle was glad because he was the last person she'd want to see in service today. But his runner-up prevented it from being the perfect Sunday.

Michelle looked up and spotted Nicola as she approached the pew. She stared at the woman and wondered what she was up to.

"Good morning, everyone," said Nicola as she stood in the aisle. "David. Michelle. Sasha." She nodded one time for each name she called.

Michelle didn't know what to say, so she said nothing at all. A weak smile was the best thing she could offer.

David spoke up. "Nicola, how are you and Davita?" he asked looking at the child.

Michelle remained quiet; she didn't trust herself to speak to Nicola. She thought David needed to ask her why she'd decided to attend this church. Why was Nicola even in their atmosphere?

Nicola's voice broke through Michelle's thoughts. "Can I speak with you in private?" she asked. "It will only take a minute."

Michelle pointed to herself. "You want to speak to *me*?" Even after Nicola nodded her head, Michelle didn't make an attempt to get up.

David leaned over to her and kissed her on the cheek." Go ahead; it'll be all right."

Michelle slowly rose from the pew like her bottom was made of concrete. Nicola began walking toward the back of the church, and Michelle followed. Nicola stopped in a rear corner, and Michelle did likewise, keeping a comfortable distance between them.

"I've really grown fond of this church and would like to join," stated Nicola. "Will that be a problem for you?"

Michelle couldn't believe her ears. Of course that would be a problem for her. Nicola and David had a child together. It couldn't help but be uncomfortable; that was a no brainer. There was no shortage of churches in Washington, D.C.

Michelle thought all those things, but what she said was, "Nicola, I can't stop you from going to any church you choose. I suppose it may get awkward at times."

"I know, but I'll try to stay out of your way. Believe it or not, I'm growing spiritually here." Nicola smiled. "Plus this would be a great place for me to meet a husband."

Is this woman mentally sound? Michelle thought. "You're supposed to come to church to hear the Word; not hunt for men."

She looked at Michelle. "I told you, in my few times at this church, I've grown spiritually. But I can hear the Word and seek a husband at the same time."

Michelle looked away from the woman. She was done with this conversation. "Continue to grow in the Lord, Nicola," she said before walking away to rejoin her family.

On Wednesday evening, Michelle and David arrived at the church for Bible study and saw Nicola was already there looking through her Bible. She looked up and nodded at them. They waved in return.

Sister Precious was there with her father. Elder Peterson looked at Nicola like he was checking her out. He had a big smile on his face, and Nicola smiled back before turning away. Michelle noticed the exchange and she couldn't help but be concerned for the older gentleman.

At the close of Bible study, Michelle and David walked across the street to Peace Diner. They took a seat in the booth. Michelle placed her hand on the table, and David laid his hand on top of hers. She looked at her husband. "I really love you," she said with a smile.

"And I really love you too," David replied just before signaling for the waitress to come over.

They just wanted a couple of glasses of ginger ale. When their quick deliveries came, the two of them sat sipping their sodas through straws.

The door to the diner opened just moments later, and in walked Nicola and Elder Peterson. Michelle almost gagged, and David just stared at them. They took a seat in a nearby booth, sitting opposite one another.

Michelle's eyes widened. She was not in the habit of staring, but she just couldn't stop herself. David tapped her on the shoulder and suggested that it was time they left for home. Michelle nodded in agreement and took a long sip from her glass before getting up. On the outside, she looked at David, and he looked back at her.

"I don't want to talk about it right now," he said as they began walking toward their house.

* * * * * * *

"Girl, we need to talk; meet me at the diner at nine this morning," said Katrina. That was an hour ago when she'd called to inform Michelle that she and her husband were finally home from her vacation in Hawaii.

Michelle walked through the door of the diner and spotted Katrina already in a booth. When she joined her, Katrina examined her friend's face carefully. Michelle didn't look too sad to her. In fact, she didn't look sad at all.

"So . . . what's been happening with you?" Katrina's question was a bit guarded, and she seemed to brace herself a little in preparation for the answer. But when Michelle filled her in on everything that had transpired when she was away, all Katrina could say in reply was, "Wow."

While Katrina took a long sip from her glass of orange juice, Michelle raised her hand in the air and motioned for the waitress to come to the table. Once she placed her order, Michelle used the palm of her hand to smooth down her shoulder length hair. Katrina was sporting braids that rested a little past her shoulders. Michelle had never seen her in braids before. "Is that just your island 'do, or are you going to keep your hair like that?" she asked.

Katrina ran her hand down her hair "As much as I paid for this, I'm going to keep it; at least for a little while."

Michelle smiled, and nodded her head in approval.

Katrina released a light sigh of relief. She wasn't sure what to expect upon her return, but she was glad to see that Michelle had not only survived, but overcome. "I've got to go to work," she said sliding out of the booth and coming to her feet. "I got to build my hours back up after this vacation. I just needed to look you in the face and know that you were okay."

"Thanks, girl; I'm fine," Michelle replied.

Katrina reached into her purse and pulled out an envelope and handed it to Michelle. "These are the photos Frank and I took in Hawaii. Hang on to them, and I'll get them back from you later." She waved and then exited the diner.

Michelle accepted the juice that the waitress brought her, and then pulled the photos out of the envelope. The beauty of Hawaii awed her. She and David definitely should take a trip there, she thought. Hopefully they'd get to do it before they got old and gray.

That evening following dinner, and after the kitchen had been cleaned, David handed her the newspaper. "Read the article about the nightclub that's turning into a church. It's on the first page of the metro section."

Michelle took the paper and spotted the article. It seemed the owner of the club had recently become saved and filled with the Holy Spirit, and he wanted others to experience what he had.

"Isn't that amazing?" said David. "Is anything too hard for God?"

Michelle looked up from the paper and smiled at him before continuing to read the rest of the article. There was a picture of the nightclub in the paper and its address. Michelle stared with widened eyes. That was the club that she and Katrina attended back in their wild days.

David looked at his wife absorbed in *The Washington Post* article. He had to admit that it was an amazing story, but Michelle seemed unnaturally engrossed. He shrugged it off. "I'll be right back," he said before walking out of the kitchen.

Michelle wondered if Katrina had seen the article. When the phone rang, she carried the paper with her to answer it. "Hello?"

"Did you see the front of the metro section in *The Washington Post*?"

Katrina's voice had a nervous tremble.

Michelle looked around to be sure David wasn't nearby before responding. "Yeah, I'm rereading it now." The article brought back memories she didn't ever want to recall. She was so different back then, and so was Katrina. What had her friend said earlier? That they were dumb as two rocks back then? The recent conversation made Michelle laughed into the phone.

"I'm glad you find this funny." Katrina was clearly ticked off. "I certainly don't."

Michelle didn't bother trying to clear Katrina's confusion. Instead, she looked at the paper in her hand and shook her head. She'd thought about coming clean with David about her past, but she knew Katrina didn't want to tell Frank. Michelle reasoned with herself that if she told David, then Katrina's husband would find out as well. But what if she were wrong? What if Katrina did want to tell Frank, but she wasn't telling him because she was too concerned about what might happen if David found out as well? "Have you ever thought about telling Frank about our hanging out at the nightclub?" Michelle asked her.

There was a brief silence on the other end of the phone. "No, not really," Katrina said. "I was so different back then; I'm not the same person today. There was another pause, and then Katrina continued. "You know sometimes I want to tell him, but I get scared because I don't like that person I used to be, and I don't know if Frank would be able to love me the same if he knew."

Michelle totally agreed with her, that's why she'd been paying Freddie not to blab to her husband about her past.

"This might sound crazy," said Katrina, "but once this club becomes a church, I'd like to walk through it one time."

Michelle smiled to herself. "Oddly enough . . . so would I."

Chapter 13

It had snowed overnight, and Washington, D.C. had received six inches of the white stuff. Sasha ran into her parents' bedroom with a smile in her voice.

"Mommy, have you looked outside and seen all that snow?"

Michelle smiled and nodded her head. David had already left for work, and Michelle didn't want to get out of bed. The D.C. public schools were closed today. Michelle pulled back the covers and patted a spot on the mattress, beckoning her daughter to lie there.

Sasha bounced like a bunny rabbit onto the bed. Michelle placed the covers over her and cuddled close. Sasha asked to be read a story, but Michelle didn't want to get from under the warm blankets, so instead of getting a storybook, she told Sasha stories about when she was a baby and details of the day she and David brought her home from the hospital after she was born. She told her what her first words were, and when she took her first step. She described to the girl exactly how she and David had felt when they first laid eyes on her.

"Tell me more stories, Mommy," requested Sasha.

Michelle had a whole bag of stories to tell her daughter. She told her how out-of-their-minds excited they were with her birth. Michelle didn't mention the part about the labor pains or the nausea early in her pregnancy. She'd have that conversation much later; when Sasha became a young lady. Right now, the only words to pass her lips would be the bliss; the wonderful and amazing experience of bringing a new life into the world.

"When your father and I first brought you home, you slept most of the time," Michelle told her.

On cue, Sasha yawned and closed he eyes halfway.

Michelle kept talking about what a delightful baby she had been. A few minutes passed, and she looked over at Sasha and her eyes were completely closed. Michelle smiled. Sasha was sleeping in her arms just like she had done when she was a baby.

The rest of the week proved to be uneventful, and by the weekend, the sun had come out. On Sunday, Michelle's family trudged to church in the melting snow. Upon arrival, they shook the snow off their shoes while they chatted with Brother Earl at the entrance doors.

"It's a cold one," the deacon said, closing the door behind them.

Michelle took off her gloves and rolled them up in a ball before placing them in her coat pocket. "It sure is," she agreed.

Sasha was still shivering, and Michelle rubbed the girl's shoulders and her back. David grabbed his daughter's hand and led his family into the sanctuary.

Just minutes later, Nicola and Davita entered the church. "God bless you all," said Nicola as they reached the spot where the Davidson family sat. David reached for his older daughter's hand and smiled at her.

"Do you mind if Davita sits with you this morning?" asked Nicola.

David nodded and pulled his daughter toward him.

"Thanks," said Nicola before walking a few rows up to grab a seat for herself.

Michelle smiled because her husband was smiling David was obviously pleased to be sitting with both his daughters. Looking toward the back of the church, Michelle saw Precious and Ed. Precious beckoned for her to join them.

"I'm going to speak to Sister Precious and Brother Ed for a moment," she whispered to David.

"Hello, Sister Michelle," said Precious when she had reached her. "Can you tell me a little about Nicola Brooks?"

Michelle bit her bottom lip, and her eyes briefly looked heavenward. "Uh, I don't know the woman that well. Why do you ask?"

"Well, for one thing, she has started dating my father. Did you know that?"

Michelle was on the verge of replying, but the sounds of music interrupted her. Morning service was about to begin. She looked at Precious. "I'll call you tonight, and we can talk all about it; okay?"

Why would a woman in her thirties be dating a man in his seventies?

Michelle thought on her walk back to her seat. She didn't have an answer to her own question, and she didn't want to dwell on Nicola long enough to come up with one either.

While the church announcer approached the podium and filled the congregation in on all of Peace Baptist's upcoming events, Katrina and Frank walked swiftly and quietly down the center aisle and stopped at the pew behind Michelle and her family. As Pastor Jenkins walked toward the podium carrying a Bible, he had the entire church's attention.

* * * * * * *

"Nicola has a child with David," Michelle said over the phone that evening, while sitting on the edge of her bed.

She decided to tell Precious all she knew about Nicola; the good (which there wasn't much of), the bad, and the ugly. Since the woman was dating Precious's father, Michelle spared no details. "She brought her daughter to my aftercare program without telling me the girl was David's child." Michelle heard Precious mumble something into the phone followed by a long sigh. But when she didn't offer any other comment, Michelle continued. "I guess she seems to be over David, but I'm not totally sure. It does appear that she's changed somewhat for the better, but you can never be too careful in cases like this."

Precious thanked her for the information and ended their conversation, but before she hung up she handed the phone to her husband.

"Hello, Brother Ed," Michelle said when she heard him on the other end of the line.

"I just wanted to let you know that Freddie is no longer in Washington, D.C.," he told her. "He bought a one way ticket to Philadelphia a few weeks ago."

The sound of "one way ticket" was music to Michelle's ears. *Maybe he's finally gone for good.* She didn't tell the detective that she had given him more blackmail money. At this point, that wasn't even important to her. It was worth it. Her husband was back home, and she, David, and Sasha were a family; that was all that mattered to her.

"Thanks a lot, Brother Ed," she told him, "and tell Sister Precious I'll be in contact with her again soon."

Michelle and Katrina pushed through the March wind, as they made their way to The Hope and Faith Center. Before the massive transformation, it was known as Dazzle Nightclub. They stood outside the building staring at its landscape. The new church was about two-thirds completed.

A man walked out of the building and approached the two women. "Are you ladies planning to visit the church once it's completed?" He looked at the building with pride. "This place used to be a nightclub. Isn't God amazing?"

Katrina and Michelle nodded in agreement. They were glad he hadn't reached out to shake their hands. With the high cold winds, it would have been hard for them to pry them from their pockets.

"Would you ladies like to come inside? I'll be serving as the associate pastor here once we get started."

Michelle and Katrina exchanged glances and followed the pastor into the incomplete church building. Michelle rubbed her hands together and let out a soft whistle as she looked around the church. Her eyes caught the giant cross near the altar, the stain glass windows, and the boxes filled with books on the floor. The edifice appeared to be complete to her.

The associate pastor walked out of the sanctuary and down the hall with them following close behind. They were taking in all they saw with widened eyes. The minister stopped walking and finally extended his hand to the women. "By the way, my name is Pastor Wynn." He shook Michelle's hand, and then Katrina's. "I hope you ladies will give this church a try."

They thanked him for the invitation, but informed the associate pastor that they already had a church that they loved dearly. The women continued to look around the building examining every aspect of the place. They remained silent for a moment before Michelle spoke.

"We were just curious; you know, about a church that used to be a nightclub."

Pastor Wynn nodded as if he knew exactly what she was saying. He seemed to sense that they were perhaps holding something back. It was probably because they seemed overly concerned about his church when they were already members of another one.

Michelle stared at all the walls around her, and Katrina was checking out every nook and cranny.

"Have you women ever been here before?" he suddenly asked. "When this place was a nightclub, I mean."

Katrina and Michelle's eyes must have given them away. "Me too," he confessed. "Years ago, I used to come here and shake everything I could. I used to dance the night away."

A half smile appeared on Michelle's face. "Us too," she admitted. "You sure are wise to pick up on that."

Katrina nodded her head in agreement, and soft laughter escaped her lips.

Michelle continued. "We used to come here back in the day, and that's something we aren't proud of."

The pastor nodded. No doubt, he wasn't proud of his time spent at the club before he gave his life to the Lord either. "Yeah, I know what you mean, but I don't look behind; I try to keep pushing forward." He began walking and they followed him again. It appeared that Pastor Wynn was going to give them a complete tour of Hope and Faith Center.

"Pastor Wynn was certainly nice, wasn't he?" asked Katrina as they drove down the highway on the ride back home.

Michelle couldn't agree more. He had given them his business card as they parted ways, and when he asked that they keep in touch, they had agreed they would. The rest of the ride home was made in silence with a million thoughts running through the women's minds. Katrina dropped Michelle off at her house and drove away. Michelle walked briskly to her house with her hands in her pockets and her coat collar turned up. As soon as Michelle was about to walk into her house, her cell phone rang and she fished it from her pocket.

"I made some hot chocolate and cookies. Want some?" Cheryl immediately asked when Michelle answered.

What Michelle really wanted to do was go into the warmth of her home, but she couldn't say no to cookies, hot cocoa, and the latest news on Freddie. She took quick steps to get to Cheryl's house, and the warmth she longed for met her as soon as she walked through the door. Michelle put her coat on the back of the chair and took a seat at the kitchen table where the cookies already sat in a plate.

Cheryl placed a Styrofoam cup of hot chocolate before Michelle and fixed herself one as well. Michelle picked up her cup and took a sip of the chocolaty flavor. "Mmmm," she moaned. "This sure hit the spot."

Cheryl looked at her for a second before she spoke. "I really feel sorry for Freddie's girlfriend."

Michelle didn't have to wonder what she meant by that. Cheryl had already told her that Freddie had four babies by his girlfriend. Michelle wondered what that woman was thinking; she should have left him a long time ago.

"I feel sorry for her," Cheryl repeated. "She calls me all the time and tells me how rotten he treats her, but she still loves him."

Michelle reached for a cookie and took a small bite. She chewed and swallowed before speaking. "What do you advise her to do?"

"I told her to leave him," Cheryl replied with no hesitation. "I don't think he's changing anytime soon.

Good advice, thought Michelle as she nibbled on the cookie.

"Every time she calls, which is a lot; I pray with her. I believe in prayers," said Cheryl. "By the way, what do you think of the cookies?"

Michelle knew Cheryl was experimenting with the different flavors because she wanted to open a cookie shop of her own. "These are good," she told her. "Bring a batch, a dozen over to my aftercare program tomorrow."

Cheryl smiled at her friend. "You can have these," she said as she reached for a food container to place the cookies in. "I told Dana she needs to love Freddie less and love God more," Cheryl added.

When Michelle exited Cheryl house thirty minutes later, she was still finishing the chewing of a cookie. When she entered her own house, she saw her husband staring at her. He walked toward her sniffing at the container in her hand before enveloping her with his arms.

"I missed you, Michelle."

She looked at David and grinned. "I missed you too." She relaxed in his arms.

Sasha ran down the stairs and toward her parents. "I missed you, Mommy."

The thought that they'd all missed each other made Michelle feel warm on the inside. The three of them were embracing one another in a group type of hug, but then Sasha spotted the container of cookies and pulled away.

"Can I have one?" the girl asked. When Michelle extended the container toward her, she took it out of Michelle's hand and dashed toward the kitchen.

"Hey, don't eat them all," said Michelle trailing behind her with David on her heels.

Chapter 14

The weather was a lot warmer on this Monday morning as Michelle stood on her front porch. She saw her neighbor's car slow down and come to a stop in front of her home. Cheryl must have had something important to say to stop when she was already running late for work.

"Guess what, or rather guess *who*?" said Cheryl when she climbed from her car and stood in front of Michelle's gate. "Freddie's moving back to D.C.; this time for good."

Michelle looked at the woman in disbelief. Would the nightmare that is Freddie ever end?

That was all she said before turning around and heading back to her car. Just before getting back in her driver's seat, she said, "I got to get to work. If you're interested in this continuing drama, be at my place at seven tonight."

At five minutes before seven that evening, Michelle walked out of her house, and down the street to Cheryl's. The front door opened before she knocked, and she followed Cheryl back into the kitchen where a small plate of cookies sat on the table. Cheryl motioned for her to have a seat, and she did. Michelle was curious as what was going on with Freddie. She hoped her friend and neighbor would get straight to the point. Cheryl reached for a cookie and took a small bite, and Michelle followed her lead.

Cheryl chewed several times before placing the cookie on the saucer in front of her. "Freddie and his girlfriend and their four children got evicted from their apartment in Philadelphia."

Michelle stared at her and continued chewing on the cookie. She wanted more information but didn't want to ask any questions. Thankfully, she didn't have to.

"He always loved Washington, D.C.," Cheryl continued, "so he's moving back here and his girlfriend and the children are moving back with her mother." Cheryl rose to go to the refrigerator and get a pitcher of punch.

Michelle reached for another cookie and began munching. Cheryl filled the two Styrofoam cups with punch and placed them on the table. She then took a seat and continued with the story.

"The good news is he's getting a place of his own. He'll only need to stay with me for a month at the most." Cheryl sat back in her chair. "He said his friend, Leo, hooked him up with a good job."

Michelle reached for her punch and swallowed half of it. Her thoughts made her subconsciously shake her head. *How could Freddie leave his girlfriend to take care of his four children without helping her at all? He was worse than ever!*

Cheryl's next words sent chills down Michelle's spine. "I told him that if he stays with me for more than a week, he must attend church. That's a house rule."

Michelle's shoulders trembled slightly. That meant he would be attending Peace Baptist. And what kind of job did Leo have for Freddie? Leo was just as crooked as he was. It wasn't a stretch to think that they might be involved in illegal activities.

"I didn't mean to bend your ear about my cousin," said Cheryl.

As much as Michelle disliked Freddie, she wanted to hear more. The more she knew about him, the better it was for her. Michelle reached for another cookie and started chewing. The entire time, she prayed that Cheryl wouldn't drop the subject. Her prayers were answered.

"Freddie's girlfriend calls me all the time discussing him. I feel truly sorry for her." Cheryl sighed long and deep before throwing up her hands in frustration.

Michelle could totally relate to the exasperation. She, too, was tired of that man's low life behavior. Freddie's moving back to D.C. was awful news for her. To make matters worse, he'd be staying two doors down from her house; at least for a while. She would not let this man spoil her bright and happy future with his blackmail. No, she would fight back! Anybody who tried to destroy her family was in for a fight; a great battle. Michelle only hoped she could be as strong as she was telling herself.

* * * * * * *

Sure enough, Freddie was back in town two days later. Ever since Cheryl told her, Michelle had been sitting on pins and needles.

"I'm going to the diner. You want anything? A muffin, maybe?" David waited for an answer, but Michelle just shrugged. "Banana-nut muffin, it is," he declared, raising an eyebrow at her peculiar behavior before he walked out of their bedroom.

A few moments later, Michelle heard David's voice coming from outside the house. He was talking to someone. A second male voice drew her closer to the window. She pulled back her curtains and saw David standing on the front porch with Freddie. Michelle leaned on a chair to steady herself.

What was Freddie saying to her husband? Why was he making her life so hard? She watched as they gave each other the brothers' handshake, and then Freddie walked back toward Cheryl's. David walked in the opposite direction, down the street. Michelle hoped Freddie hadn't told David anything about the two of them. She had paid the man not to tell her husband what he knew about her past. Had Freddie double crossed her and spilled the beans?

David returned with her muffin and coffee thirty minutes later. They sat at the kitchen table eating and reading the newspaper. Actually Michelle was using the paper to hide behind, thinking about the exchange between Freddie and her husband. The more time that passed, the more she relaxed. If Freddie had blabbed, David wouldn't be sitting calmly reading the paper. She took a big bite out of her muffin, wanting to finish it in a hurry so she could go somewhere and be alone with her thoughts. She took in another mouthful.

"I didn't know you were so hungry," David teased. "I would have bought you a full breakfast."

Michelle smiled weakly at his comment, then took another bite from her muffin and chewed. She folded her section of the newspaper and placed it on the table, ate the remains of the muffin, and wandered out the kitchen.

Sasha was coming down the stairs as she was going up. "Mommy, can we go to the park?"

Michelle looked at her daughter and sighed. "Sasha, I'm tired right now. We can go in about an hour." She took two steps at a time and hurried into her bedroom, closed the door, and plopped on the bed. At some point, she dozed off. Forty minutes later she rose from the bed and was surprised at how refreshed she felt.

Michelle slipped into a pair of jeans, an old blouse, and her comfortable sneakers, and prepared to go to the park with her daughter. She held Sasha's hand, as they walked, and made a heartfelt confession. "I need to spend more time with you. Sometimes I feel we don't spend enough quality time together."

Sasha smiled and squeezed her mother's hand. "Yeah; we need to go to the park more."

Michelle smiled, bent down, and kissed her daughter on the forehead. Her words were sincere. She planned to spend more time with her child doing all kinds of things. Sasha was always going places with her father. Michelle loved watching the way Sasha and David interacted with one another.

When her cell phone rang, Michelle reached in her jacket to retrieve it. She looked at the caller ID and smiled before pressing the button to answer. "Hello, David; we're almost to the park."

"I know," he replied. "I'll be there to join the two of you soon."

Less than half an hour after Michelle and Sasha reached the park, David joined them as promised. The Davidson family spent Saturday afternoon together at the park as a unit.

* * * * * * *

"What? What?" Michelle sat in a booth at Peace Diner with Katrina and Cheryl, the following day. Her neighbor had just informed her and Katrina that Freddie sent money to his girlfriend so she and his kids could join him in Washington, D.C.

"Is that a good idea?" asked a stunned Katrina.

Cheryl shrugged. "I don't know. It could mean he's trying to do the right thing."

Michelle and Katrina exchanged terrifying glances. According to Cheryl, Freddie planned to rent a house, and have Dana and their four children live there with him. Cheryl informed them that he had steady work with the job that Leo had helped him get. Apparently, Leo had also loaned Freddie some money.

99

Cheryl finished her coffee and scooted out of the booth. "Ladies, if you'll excuse me: I got to run. I'll give you the latest installment in the saga of Freddie next time we meet." She waved before walking out of the diner.

"I never thought Freddie and Leo would settle in D.C. for good." Katrina nervously looked at Michelle while speaking in low volumes.

Michelle's head was so full of thoughts that she couldn't even nod. At first she simply shrugged her shoulders, but moments later the words she wanted to say seemed to fly out of her mouth. "This is bad news; really bad news."

Katrina nodded her head up and down in rapid motions. They sat in the booth finishing their food in complete silence for the next ten minutes, then Michelle slid out of the booth, and Katrina followed right behind her. Without a word, they walked right out of the diner.

As it turned out, Michelle was right. It was *real* bad news for Cheryl's household. Freddie didn't get the house he planned on renting for his family. Dana arrived in D.C. and had no place to stay. So Freddie, Dana, and their four children were all living with Cheryl. Freddie paid her some money because he was working, but it was never enough. Cheryl was boiling mad and trying not to boil over. Dana was also steamed at Freddie, and she was barely speaking to him.

Cheryl sat at Peace Diner in a booth next to Michelle and across from Katrina. "Michelle and Katrina, I want y'all to know that I'm in over my head, and I'm going bonkers."

Michelle reached over and patted Cheryl on the shoulder. Katrina cast her eyes down toward the table.

Cheryl sighed. "I've got Brother Ed, Sister Precious and Brother Earl coming over to pray with me." She slumped down and allowed her head to rest on the table.

Michelle really felt for her. How could some people be so inconsiderate?

Cheryl returned to an upright position. "I've given all of them two months; then they have to move. I'm sorry, but I can't handle it."

Michelle completely understood how Cheryl felt. As far as she was concerned, Cheryl was a saint for letting them stay that long. She looked at her neighbor and wondered how she possibly could be holding up from all the pressure coming from her household.

Cheryl scooted out from the booth and stood. "My intercessors will be over to pray with me soon, so I got to go." She gave a wave before heading for the door.

Katrina looked at Michelle and softly said "I wouldn't want to be her," and Michelle nodded her head in agreement.

The next evening, curiosity got the best of Michelle and Katrina. They stood on Cheryl's porch, knowing that Freddie was still at work, making it a safe time to come over. Michelle and Katrina had never met Dana and the children; they had only seen them from a distance.

When Michelle knocked on the door, Cheryl quickly opened it and ushered them inside. The two women's eyes widen as they entered the house. Cheryl's home appeared as though it had been transformed into a daycare center.

Dana sat in a chair in the front room holding a baby. The other children sat nearby on bean bags. From all appearances, not more than one year separated the children's ages. Earl was there, and he sat near Dana talking to and smiling at the children. Cheryl walked toward the kitchen and motioned for Michelle and Katrina to follow. Once in the kitchen, they took seats around the table.

Cheryl sighed. "You see what I mean? Don't get me wrong. I like Dana and the kids, but . . ." Her words trailed off. She didn't have to say anymore; they totally understood how she felt. "What brings you ladies over?"

"Uh, we were just curious," admitted Katrina.

Cheryl nodded as if she completely understood. Dana was a tall, slim woman with a medium brown complexion. Her clothes looked expensive, and she was well groomed. She had the build and appearance of a model.

"Brother Earl has been spending a lot of time at the house," Cheryl told them. "He's been praying with Dana and the kids. Every now and then, he takes them to eat at the diner."

Michelle knew Freddie worked until late and that Dana was still mad at him for not having a place for them to stay. "How does Freddie feel about Brother Earl spending so much time with Dana and his kids?"

"Freddie is gone most of the time, and when he's home he's drunk or something," Cheryl explained. "Brother Earl is just a nice man; he helps lots of people."

Michelle looked at the clock on the wall. She wanted to leave in plenty of time before Freddie got home. "We just wanted to stop by," she said before rising from her chair.

"Yeah, that's right." Katrina got up as well.

Cheryl walked to the refrigerator and pulled out two small plastic containers and handed one to each of the women. "Taste these cookies, and give me your feedback," she said before hugging them individually. "Thanks for dropping by."

Chapter 15

Cheryl danced around her house to the gospel music that blasted from her stereo speakers. Two months had passed since she'd had that conversation with her friends, and she finally had a reason to rejoice. In jubilant motions, she twisted and turned out of the kitchen into the hallway and quickly twisted back into the kitchen. She threw her arms in the air praising the Lord.

"Whew!" She took a seat at the kitchen table. Cheryl was out of breath but she was full of glee. The telephone rang, and she bounced up to answer it. "Hello?" she said over the loud music.

Michelle was on the other end of the line. "It sounds like you're having a party over there."

"Yeah, that sounds like a good idea," Cheryl responded. How fast can you, Katrina, and Sasha get over here?"

Michelle laughed into the phone. "You're joking, right?"

"No. I'm not kidding; I'm for real."

Michelle chuckled and thought she might take Cheryl up on her offer. The music sounded good, plus Cheryl made delicious cookies. Rounding everybody up wouldn't be a problem. Sasha was upstairs in her bedroom, and Katrina was sitting in Michelle's kitchen at that very moment. "We'll be over in fifteen minutes," said Michelle.

"Welcome, welcome," Cheryl said when Michelle, Katrina, and Sasha showed up at her door. As the music blasted, the hostess danced her way to the kitchen, followed by her three dancing guests.

Cheryl dropped in a seat at the table and caught her breath. "Want to know why I'm so happy?" She didn't give them time to answer. "Because Freddie, Dana, and all their children moved out last night."

Michelle and Katrina looked at each other, and then back at Cheryl.

"They still live in D.C.," Cheryl clarified, dashing their unspoken hopes. "Freddie 's rental house finally came through."

Michelle gave a weary smile. Heck, she thought he was finally leaving her hometown. Cheryl bounced from her chair and danced to the refrigerator. She pulled out a small tray of sandwiches and a container of cookies and placed everything on the kitchen table. She bopped back to the refrigerator for a two liter bottle of punch.

Katrina spotted the Styrofoam cups still in plastic, opened them, and placed them on the table. Sasha had been dancing to the music in the middle of the room, but when she saw the food being brought out, she rushed to the table to eat. Cheryl continued to twirl around the kitchen as her guests ate.

Michelle didn't want to upset Katrina, but she told her what Cheryl had said about Leo. Leo had two kids with his girlfriend, and they had two kids each from other relationships. Katrina was interested in the information, but she was having a good time and didn't want to think of him. Freddie was the thorn in Michelle's side, and Leo was a thorn in her side. Little Sasha was dancing with Cheryl and having a supreme time. Sasha always loved a good party. They stayed another hour before leaving a still jubilant Cheryl all by herself.

Two hours later, Michelle was alone in her home. Katrina had gone, and David had taken Sasha and Davita to the park to spend some time together. Michelle looked out of her living room window and took in the sights of her neighborhood. Like most days, it was quiet outside with not much movement going on. She was preparing to leave her sightseeing post when she saw Dana and Earl walking down the street together.

Is Brother Earl getting sweet on Freddie's woman? Michelle shook off the thought. She was probably reading too much into the situation. Like Cheryl had said before; he was just a nice man. Michelle pulled the curtains closed when she saw David and Sasha enter the yard.

"Is it all right if Davita comes over?" David asked his wife when he walked inside.

Michelle was supportive of the time David spent with his children. "Sure," she said before hugging her husband, and giving him a peck on the cheek. She bent down and gave the same to Sasha before walking upstairs and lying across her bed.

An hour later, Nicola delivered Davita to their home and left. Precious's father had accompanied Nicola. He'd gotten out and opened the door for her to get back in the car as they prepared to leave.

"Wow," Michelle said aloud. The thought that they must really be a couple made her jaw drop. It was hard to believe with that big forty-year age gap between them.

The next morning, Michelle walked out on her porch just in time to see Cheryl as she walked past her house.

"I'm heading to work," informed Cheryl. She sighed and shook her head. "I thought I was free of Freddie and his drama, but I guess Dana's going to keep coming over even though they have their own place now."

"At least Dana has Brother Earl to talk to," offered Michelle.

Cheryl nodded and added, "Yeah, they're getting really close." She waved before hurrying down the street.

Michelle walked back into the house and up the stairs to her bedroom. When she reached the landing, the telephone rang. Michelle quickened her steps and grabbed the phone on the third rang. "Hello?"

"Hello, Michelle; this is Precious." The woman stopped talking, like she was almost choking up. Was she crying? Precious continued. "You won't believe what happened," she said before taking a pause. "My father and Nicola eloped! They eloped last night and I'm so—"

"What?" Michelle cut in. "I can't believe it." She could tell that Precious was about to lose it, so Michelle softened her tone. "Are you all right?" There was silence on the other end of the phone for a few seconds.

Precious finally cleared her throat and asked, "Can you meet me at the diner?"

All kinds of thoughts swam through Michelle's mind as she changed her clothes and got ready to leave. They were those drowning kind of thoughts. Should she call David first and tell him about Elder Peterson's marriage to Nicola? Should she call Katrina? Calling Katrina first sounded like a good idea. She might need her to help encourage Precious.

A half hour later, Michelle walked through the door of the diner. The place was crowded but she spotted Katrina sitting in a booth and walked across the floor to join her. Precious hadn't arrived yet.

"I cannot believe Nicola and Elder Peterson eloped," were the first words out of Katrina's mouth when Michelle sat in the space beside her. "What was he thinking? He's old enough to be her grandfather." She stopped talking when they spotted Precious dashing through the door.

Precious joined them and plopped down on a seat in the booth. Michelle and Katrina waited quietly, giving her a chance to initiate the conversation. In the interim, they offered sympathetic looks.

Michelle looked away from Precious and allowed her eyes to scan the diner. In a cozy corner near the restrooms, she spotted Dana and Earl sitting in a booth. She shook her head and Precious's voice pulled her attention back to her own table.

"Thank y'all for coming," she started. As Precious went on to fill the two women in on the details of her father and his new wife, tears began to stream down her cheeks. Katrina reached over and held her hand for comfort.

Minutes later, Precious was using a napkin to dry her eyes. "Ain't nothing I can do about it now." She parted her lips and blew out a lung full of air. "How can that woman be my stepmother?"

Michelle reached forward and grabbed Precious's hand, and then Katrina's. Together, the women prayed to God for strength, encouragement, and the wisdom to understand.

Afterward, Precious did look somewhat better. Michelle and Katrina insisted that she have a meal, and the three women dined together. When the meal was done, Precious called for a cab and they walked her to the restroom so that she could freshen up before riding back home. The women waved at Earl and Dana as they walked past them. When the cab arrived, Precious hugged Michelle and Katrina before leaving.

"I sure wouldn't want to be in her shoes," said Michelle. She and Katrina had returned to their seat in the booth.

Katrina nodded her head in her agreement. "Does David know Nicola and the elder eloped?"

Michelle nodded. "He was pretty shocked at the news."

Katrina intertwined her fingers and displayed a toothy grin. Michelle looked at her friend and wondered what was going on. She knew she wasn't happy about the marriage, so it had to be something else.

"What are you grinning about?" asked Michelle.

Katrina smile grew even wider. "I'm with child," she announced. "Girl, I'm going to have a baby."

Michelle opened her mouth, and then closed it a couple of times. She placed her hand over her mouth, and then removed it. Finally, she found her words. "Oh, I cannot believe it. Congratulations, Katrina."

"Thanks," Katrina replied.

Michelle raised her hand to signal the waitress over. "Can I get two glasses of ginger ale, please?"

The waitress nodded and said, "Right away."

Katrina placed her elbows on the table and leaned forward. "You remember when Frank and I went to Hawaii for Valentine's Day? Well, that's when this baby was conceived."

Michelle's grin was as wide as her friend's. The waitress returned with the ginger ale and placed the glasses on the table in front of them before walking away. Michelle reached for her glass and held it up, and Katrina followed suit. "I'd like to make a toast to Katrina and Frank Beckett. May they have a happy and healthy baby." They clicked glasses and took a sip of the soda.

Twenty minutes later, they left the diner and went back to Michelle's house to continue their conversation. The phone was ringing as they walked in the front door, and Michelle ran to answer it.

"Hello? Hello?" She was out of breath.

"Hello, Michelle; this is Nicola. I'd like to invite you and your family to my wedding celebration."

Michelle was stunned. *Why is this fool . . . Sorry, Lord.* She corrected her thoughts. Why was this woman, who was a former girlfriend of her husband and shared a daughter with him, inviting her to a wedding celebration she was having? Michelle was at a loss for words; for *nice* words, that is. She bit her tongue and said, "Uh, thank you, Nicola, but my family and I will be unable to attend your celebration." She closed her mouth after that before something bad and unchristian fell out.

"Oh, that's too bad," cooed Nicola. "I'm very fond of your little family."

Michelle wanted to get off the phone badly. "Bye now. I'll see you at church," she said. After hanging up the phone, she paced back in forth in the kitchen shaking her head before returning to the front room to join Katrina.

"Who was that on the phone?" asked Katrina as Michelle entered the room.

"Get this. It was Nicola inviting David, Sasha, and me to her wedding celebration."

Katrina's eyes widened in total disbelief. They soon changed the subject because Nicola was the last person they wanted to discuss for any length of time. Katrina visited with Michelle for the entire evening, even helping her with her aftercare business. After the last charge had left for the day, they hugged, and Katrina headed home.

Michelle began the task of tidying up the family room where the children stayed until their parents came to collect them. There really wasn't much to do; she had taught the kids to pick up after themselves. Michelle walked over to the table and placed the lid back on the checkers game before putting the game away. After that, she walked into the kitchen to retrieve a broom to sweep the floor.

She heard a key in the door and turned around to see her husband let himself in. She smiled at him from the hallway, and David followed his wife into the family room. He took a seat in a black, lazy-boy recliner.

"How was your day?" asked Michelle.

David blew a stream of air from his mouth. "Okay, I guess. I still can't believe Nicola married Elder Peterson. What would possess her to marry such an old man?" He rubbed his forehead and continued. "I hope they take good care of Davita." He rose from the recliner and walked out of the room.

Michelle kept sweeping and thinking about what her husband had said. Why was he so upset because Nicola had gotten married? Michelle realized that no one seemed happy with the union, but she still couldn't help wondering if David was a little bit jealous that his ex-girlfriend had gotten married. Of course, it could be that he was only concerned with the wellbeing of his daughter. Either way, it gave her the creeps when he showed deep emotions about the situation. She gripped the broom handle tightly and continued sweeping the room. As she did so, she also tried sweeping the thoughts of that woman out of her mind.

* * * * * * *

A week later, while the Davidson family sat together in the kitchen, the phone rang. David was the closest to the phone so he answered it. "Hello?" He stood with the phone to his ear.

"Hello, David."

He immediately recognized that voice and quietly listened to what she had to say.

"My husband and I are going to Hawaii for our honeymoon," Nicola began.

David sighed. He didn't know why this information disturbed him so. He loved his wife, but still he wasn't happy that Nicola had gotten married. He remained silent while she continued.

"I was wondering if you'd like to keep Davita while we're gone."

David perked up. "Oh yes, Nicola; I'd love that."

Michelle looked up at him. It was obvious that she was wondering what Nicola was saying that had suddenly made her husband so happy.

"Of course, I have to check with Michelle first," he added.

His wife stared at him even harder with the mention of her name. When David ended their conversation and hung up the phone, he walked back to the kitchen table where Michelle and Sasha still sat. David looked at Michelle, and then at Sasha, and then back at Michelle again. "Nicola wondered if we could watch Davita while she's on her honeymoon."

Sasha jumped up from her seat and ran to her father. "Can Davita stay with us? Please, Daddy?" begged the six-year-old.

"If your mother says it's okay," he answered.

Michelle narrowed her eyes. Why was he making her the heavy? "I don't have a problem with Davita coming for a visit," she finally said.

Sasha started clapping her hands together with glee and David joined in the celebration.

Michelle shook her head at the scene. "Sasha, when you're done celebrating, I want you to finish your sandwich."

Sasha bounced into her chair and began eating again, taking big bites.

Michelle patted her daughter on the shoulder and rose from her chair. She walked out of the kitchen; she needed time to think and to talk to Katrina. As Michelle walked away, she overheard David tell Sasha that he was going to take the entire week off from work to spend with his two daughters. It was clearly a dream come true for him. Michelle couldn't remember the last time he had taken off from work.

Chapter 16

David and his girls had gone to breakfast at Peace Diner this morning before he took them to school. Michelle didn't want to infringe on the outing he planned for his daughters, so she decided to stay home. It was now seven in the evening, and they were still out. Dinner and a movie were on the agenda for this evening.

Michelle sat alone at the kitchen table drinking herbal tea and eating oatmeal-raisin cookies. She had been feeling kind of lonely ever since Davita had come to stay. She was really fond of the girl, and David had invited her to join them on their adventures, as he called them, but Michelle had declined the offer. She knew she had no one but herself to blame for her loneliness. She got up from her chair and walked over to the telephone, she needed to talk to her best friend.

"Hey, Michelle; what's happening?" Katrina said with glee in her voice.

"David and the girls are out, so I decided to call my best friend." Michelle tried to sound just as cheerful. "How are you doing?"

Katrina was two months into her pregnancy and had been experiencing nausea. Morning sickness had become a part of her daily routine.

Michelle heard a knock on the door and excused herself temporarily. "Yes? Who is it?" she asked when reaching the front door.

"It's Cheryl," returned her neighbor. Michelle unlocked the door and opened it. Cheryl's eyes were wide and sort of scary looking, and her voice was panic-stricken. " Dana has been shot, and I'm headed to the hospital to see her now."

Michelle tried to process the information, but was at a loss for words.

"I got to go," said Cheryl. "Do you want to come with me?"

Michelle didn't know what to say or do. She needed to think, but she found herself agreeing to going to the hospital. She remembered that Katrina was still on hold, so she signaled for Cheryl to wait for her while she walked into the kitchen to grab the phone.

"Katrina, Freddie's Dana has been shot. I'm leaving for the hospital with Cheryl now." Without giving Katrina time to reply, Michelle hung up the phone and dashed back to join her neighbor. As they walked to the car, she realized that she needed to contact David. He needed to know what had happened and how to contact her.

As Cheryl drove, many thoughts ran through Michelle's mind. "Do you know who shot Dana?" she asked.

Cheryl shook her head. "No, I don't. Brother Ed called and told me, but he didn't supply any details."

Michelle became more confused. Ed was the same police detective Michelle had asked to assistance in stopping Freddie from blackmailing her about their past relationship. Ed had said he would keep an eye on him for her. Michelle looked over at Cheryl. She had a tight grip on the steering wheel and was looking straight ahead. Cheryl didn't look like she wanted to have a conversation and neither did Michelle, for that matter.

Suddenly Cheryl began praying aloud. "Dear Father, I come to you with a heavy heart. a friend of mine has been shot."

"Yes, Lord," inserted Michelle.

Cheryl continued. "I pray that you heal her wounds and restore her health."

When Cheryl stopped there, Michelle took over. "I pray that you be there in her sick room and work a miracle so that you will get all the glory. In the name of Jesus Christ. Amen."

"Amen," Cheryl echoed.

The prayer had released the tension that was there just minutes, ago. A small smile appeared on Michelle's face and as they entered the parking lot of the hospital, she saw a more peaceful look on Cheryl's face too..

Ed was waiting for them as they walked through the doors of the hospital.

"Brother Ed," said Cheryl when they neared him, "what happened to Dana? Who shot her?"

He pointed toward some pale blue chairs that were on the other side of the room. "Let's talk over there." When they were all seated, he looked at them and in a solemn tone said, "Dana was shot by Freddie."

Michelle made a grunting sound, and Cheryl closed her eyes and mumbled something under her breath.

Ed continued. "I had been watching Freddie for a while . In fact, I was outside his house when the gunshots rang out." He paused for a few seconds. "I then ran to the house. The door wasn't locked, so I didn't have to try to break it down; I was able to just push it open. I grabbed Freddie, forced the handcuffs on him, and dialed 911 for emergency assistance." Ed sat back in his seat and let the women absorb all that he had said.

Michelle and Cheryl looked at one another. The sounds of approaching footsteps made Michelle turn around. She smiled when she saw it was Katrina. "What are you doing here?" asked Michelle.

"Did you think I could stay home after hearing the information?" she returned.

Ed rose to his feet. "Ladies, Dana was extremely lucky . . . I mean she was extremely blessed to only have been shot in the leg. She's in surgery having the bullet removed." He nodded at the three women. "I'm going to head out now.

Michelle broke the silence once the detective was out of view. "We won't be able to see Dana tonight. We all probably need to head home," she said before rising from her seat.

Cheryl and Katrina agreed, and they all walked out together. Cheryl drove while Michelle sat in the passenger seat. They waved at Katrina as she pulled out of the parking lot before them. Cheryl and Michelle trailed her home to make sure their pregnant friend got home safely. Then Cheryl dropped Michelle off at her front gate before making the short drive down the street to her own home.

Michelle's mind was swirling with thoughts. She couldn't believe what Ed had said about Freddie. She knew he was a wretched person, but she never would have thought he'd shoot the mother of his children. Michelle put her key into the door and opened it. David and Sasha were on the other side of it staring at her.

"Where were you?" asked David.

Michelle had gotten so caught up with the shooting that she'd forgotten to follow through and contact her husband. "I'm sorry." She began walking to the kitchen, and David and Sasha followed behind. Michelle didn't explain everything in detail until her daughter went upstairs.

"Wow," was all David was able to say upon hearing the whole story.

Michelle was feeling a lot of sympathy for Dana and found herself praying for her recovery. And there was a bright side to this whole ordeal. Michelle couldn't help but think that she was finally done with Freddie for good. He was locked up now and could no longer bother her. She was finally done with him blackmailing her for something she had done in her past. A small smile appeared on her face, and the more she thought of it, the wider her smile became.

"What in the world are you grinning about?" asked David. "How can you be happy after what happened this evening?"

Michelle quickly sobered and rose from her seat at the kitchen table. "I'm going to check in on the girls." She walked out of the kitchen and took the stairs to her daughter's bedroom that was temporarily being shared with her half-sister.

The next morning Michelle, Cheryl, and Katrina were at the hospital to see Dana. Cheryl had taken the day off, Michelle's aftercare business didn't start until later, and Katrina's job had flexible hours. Ed entered the hospital and walked over to meet the women.

"Hello, ladies," he said. "Dana is doing fine; doctors were able to remove the bullet from her leg without any complications."

"Praise the Lord," said Cheryl rising from her seat.

"Praise the Lord," echoed Michelle and Katrina.

They decide that they would go in Dana's room two-at-a-time. Cheryl and Michelle went in first, while Brother Ed and Katrina stayed in the waiting room. The two women walked down the long hallway and into the room where Dana lay in bed with her eyes open and her right leg wrapped in white bandages. A smile came to her face when she saw her visitors.

"How are you doing?" asked Cheryl as she reached for the woman's hand.

"I'm doing okay," returned Dana. "Doctors say I can probably go home in a week."

"I'm glad you're doing better," said Michelle looking Dana in the eyes. She hardly knew the woman; nevertheless, she was still concerned with her health.

"Thank you," said Dana. "I can't wait to get out of this hospital and go home."

Cheryl wondered where home was for the woman now that the one who paid their rent was locked up. She knew Dana's parents lived in Philadelphia. Was she going back to Philly? Was that where she was calling home? Cheryl's heart ached for the woman whose four children had temporarily been placed in the hands of the city.

Dana's voice broke through Cheryl's thoughts. "I was wondering if I could stay with you for a little while."

Cheryl was speechless at that moment. Her first thought was no way would she let Dana and her four children stay in her house. She thought she would go plum crazy with all of them in her house again; she'd barely survived the first time. Dana looked at her waiting for an answer.

Cheryl cleared her throat and said, "I'll need a little time to think about that one."

Dana smiled and nodded; she knew that she was asking for a lot.

"We're leaving now because you have more visitors outside," Cheryl said before exiting the hospital room followed by Michelle. On the other side of the door, Cheryl released a stream of breath from her puffy jaws. Michelle looked at her, and then looked away as they walked back toward the waiting area.

When they reached Ed and Katrina they took a seat next to them. Like clockwork, their friends stood and walked down the hallway that would lead them to Dana's hospital room.

Was Cheryl really considering taking Dana and her children in again?

Cheryl turned in her seat, and as if reading Michelle's mind, offered the information. "Maybe I could take them in for a little while. I'm getting married in six months, so maybe just until then."

Michelle's eyes grew larger just thinking about such a full house. "If that's what you want to do, I guess," she concluded. Quite frankly, she didn't know what else to say, so she just sat and looked straight ahead.

Cheryl had less than a week to make her final decision. Katrina and Brother Ed returned in twenty minutes, and they all walked out of the hospital together. Cheryl invited everyone back to her house for cookies and punch. They sat around the kitchen table talking about the situation with Dana and Freddie.

"Freddie was jealous of Brother Earl because he was spending so much time with Dana," explained Ed, reaching for a cup to pour his punch.

Michelle gasped. Earl was a good Christian man, and she was sure that he wasn't having an affair with Dana. Sure, he might have a crush on her, but Michelle suspected that's as far as it went.

Katrina's next words offered insight. "Those drugs that Freddie was taking made him paranoid." She rose from the table. "Can I use your bathroom, Cheryl?"

"Sure. You know where it is." As Cheryl watched Katrina walk out she thought more about Dana's request of her. She knew the woman wasn't a bad person; just a foolish one in her opinion. She had had four children with her boyfriend. *Four!* How foolish was that? One thing for sure, if she decided to let Dana and the kids stay with her for a while, there would have to be ground rules. They had to go to church; all of them, all the time.

The plate of cookies was nearing empty. Brother Ed was pouring himself another cup of punch, and Michelle was chewing on a cookie. Cheryl had had plenty of conversations with Dana; usually when the woman called her because Freddie was being abusive. Cheryl hated that her cousin was beating up on Dana. She felt kind of guilty because he was related to her.

Katrina walked back into the kitchen. "I'm going to work for a little while today," she announced

"I'd better be going too," Ed said as he stood. "I'll walk you out." Cheryl and then Michelle rose from their seats to hug their departing friends. Michelle stayed for another twenty minutes before leaving for home.

At the end of the week, Davita's visit came to an end. Nicola was back from her honeymoon and had come to pick her up. . On Saturday morning, David, Michelle, and Sasha sat at Peace Diner eating breakfast.

"I had a great time with Davita," said David. "I hate that she had to go home." He gave Sasha's hand a little squeeze as he spoke.

Michelle nodded in agreement. She had to admit that she had grown fond of David's daughter, and she was proud to be Davita's stepmother.

"When is she coming back?" asked Sasha before putting a forkful of pancakes in her mouth.

"Real soon," said David fiddling with his spoon.

"I really enjoyed her stay too," admitted Michelle, smiling at David, and then at Sasha

Upon finishing their meals and leaving the diner, they decided to go for a family walk and take advantage of the warm May morning. Sasha walked between her parents holding David's right hand and Michelle's left.

"Are we going to the park?" asked the six-year-old. When David nodded his reply, Sasha smiled, showing her missing front tooth. She ran straight for the toys when they arrived.

Michelle and David sat at a nearby bench and enjoyed watching their beautiful daughter. David was the first to speak.

"I still can't believe Freddie shot his girlfriend. I didn't think he was that bad of a person."

Michelle was caught off guard by her husband's remarks and stiffened her shoulders. She knew all-too-well what an awful person Freddie was. She looked at her husband. "Freddie isn't a good person."

"I guess you're right, but still." David stood up and stretched. "Sasha's not having much luck getting that swing going," he said. "I'm going to go and give her a push.

They were cute together, Michelle thought as she sat alone for a while and watched David and Sasha interact with one another. Desiring to get in on some of the fun, she got up from the bench and joined her husband and her daughter.

On Sunday morning, Michelle and her family walked to Peace Baptist Church, looking quite unified in their navy blue outfits. They exchanged greetings with Brother Earl at the door, who was still puzzling over Dana being shot by Freddie. They walked into the sanctuary and to the third pew from the front. Cheryl was sitting there with Dana and her four children.

She looked at Freddie's children. Dana was holding the infant in her arms. Two of the children bore a strong resemblance to Freddie.

The woman in charge of the nursery walked down the aisle to their pew. "Would you like to bring the little ones to the nursery?" she offered.

Deciding that it was a good idea, Dana rose from the pew. The caretaker gently took the infant out of Dana's arms so that she could lean against her cane as she walked. Cheryl rose to help guide the other children to the nursery.

Michelle watched the scene and subconsciously shook her head. She didn't realize her own reaction until David nudged her and gave her the eye. It was then that Michelle straightened her demeanor.

Cheryl and Dana were slowly making their way back to the pew Just as Pastor Johnnie Jenkins walked to the pulpit with a large Bible in his hand.

"Good morning, saints," he said in an uplifted voice. "This is a Holy Ghost morning that the Lord has made. We will rejoice and be glad in it."

"Yes, Lord; you got that right!" said a man in the second pew.

Other shouts of "Amen" echoed throughout the church.

The pastor continued with, "Please turn to the book of 2 John in your Bible."

Chapter 17

On Monday morning, David Davidson returned to work after a week off. "I'm going to miss being home with you," he said to his wife before leaving for the office, "but I sorta-kinda miss my job too."

Michelle feigned injury as if her feelings had been hurt for a moment, and then broke out in a big smile. They had confirmed their plans to have dinner at the diner, and then she told him to have a marvelous day. The day passed without any abnormal happenings. Katrina stopped in that afternoon and worked with her in her aftercare program.

"How are you feeling?" Michelle wanted to know.

Katrina was nearing the end of her first trimester and was throwing up a little less. She looked at Michelle and covered her mouth with her hand while she yawned. "I'm okay. Just a little tired."

Michelle had been pregnant before; she knew exactly how her best friend felt. She sighed and looked at the children that remained in her care. They had already gone over their homework, played board games, and prayed, as they did every day. The last two now sat waiting for their parents to pick them up from after care. Michelle began straightened up the family room. She wanted her aftercare children to participate in more activities. She had already made plans to begin taking them to the library two times a week.

"Wow, I can't believe Cheryl is letting Dana and her four kids live with her," said Katrina, shaking her head in disbelief.

"Me neither," Michelle admitted, "but it is a Christian thing to do." She thought about Dana's constant visitor. "Do you think Brother Earl is interested in Dana?" she asked. .

"Yes I do." Katrina laughed. "He's over the house practically every day."

Michelle laughed too. Could he possibly be interested in a woman with four small children? The doorbell rang cutting into her thoughts. While Katrina put books in their rightful place, Michelle stood opened the door for the last two parents who had finally arrived. Katrina visited with her for another half hour before leaving for home.

* * * * * * *

Michelle and Sasha were in the kitchen when David walked with a white envelope in his hand.

"Hi, honey," said Michelle as she prepared to meet and embrace him. She stopped dead in her tracks when she saw the expression on his face. David's eyes began to narrow and his nostrils were flailing wildly. "David, what's wrong?" asked Michelle "What did I do?"

He walked closer to her filling the gap between them. When he stopped, he stared at her, holding the white envelope up in the air.

"Sasha would you please leave Mommy and Daddy alone for a minute," Michelle said looking at her daughter. She didn't know what had David upset, but whatever it was, their daughter didn't need to be caught in the middle of it.

Sasha had been looking at a book and hadn't noticed her father's strange behavior. With a carefree bounce, she rose from her chair and walked out of the kitchen carrying her book with her.

David never broke the glare that his eyes had locked on his wife. He took a step closer to her, putting the white envelope in her face and said, "Did you have an affair with Freddie?"

Michelle rocked back and forth; suddenly feeling like her head had spun around. She had to sit down or she might fall down. Michelle walked over to the kitchen table and took a seat. Did David just ask her if she and Freddie had had an affair? Yep, that's what he'd said; she'd heard it with her own two ears. How in the world had David ever found out?

"Were you and Freddie ever in a relationship?" David asked again, and this time his eyes demanded an answer.

Michelle nodded, yes. "But that was so long ago," she quickly said. "I made a mistake." David stared at her a little longer, and Michelle looked down at the floor in shame. He handed her the white envelope he was holding and stomped out of the kitchen and up the stairs. Michelle opened the envelope and pulled out a sheet of paper. She began reading, and what she saw made her gasp for air. Her mouth felt as dry as the Sahara Desert, and tears came to her eyes.

She exited the kitchen and walked into the family room and took a seat in the black leather recliner. Michelle released a loud scream, crumpled the letter, and threw it across the room. She balled up her fists and struck the leather chair.

Sasha ran into the room. "Mommy, are you all right?"

Michelle rose to pick up the letter and stuffed it in her pants pocket. She put her arms around her daughter and held her tight. Michelle released Sasha when they heard David run down the stairs. They walked into the hallway and saw him carrying a duffel bag.

"I'll be staying with my mother if you need to reach me," he said before kissing Sasha on the forehead and walking out the front door.

"Why is Daddy leaving?"

Michelle wanted to answer her daughter's question, but she couldn't. Freddie had sent the letter to David's place of employment. That snake had taken another bite out of her, and she was on the verge of collapse. "Sasha, we're going somewhere right now," she told her.

"Mommy, where are we going?" Sasha asked half an hour later as they walked down the street together holding hands.

"It's a surprise, honey," returned Michelle. She didn't want to go to her best friend's house and burden Katrina with her problems. Katrina was pregnant and didn't need the agony.

They didn't stop walking until they reached the bus stop. Ten minutes later the bus pulled up and Michelle and Sasha got on. Twenty minutes after that, they exited the bus and began walking again. They walked past a convenience store, and then Michelle backed up and they went inside. Michelle purchased some snacks, and Sasha begged to carry the bag. They walked an additional block and crossed the street to the yellow house. Sasha smiled; she knew where they were going and loved going there. They walked into the yard, up the steps, and knocked on the door. A minute later, the door opened and they were ushered inside.

"Hello, Mama," Michelle said. "Sasha and I decided to visit with you."

Bethany looked at her, and then at Sasha. "It's about time you dropped by. I was about to start thinking I didn't have a daughter."

Michelle looked down because she knew her mother was correct. She should visit more often. Sasha walked to her grandmother and hugged her on the leg. Her grandmother pulled her even closer and bent down and kissed her on the cheek.

"Let's go in the kitchen," Bethany said. I have a treat that I know my wonderful granddaughter will love."

Michelle walked ahead of them. It was hard for her mom to walk fast with Sasha still hanging on to her. Once inside the kitchen, they all sat around the kitchen table as Bethany cut the devil's food cake. She put the first slice on her granddaughter's plate.

Sasha cut a piece off with her fork and placed it in her mouth. "Mmm, this is some good cake, Grandma."

Bethany smiled and said, "Sweets for the sweet."

Michelle enjoyed her slice of cake, as well, but her mother knew something serious was going on for her to make an unannounced visit. Bethany kept toys in her backyard for Sasha to play with whenever she came over. When she saw Michelle place her fork down and stare off into space, she knew her daughter needed to talk.

Bethany turned to her granddaughter who had just taken in a forkful of her cake. "Sasha, baby; you want to go out back and play on the toys?"

Sasha jumped up from her chair, and Michelle took a napkin from the table to wipe her daughter's mouth and hands. As soon as Sasha dashed to the back door and went outside, Michelle and her mother's eyes met.

"What's wrong, honey?" asked Bethany.

Michelle explained in detail all that had gone on between her and David. She told her mom about Freddie and what had transpired with them. She told her everything. It was a story that Michelle had never divulged to her mother, and as she spoke, Bethany's eyes filled with sympathy.

"Oh, I didn't know," replied Bethany as she rose from her chair to look outside and check on Sasha. She then returned to her seat at the kitchen table.

Michelle let out a soft sigh. "It's pretty bad, isn't it, Mama?"

Bethany reached for her hand." Let's pray on it."

The prayer was brief, but after it was said, Michelle felt lighter; less stressed.

"Sweetie, you've got to learn to take your problems to the Lord and leave them there," spoke her wise mother.

Michelle nodded because she knew Bethany was right. They heard a key in the lock, and then the door opened. Michelle's eyes grew large when a man walked through the kitchen door a minute later.

"Joe," Bethany said. "Look who's here."

"Who's this stranger?" he asked smiling.

Michelle rose from her chair and walked over to hug him. "Hi, Daddy. I didn't mean to stay away so long."

They stayed in a warm brace for a few seconds before her father pulled away. He then, looked at the cake on the table and his face brightened. He took Michelle's hand and led her to the kitchen table, and they both took a seat. "Let's have a piece of cake," he said.

Michelle could agree with that; she didn't mind having a second slice of cake.

"How are my wonderful daughter and granddaughter doing?" he asked before forking cake into his mouth.

Michelle explained to him a little of what was going on in her life, but not everything. When Bethany asked if she and Sasha wanted to spend the night with them, Michelle politely declined the offer; she had an aftercare business to tend to. Being in her childhood home made Michelle want to be ten years old again. It made her long for the days when she just ran and played without a serious care in the world. She shook her head and snapped out of her longing. She couldn't go back. She was Michelle the adult, with a boatload of problems.

Before they left for home an hour later, Michelle made several promises to her parents. One was to visit more often, and another was to let Sasha spend more time with them. They reminded her that children grow up quickly, and they didn't want to miss their granddaughter's childhood.

Bethany also insisted in helping with the aftercare business for a while; at least until the situation with David quieted down. Michelle agreed to that. Her mother was a retired D.C. government employee and wanted to keep herself busy until she determined what she wanted to do next.

Michelle thought about her mother as she and Sasha walked to the bus stop. She and Bethany bore a strong resemblance. They both had the same facial features and skin complexion. The strange part was that Michelle didn't realize she looked so much like her mother until several people brought it up. Now when she looked in the mirror, she, too, could see her mother's face.

Michelle and Sasha boarded the bus heading for home. Sasha was still carrying the bag of snacks. On the bus, she laid her head on her mother's shoulder, and Michelle held it there with her hand as they rode.

Michelle's mother showed up at her house bright and early the next morning. She brought breakfast with her; more than enough for everyone. She motioned with her index finger for Michelle to follow her into the kitchen, and she obeyed. Once in the kitchen Bethany laid out on the table all the food items she'd brought. There were five Styrofoam containers filled with pancakes, eggs, sausages, cheese biscuits, and cinnamon rolls. There was also a tray of coffee and bottles of orange juice.

Bethany surveyed the food and with a grin on her face asked, "Did I bring enough?"

Sasha ran down the stairs and into the kitchen. She smiled when she saw all the food spread out on the table, "Hi, Grandma. Did you bring all this food for me?"

Bethany smiled and bent down to hug her granddaughter. "Not all of it, honey, but some is for you."

Satisfied with that answer, Sasha took a seat at the kitchen table, and her grandmother chose to sit in the chair next to her. Michelle was already seated, and they joined hands and prayed over the food.

"I'd like to take Sasha to school today" said Bethany glancing at her daughter.

Michelle nodded her head in approval. She knew Sasha would like that too, but right now, the child was too busy attacking her pancakes to take any interest in their conversation. Bethany announced that after she took Sasha to school, she would head for the employment office to seek work. Michelle knew her mom was growing restless sitting at home, so it didn't surprise her to know that retired life wasn't working out for Bethany.

An hour later, Michelle sat in the family room alone. It was going to be a long Tuesday. David had not come by or called since he stormed out yesterday. She wished she had told him about Freddie from the get-go. If she had, she wouldn't be sitting alone lamenting about the whole, ugly ordeal.

Michelle dragged herself out of the chair and over to the window. She pulled back the curtains and stared at the world outside. Her mind drifted to Dana who'd just had a baby three months ago. And her other children were ages four, three, and two years old. How could someone have that many kids with a man who wasn't her husband? Did the woman have rocks in her head or something? Cheryl had called Dana a foolish woman, and Michelle had agreed with her totally. Michelle shook the judgmental thoughts from her head and decided to pray for the woman instead.

A cab pulled up and stopped in front of her house. She wondered who would be coming to her home in a cab this time of day. A few seconds later, Katrina emerged from the car and began walking toward her house. Michelle let the curtain panels close and went to greet her best friend. Michelle opened it before Katrina could even knock.

"What's wrong?" asked Michelle when she saw the faraway look in her friend's eyes. She stepped aside to let the woman enter the house, and then closed the door behind them and stared at her friend. "Is the baby all right?"

Katrina nodded her head and reached into her pocketbook and pulled out a white envelope. "Leo sent Frank a letter to his place of employment, telling my husband about me and him,"

Michelle opened her mouth wide and covered it with her hand. With her free hand, she accepted the envelope that Katrina handed her. They'd both been blindsided in the same manner. Michelle ushered her friend into the house where they each took a seat on the couch in the family room.

"This don't make no sense," said Katrina. "I paid Leo all that money to keep my past in the past."

Michelle could only sit and stare. She had paid Freddie money to keep her secret from her husband too.

"Frank left me," Katrina blurted through a sudden sob.

Michelle didn't want her pregnant friend to become too upset, and she placed her arm around her to try and offer some level of comfort. As Katrina's tears subsided, she reached into her pocketbook and pulled out a tissue to wipe her eyes and blow her nose.

"Why did we think we could trust two guys who were blackmailing us?" asked Katrina.

Michelle looked as puzzle as she did. All the women could do was shake their heads at their own stupidity. Katrina stuck around and joined Bethany in helping Michelle with her aftercare program. Bethany sat at the table coloring with two children in Bible themed coloring books. Michelle sat in the corner reading a book with two children. Katrina sat on the couch playing a card game with a child.

As Michelle turned the page of the book she was reading, she thought of David. Thoughts of him had been filtering in her mind throughout the day. Eventually, she lost concentration and told the children to take turns reading the rest of the book themselves.

At the end of the day, the three ladies sat around the table in the family room. The children had all gone home and the room was tidy now.

"Why don't you spend the night here?" Michelle asked Katrina.

She didn't answer right away; Katrina only looked up and smiled as if she was contemplating the offer.

Michelle's mother spoke up. "That's a wonderful idea; you being pregnant and all."

It didn't take too much coaxing. Katrina agreed to spend the night at Michelle's house. It would give her somebody to talk to and somebody for Kayla to play with too.

Bethany rose from her seat. "I've got to go," she said "I'll see you all tomorrow." She gave each of them a hug before heading out the front door.

Michelle looked at Katrina, "Are you tired?"

Katrina smiled and shook her head no. "Michelle, I'm pregnant; not disabled."

Michelle chuckled and said, "I'll go get the guestroom ready for you

David called that night as Michelle lay in bed.

"How are you?" he asked. "And how is Sasha?"

There was dead air on the phone for a few seconds as Michelle struggled to put her thoughts into words. "Uh, I'm okay, I think," she said. "And Sasha is fine too." Inwardly, she thought, *You've got to be kidding. What a stupid question to ask.* Did he want her to say she was happy and had been dancing around the house? She had been hurt that he hadn't called earlier to straighten out their problem. Did he think he could call now, and she would be overjoyed with glee and gratitude? Michelle had to admit that she was glad to hear his voice, but still . . .

He broke into her thoughts. "Michelle, are you still there?"

"Yes," she answered, and then listened to all he had to say.

The conversation was fairly brief, and in the end she agreed with everything he had said before they said their goodbyes and hung up. She lay in bed reviewing it all in her mind. David told her that he had spoken to Pastor Jenkins about getting marriage counseling through the ministry. Michelle thought that was a good idea. David also mentioned she should get individual counseling from First Lady Mary Jenkins Michelle still had thoughts of her husband crowding her mind, as she drifted off to sleep.

Chapter 18

The next morning, she, Bethany, and Katrina sat in the family room together, after taking Sasha and Kayla to school.

"I'll treat for breakfast," announced her mother. "Do you want to go to Peace Diner?"

"Let's go," Michelle said with an appreciative smile. Katrina rose from the sofa to follow, and they all headed toward the front door. The phone rang, interrupting their departure; Michelle ran to the kitchen to answer it.

"Hello?"

"Hi. It's Frank. Nobody's answering the home phone, so I thought maybe Katrina was at your place."

Michelle looked toward the door where the others waited. Breakfast was going to have to wait a minute longer. "Yes, she's here. Hold on." She spotted Katrina and held up the phone, covering the mouthpiece with her hand. "It's Frank," she whispered.

Michelle and her mother waited at the front door as Katrina spoke on the phone to her husband. Frank's calling was a good sign. It meant that he was talking to her again. Michelle hoped they could get back together soon, and she knew Katrina prayed for the same.

Katrina exited the kitchen and walked to join them. A small smile inched its way across her face. "Frank wants to talk to me about our problem."

Michelle raised an eyebrow and tilted her head to the side, curious to know more about what had just occurred with her friend.

Katrina eyed Michelle and said, "Frank wants to meet me at Peace Diner in a half hour." She smiled because that's where they were heading anyway.

After Michelle locked the door behind their exit, the three women walked to the edge of the property to begin their walk to the ministry's eatery. From the sidewalk, they had a pretty good view of Cheryl's house. Sitting on her porch were Dana, her four children, and Earl. Earl looked up and caught their eyes and waved at them.

"We should go over and speak," Katrina said.

They walked two doors down to the house. The three women waved as they made their approach.

"How are you Brother Earl, and how are you doing Dana?" Michelle glanced at all the children in the yard as she spoke. Katrina and Michelle's mother smiled at the scene.

"I'm blessed and highly favored." Earl replied, beaming the entire time.

Dana was a little less enthusiastic. She looked down at the three-month-old that she held in her arms and shrugged her shoulders. "I'm okay, I guess."

"This lovely lady is more than okay," added Earl, as he looked into Dana's eyes.

"We have to get going," Katrina said. "I have a meeting to get to, but we just wanted to come over and speak."

"We're sure glad that you did," replied Earl with Dana nodding in agreement.

The three women waved goodbye and began walking down the street. They walked in silence for another block, but Michelle knew they were probably thinking what she was thinking.

"Brother Earl seems to be sweet on Dana," she said.

Katrina laughed. "I'm sure Freddie could see it too. That's why he was jealous of Dana and Brother Earl," she said.

Michelle knew she was right, but how could he shoot the mother of his children over his jealousy. Who did he think was going to take care of those four kids if Dana wasn't around to do it? That man needed to pay for his dirty deed. Jail was definitely where he belonged. They stopped on the corner waiting for the light to turn green.

"Do you think Brother Earl might pursue a relationship with Dana?" asked Bethany. The light changed to green and they began walking, again. "After all she has four children," she continued.

Michelle thought over her mother's question. Earl was a good God-fearing Christian man, but was he up for the responsibilities that would come with pursuing a relationship with Dana? Michelle didn't know the answer to that, but she knew he visited the woman practically everyday.

"I don't know," Katrina said, voicing Michelle's thoughts.

Frank was waiting for her in front of the diner. "Ladies," he said when they approached him.

Michelle and her mother waved and walked inside the diner together, leaving Katrina alone with her husband. The women slid into a booth and sat facing one another.

"I guess it's just the two of us," said Bethany smiling.

After eating breakfast, the two women prepared to leave the diner. En route to the door, they saw Katrina and Frank sitting in a booth off to the side of the eatery, and they waved at them before exiting the diner.

Dana, Earl, and the children were still on Cheryl's porch when Michelle and Bethany returned home. Earl waved to them, and the ladies decided to once again walk over to the yard to fellowship briefly with him and Dana. Michelle eyes grew large when she noticed that Earl was holding Dana's hand. The broad smile on Dana's face said she didn't mind it one bit. Michelle's eyes wandered to the children, and a shiver rushed up her spine.

"It's a shame most of my children looks like their daddy, "Dana suddenly said. "Don't get me wrong; I love all my children, but still . . ." She allowed her sentence to go unfinished.

Michelle stepped closer and greeted both Earl and Dana with a hug. "You two look very serious holding hands and everything." Michelle couldn't believe she had said that aloud.

Bethany tapped her on the shoulder letting her know her words were a little too direct, and it was time for them to leave. Michelle looked down at the ground; embarrassed by her own actions.

"We're not serious yet, but we're getting there fast," Earl's revelation made Dana break out in a child-like giggle.

Michelle looked at them and gave a weak smile. "Well, we'll leave you two lovebirds alone with the kids." Both she and her mother waved before walking away and back to her house.

They saw Katrina walking in their direction and waited on the porch for her to catch up before going inside the house. Katrina had a wide grin on her face. It was evident that her meeting with Frank had gone well.

"I'm going home to my husband tonight," informed Katrina as they sat around the table in the family room.

Michelle gave her the thumbs-up sign, and her mom patted Katrina on the shoulders.

"We had a marvelous discussion," Katrina continued. "He wants us to bring our unborn baby into a united family."

Michelle smiled. She was genuinely happy that Katrina had worked things out with her husband. David wasn't living at home at this time, but she believed that they were on the mend as well.

"I have loved working in the aftercare program," said Bethany, changing the subject. "And I love spending time with my daughter, my granddaughter and you too, Katrina."

The phone rang, and Michelle scrambled to the kitchen to answer it. "Hello?"

"Hello yourself, stranger," was the reply. It was Mary Jenkins on the line.

"Hello First Lady," return Michelle. "To what do I owe this pleasure?"

The pastor's wife informed her that David had called and asked if she'd consider offering counseling to her. Her words didn't surprise Michelle; they had agreed that she would get individual counseling from the first lady, and that she and David would get it jointly from the pastor. In their brief telephone chat, Michelle and the first lady set up a time and date for her to begin her sessions.

Michelle smiled after hanging up and walked back into the family room thinking what a wonderful person her pastor's wife was. Before she could get settled back in her seat, a knock came to the door and Michelle went to answer it. On the other side of her door was Dana, who identified herself she was standing outside without any of her children. Michelle opened the door for her and turned to the side so that the woman could enter the house. She closed the door behind Dana and looked suspiciously at the woman standing with a cane in the hallway.

"I know you don't know me well," said Dana as Michelle ushered her into the family room and offered her a seat, "but I was wondering if I could work in your aftercare program."

Michelle stared at the woman and said absolutely nothing. Katrina and Bethany weren't saying anything either. Michelle couldn't put her thoughts into words. The ex-girlfriend of the fool who had blackmailed her and nearly ruined her marriage was asking her for a job. She couldn't believe her ears.

Dana stared at her waiting for an answer. When none came, she said, "I probably need to give you some time to think it over." She smiled and gave a little wave before using her cane for support as she struggled to her feet.

Bethany got up and walked Dana to the front door. Katrina walked over to talk to Michelle as her mother made her way back into the family room. Michelle hoped she hadn't been rude to the woman, but she had literally become speechless.

Shortly after Dana left, Katrina's husband came to get his family and they all went home together. They'd given Bethany a ride home as well. Sasha was upstairs in her room taking a nap before dinner, and the house was quiet again. Michelle felt in her heart that David would return to his home and his family very soon.

The following day, she received a visit from Earl. "Come in," she said ushering him into the house.

He came bearing gifts; breakfast food and a handful of flowers. He extended the bouquet to Michelle and she gave them a sniff.

"Wow. Are these for me?" She beamed and walk to the kitchen motioning for him to follow her. Michelle placed her gifts on the kitchen table before she and Earl took a seat.

"Let me get to the point, Michelle," he said "I'm here on Dana's behalf."

Michelle looked at him and nodded. She hadn't had time to seriously consider the woman's request to work in her aftercare program. There were five children in her program, and she hadn't had a problem in meeting their needs. Katrina helped her sometimes, and now her mother was assisting temporarily.

"Consider it a personal favor to me if you can hire her for a while," he said sincerely. The man was such a good, upright Christian. He taught Sunday school at the church, and he made sacrifice after sacrifice for the members of Peace Baptist Church.

It would be hard to turn him down, but if Dana did get hired, she would have to bring her four small children with her. Michelle rose from the chair and searched for a vase for the flowers. She located one and then turned to look at Earl. "I guess she can work two days a week to start off."

Earl's entire face lit up. "I really appreciate this, Sister Michelle," he said before rising from the chair. "I got to get to work. I'll have Dana call you," he added before walking out of the kitchen. Michelle walked him to the front door. She suddenly became hungry when she walked back into the kitchen and sniffed the bag of food he had brought.

The following evening Dana reported to Michelle's house for work. They had talked on the phone the previous evening, and the woman had practically begged to begin working immediately. Dana leaned her cane against the chair and began limping as she walked across the floor.

"Why don't you use your cane?" asked Michelle

"I don't want to get too dependent on it," Dana explained. "I can work without it most of the time."

Michelle lined up the five school-aged children to go to the kitchen for a snack. Dana and her four little ones stayed in the family room; they would get their snacks once the first group returned. Dana was setting out coloring books and board games for the big kids to play with when they returned to the family room. Two of her children were asleep, and the others sat on bean bag chairs playing with their number cards.

"Do you want me to get that?" Dana called out after hearing someone knocking on the front door.

"Yes, please," shouted Michelle reply from the kitchen.

It was Earl, and Dana smiled from ear to ear when she saw him. He kissed her on the cheek and followed her to the family room and took a seat in a chair just as Michelle and her five charges returned to the family room. Earl stood up to greet Michelle, and then Dana gathered her four children with help from Earl, and they all went into the kitchen. Earl stayed the rest of the evening, helping Dana with the aftercare program and her tasks.

Michelle had to admit the woman was a good worker, even with her physical limitations. That evening Michelle took Sasha to Peace Diner for a meal of sloppy joe and coleslaw. The church owned diner was crowded this evening. They were sitting in a booth eating their meals when Mary Jenkins approached their table and greeted them.

The first lady looked at Michelle. "Are you ready for tomorrow?"

Michelle knew she was referring to their marital counseling session. "I'm ready and I can't wait." She motioned toward an empty space in their booth. "Would you like to join us?"

"I can't today, but one day soon." Mary reached over and patted Sasha on the shoulder before pointing to her watch and waving goodbye.

Sasha picked up her sandwich and wasted half of the meat on the plate before taking a bite. Michelle bit into her own sandwich and savored the spicy flavor. She nearly choked when she looked up and saw David in the diner. At first she stared, not certain whether it was actually her husband or just an image conjured up by her wishful thinking. He looked around the diner and spotted her and Sasha.

When Sasha saw him approaching the table, her eyes bulged and the first words from her lips were, "Daddy, when are you coming home?"

Michelle wanted to know the answer to that question as well.

David took a seat next to his daughter in the booth, across from Michelle. He picked up a napkin from the table and wiped his daughter's mouth. "I'll be home tomorrow." he said, he was speaking to Sasha, but looking at Michelle. David returned the smile that his wife gave him. "That sandwich sure look good," he remarked before calling over a waitress and ordering one for himself. "I'll be over early tomorrow so I can walk you to school," he said to his daughter.

Michelle was ecstatic about what she'd just heard. David informed them that he planned to take both of his daughters to school on tomorrow morning. Sasha was overjoyed that her half-sister was also coming with them.

After they finished their meals, David walked Michelle and Sasha home and waited until they were safely inside the house before turning and walking away. That night Michelle prayed with her daughter and tucked her in bed, as usual. She then skipped back to her own bedroom with glee. God was good, she thought to herself. She slept long and peaceful like a newborn baby that night.

David arrived early the next morning holding Davita's hand. He decided to take both of his daughters to the diner for breakfast before ushering them to school. Michelle went along with them. She loved the fact that David was creating memories for his girls to cherish for life. An hour later they had left the diner, and now Michelle sat alone at the kitchen table feeling loved and in love.

Chapter 19

"Turn to Proverbs 31:10," said First Lady Mary Jenkins as she sat in her office with Michelle. David was across the hall in the main office getting counseling from the pastor.

The first lady began to reading from the Amplified version, and Michelle followed along. *"A capable, intelligent, and virtuous woman— who is he can find her? She is far more precious than jewels and her value is far above rubies or pearls.* Verse 11: *The heart of her husband trusts in her confidently and relies on and believes in her securely, so that he has no lack of gain or need of spoil."* The first lady paused for a moment and instructed Michelle to read the next verse.

Together they read and discussed five verses from Proverbs. Michelle was soon enveloped into a spiritual zone where her worldly problems seemed the size of ants. She felt good, relaxed and totally in tune with the peaceful message of the Bible. Not wanting the first session to last too long, First Lady Jenkins closed it out in prayer, and Michelle was given additional scriptures to study for their next session. The two women hugged before Michelle exited the first lady's office.

Michelle and David left the church holding hands. Michelle looked up at her husband and jokingly said, "Maybe the one session did the trick, and we don't need to go again."

David nodded and stopped walking long enough to give his wife a kiss on the forehead.

Cheryl was babysitting Sasha for them. Michelle thought that Cheryl certainly had a houseful today with Dana, her four children, and Sasha as well. She and David agreed to go to the diner as soon as they picked up their daughter. When they arrived home, they saw Cheryl sitting on her porch with all the children. Michelle and David walked over to her house and entered the yard.

Cheryl's mouth was turned down and her eyes were stretched wide. "You won't believe this," she said. Cheryl stood and walked closer to them, and in a soft voice said, Freddie was stabbed in jail." She paused for a moment and looked upward. "It doesn't look good; he may not make it. Dana ran to the jail to see about him."

David's eyebrows went up and he shook his head. Michelle opened her mouth to speak, but no words came out. Cheryl grabbed their hands and began praying with them right there in the front yard for the healing of her cousin. They all hugged afterward, and Michelle and David retrieved their daughter

"Call us if you need anything or if there is news," said David just before they began slowly walking toward their house.

Michelle felt numbed and dazed as she entered their home. They walked into the family room and Michelle stiffly took a seat in the chair and stared into space.

"What's wrong, Mommy; are you sick?"

Michelle didn't answer her daughter. All she could think was, *Is Freddie going to die?*

David tapped her on the shoulder and reminded her that they still needed to eat dinner. Sasha was probably hungry and needed a meal. Michelle shook her head. No way could she walk to the diner. She could barely sit up straight in her chair.

David looked at his stunned wife and a bright idea popped into his head. He walked out of the room and into the kitchen and reached for the telephone. A few minutes later, he returned to the family room to rejoin Michelle and Sasha. "I placed an order at Peace Diner and persuaded them to deliver the food," he said. "Is that okay?"

Michelle slowly nodded her head in reply. David walked out of the room and into the small downstairs bathroom, grabbed a wash cloth and wet it under the faucet. Returning to the family room, he placed the cold, wet washcloth on Michelle's forehead and reclined her chair back for comfort. Then he gently escorted Sasha out of the room. He wasn't sure if Michelle cared for Freddie or simply wished him to pass away.

An hour later, Michelle was almost back to normal and was as hungry as a bear. She sat in the kitchen at the table eating dinner. The delivered food from the diner was superb. The meatloaf was juicy and tangy, with the garlic mash potatoes were perfectly creamed, and the string beans had a delightful snap to them.

David and Sasha had already eaten, but had saved the desert to eat together as a family. They sat around the table waiting for Michelle to finish her meal, and then David pulled out the cheesecake. Sasha smiled because she loved her some cheesecake.

Michelle was so glad that David was back at home, and she looked into his face for a long while.

"What?" he said as he caught his wife staring at him.

She looked away, reached for her fork, and dove into the slice of cheesecake. Thoughts of Freddie reentered her mind. She wondered how he was doing? Was he dead or alive?

The following morning, she walked to Cheryl's house and knocked on the door. Cheryl opened it once Michelle identified herself, and then turned to the side so, her friend could enter the house.

"How is Freddie doing?" asked Michelle when Cheryl had closed the front door.

Cheryl shook her head. "He's not doing good." She motioned for Michelle to follow her into the kitchen. "Dana is at the hospital with him," she added once they were seated at the kitchen table. "I'm watching the children for her; they're all still asleep."

Michelle sat at the kitchen table thinking about what her neighbor had just told her. Freddie may not make it. He could die as a prison inmate, unsaved and on his way to hell. She didn't want that; not even for him. She closed her eyes and said a prayer aloud for Freddie's recovery and his redemption.

Cheryl reached down and squeezed Michelle's shoulder. "Thanks." She moved her head in the direction of the door; she needed to go check on Freddie's kids. Michelle followed her into the room, where several of the children were just beginning to wake up. Michelle picked up the little boy who looked just like his dad and carried him to a chair and sat him in her lap. Cheryl smiled at her and reached down to pick up the baby from his crib and cradle him in her arms.

"I can help you with the children," said Michelle looking into the little boy's eyes. She couldn't help but think he might not have his father much longer.

There was a knock on Cheryl's door and she walked out of the room to answer it. When she returned, Michelle's mother was with her.

"I went to your house and there was no answer, so I figure you might be here," said Bethany as she entered the room.

"I'm sorry, Mama," said Michelle.

Bethany waved her hand in the air as if it was no big deal. She placed her handbag on the table and reached down to pick up a child. She smiled and took a seat and placed the little one on her lap. Michelle and her mother stayed to help until her aftercare program began.

Cheryl walked them to the door as they prepared to leave. "Thanks, ladies. I'll keep you all updated on Freddie's situation," she promised.

Earl passed them in the front yard. He was coming to help with the children. He hugged Michelle and Bethany before walking into the house.

Brother Earl must want a future with Dana and her kids, thought Michelle while she and her mom walked to her house. *But why would he? Dana is at the bedside of her former boyfriend.*

"Brother Earl looks like a man in love," commented Bethany as Michelle closed the house door behind them. "I hope he doesn't get his heart broken."

* * * * * * *

The next morning while standing on her porch, Michelle saw Dana leaving the house and flagged her down. The woman walked over to Michelle and sighed heavily.

"I don't mean to keep you," said Michelle, "but I'm just curious about Freddie's health."

Dana looked at her and began sobbing. "I don't think . . ." She wiped her eyes with the backs of her hands. "I don't think Freddie is going to make it. The doctors say it doesn't look good. Please pray for him," said Dana before walking down the street leaning on her cane.

Michelle watched her until she disappeared, and then turned to walk into her house. The telephone rang a few minutes later. It was her mother calling saying she wouldn't be able to make it over today because she had a job interview. Michelle would really miss her mother's extra pair of hands. She needed to get ready and help Cheryl take care of Dana and Freddie's children.

While preparing to leave, she thought about her best friend and picked up the phone.

"Hello?" Katrina answered on the second ring.

"Hello, Katrina. What are you doing today?" Michelle balanced the phone between her shoulder and her ear. "I sure could use your help this afternoon if you can drop by."

"I have to work a half day today. I can meet up with you later."

Michelle thanked her friend, and as soon as she hung up the phone, it rang. "Hello?" Michelle waited for a response on the other end of the line.

"Hello, Michelle; how are you doing?" It was Nicola. Before Michelle could say anything in response, she added, "We're doing marvelous at our house."

Michelle remained silent. She wanted to say, "Things can't be all that marvelous being married to a man who's forty years older than you." But she didn't. Inwardly, Michelle just wished the woman would get to the point so that she could get off the phone with her.

"I'm calling to invite Sasha to a sleepover I'm hosting for Davita. Would Sasha like to attend?"

There was dead air on the phone for a few seconds. Michelle knew that David loved Sasha to spend time with her half-sister. "I guess it should be okay," Michelle finally said. "I'll have to check with David first." She didn't want to spend a lot of time chatting with Nicola for sure. "I've got to go," Michelle said. "I'm helping Cheryl out with the children."

"Wait, wait," Nicola called just before Michelle hung up the phone. "I want to help Cheryl too. Dana goes to our church, and I want to volunteer also. I'll be over in a half an hour," said Nicola before hanging up her phone.

Michelle called out her name into the phone, but it was too late. The woman was on her way to Cheryl's house. Michelle pushed those thoughts away and proceeded to get dressed. A woman of her word, Nicola showed up at Cheryl's door half an hour later with a flower in her hair. Michelle stared at the flower once the woman was inside the house.

Nicola reached up and touched it with her finger. "I wore a flower in my hair my entire honeymoon in Hawaii. I decided to keep it when I returned to D.C."

Michelle shook her head. She hoped she would be able to tolerate the irritating woman for an entire afternoon. Cheryl was using several of her accrued paid time off days to assist with the children, and she thanked Michelle and Nicola for helping her. Dana was so often at Freddie bedside, and Cheryl feared that if she didn't get help she might snap or something. Although she had never experienced childbirth, Cheryl felt like she was the mother of four small children.

They went straight to the family room, which had gone back to resembling the makeshift daycare center it looked like before Dana and Freddie ever moved out into their own place. Nicola scooped up the youngest child in her arms while Michelle and Cheryl sat on the couch watching children simply being children. Michelle had been sure that by noon she would want to choke Nicola, but she was wrong. The woman had actually been a source of comfort. Nicola sat with the baby in her arms making cooing sounds to him.

Katrina came by around one as promised, and immediately began interacting with the children. "I'll help you with the aftercare program later," she said to Michelle.

The sound of a key in the door got all of the ladies' attention. A distraught Dana entered the house with tears in her eyes. She slowly walked in the room assisted by her cane and stiffly took a seat in a chair. Michelle, Katrina, and Nicola stared at the woman who was gazing into space. Cheryl had gone in the kitchen to get something to drink.

Michelle approached Dana and took her hand. " Are you okay?"

The visibly shaken woman looked at Michelle, but didn't respond.

Michelle released her hand and joined Cheryl in the kitchen. She didn't know what else to do. The two women spoke in low volumes to each other trying to decide how to deal with Dana. When they returned to the room, Dana was finally talking. She was conversing with Nicola. Michelle and Cheryl stood in the entrance of the room and watched them.

"You say doctors don't believe Freddie will be alive in the next forty-eight hours?" asked Nicola.

When Dana nodded in confirmation, Cheryl leaned against the door frame for support, and Michelle covered her face with her hands.

"You still can't give up," encouraged Nicola. "Doctors aren't God."

Dana shook her head. "There's no hope. He'll be dead in two days."

Nicola wouldn't give up. "Look, my husband is a deacon in the church." Her words got every eye in the room directed at her. Nicola continued. "He . . . we can organize a prayer group and go pray at Freddie's bedside."

Michelle thought for a moment, and then began nodding her head in agreement. Katrina was nodding too.

"Why not?" said Cheryl. "We've got nothing to lose."

Nicola stood in an organizational mode. "I'll call my husband, and then I'll go to the church. I'll keep everyone informed," she said before walking out of the room and out the door.

Nearing three o'clock, Michelle and Katrina left as well so that they could get ready to tend to the aftercare program. That evening twenty members of Peace Baptist Church prayed at the bedside of Freddie in the hospital, where a police guard stood outside the door. Pastor Jenkins and the first lady were among those who were there sending up fervent prayers. They went into his hospital room in twos, holding the man's hand, anointing him with oil, and reading the Bible to him. This went on for several hours, and Freddie was lifeless most of the time

"God, I love you people," he mumbled once before going back into an unconscious state.

Michelle touched the man's arm as she prayed for him. She had once wished that Freddie would go away, maybe even die. Now she was begging God to save the life of this lost soul. The man had blackmailed her repeatedly and made her life a waking nightmare. That was all forgiven now, and she didn't want him to spend eternity in hell.

Once the flock of Peace Baptist Church was all prayed out and all cried out, they left the hospital with a sense of peace. They had done all they could do; it was now in the hands of their Heavenly Father. Whether Freddie lived or died, God was still in control, and God was still good.

Two weeks later, Freddie was conscious and making daily progress. "I think he's going to live," said Dana to Cheryl, Michelle, Katrina, and Nicola as they sat around Cheryl's kitchen table eating cookies. "He told me he's not going to die and asked me to marry him."

Michelle almost choked on the peanut butter cookie she was chewing. Cheryl reached over and patted her on the back.

"So, you and Freddie plan to get married?" asked Nicola, as if nothing was wrong with that idea.

"You've got to be kidding, Dana; The man shot you," said Cheryl. "He's my cousin, but use the brains God gave you, okay?"

Dana looked at Michelle. "What do you think about it?"

Michelle closed her eyes before answering. "It doesn't sound like a good idea to me." She thought she had put it lightly. Why would this woman even consider marrying Freddie? He'd shot her in a jealous rage. The man had had four children with her without marrying her, but now that he had spent some time at death's door, he suddenly wanted to make a serious proposal to her. This is a no brainer. Of course the woman should not marry him. He might not even be alive tomorrow.

Nicola was the only person in the room who thought Dana's marrying Freddie was a good idea. Katrina sat quietly listening to the exchange, and sitting quietly was so unlike her.

"I'm going to check on the children," announced Cheryl.

Michelle popped up from her seat to join the woman, then Katrina did the same, and they all walked out of the kitchen together. Nicola stayed to chat with Dana.

The next day at Cheryl's, Michelle glanced over at Dana's left hand and spotted a ring. She hadn't seen it there yesterday.

Dana noticed her staring and raised her hand in the air displaying her ring. "Freddie and I got married last night." She beamed with delight.

Michelle began coughing, and her hacks got harder and louder. She felt like her throat was closing.

"Wasn't that foolish?" spat out Cheryl. "She told me that mess this morning."

Nicola chimed in. "It may not be as bad as you think."

Michelle and Cheryl stared her down in unison.

Dana began sobbing. "I'm sorry, but I always wanted to be Freddie's wife."

Michelle couldn't stomach the woman or the situation any longer. She rose from her seat at the kitchen table. "I got to go. I got stuff to do at home," she said before walking out of the kitchen, and then out of the house. Once inside her own house, Michelle took a seat on the bottom step of her staircase.

Dana had really messed up her life. Earl was a good Christian man who had been pursuing a serious relationship with her. Michelle couldn't believe Dana threw all that away for the likes of Freddie. Earl was willing to be a father to four children that weren't even his own. Michelle shook her head in disbelief. She needed to talk to her best friend, and Katrina soon walked to the door from Cheryl's house.

Chapter 20

"That's the craziest thing I've ever heard," said Katrina with a faraway look in her eyes.

It was Saturday morning, and Michelle and Katrina were at the park with their daughters. The two girls were playing on the toys, as their mothers chatted on a nearby bench.

"How long does Freddie have to live?" Katrina asked.

Michelle shook her head. "Doctors thought he'd already be dead by now. I don't know." When she rose from the bench, Katrina did the same, and they walked over to join their daughters on the toys.

* * * * * * *

"Freddie's getting better. Doctors say he's breathing on his own," was the news Dana delivered to the gathering at Cheryl's house. " I'm taking the children to see him soon."

Nicola jumped up and hugged Dana, and then went around hugging everyone in the room. "God is good. God is awesome!" she declared loudly.

Michelle agreed that God was good and awesome, but she still believed that Dana had made a mistake by marrying Freddie. She rose from the couch and stretched her tired body. "I got to go, but the best to you and Freddie," she said before waving goodbye. She was out of there.

Inside her house, Michelle walked barefooted to the kitchen, blowing air from her cheeks as she walked. The phone rang, and she reached to pick it up. "Hello?" Her tone was lazy.

"Are you all right?" asked the first lady.

"I'm fine," Michelle told her. "Just a little tired, I guess."

"I'm calling to remind you that our next counseling session is in two days."

Michelle's disposition changed rapidly. "Great. I look forward to it." A sudden idea prompted her next statement. "First Lady, I'd like to buy you lunch, today, if your calendar is clear."

There was a brief silence on the phone, and then her pastor's wife answered, "I can do that. Peace Diner in an hour?"

Michelle agreed to those conditions before hanging up the phone, and then dashing up the stairs. Mary Jenkins always had such a positive effect on her

"How is the communication going between you and David?" asked the first lady sitting across from Michelle in a booth in the diner.

Michelle took a sip from her grapefruit juice and puckered her lips at the tart taste. She sat back and smiled. "Communication with David is great these days. Thanks to God and you," she added.

The first lady looked pleased. "Is there anything in particular you wanted to talk about?"

Michelle thought of what had transpired in the past couple of days. "Did you know that Freddie and Dana got married?"

When the first lady shook her head no, Michelle began telling her all about the newly married couple. Mary Jenkins was a good and compassionate listener. Michelle felt comfortable telling her all that was on her mind. They talked for an hour and a half, before the first lady offered her some scriptures to read. They hadn't planned it, but somehow the talk became Michelle's marriage counseling session. They held hands and prayed together before First Lady Jenkins had to leave for another appointment.

Shortly after her pastor's wife left, Michelle saw Dana and three of her children entering the eatery. She didn't want to be mean, but if the woman didn't happen to see her, Michelle decided that she would slip out and avoid any interaction. She'd had enough of Dana for a good while. She watched as Dana sat in a booth with her children. When she felt that the coast was clear, Michelle quietly scooted out of the booth and walked slowly to the door.

"Michelle."

She heard her name called, and she turned around to wave in hopes of still making a clean getaway. But Dana motioned with her index finger for Michelle to join them. With a sigh, Michelle dragged her feet over to the booth and stood. "Hi," she said dryly. "What's up?"

"I'm taking the children to see Freddie in D.C. jail."

Michelle looked at her in silence.

Dana continued. "Freddie is writing a letter to you, and I'll deliver it when he's done."

That revelation got a reaction out of her. Michelle's mouth opened and closed several times, but no words came out. She didn't know what to say, and saying nothing felt like the best decision. She forced a smile, and then waved before making her way out of the diner.

The walk home was terrible. Michelle constantly thought of the letter that Freddie was writing to her. What could he possibly have to say? Just the thought of it agitated her.

* * * * * * *

The month of June had arrived, and school would be out in a couple of weeks. Michelle's aftercare program would be closed for the summer; too many kids going away on vacation or camp. She needed something to do with all the free time she would have on her hands.

David walked through the front door with his arms loaded. He had carry-out food in one hand, and a bouquet of flowers in the other. David walked over to Michelle with a big smile on his face, and she returned an even bigger smile. "Which one do you want?" he asked, holding the food in one hand and the flowers in the other.

Michelle grabbed for the flowers and sniffed them while David sat down on the couch and placed the bag on the coffee table in front of him. He clutched her hand, and Michelle sat on the space beside him. She kicked her foot in the air in joyful contentment. The marriage counseling was working miracles.

They heard Sasha coming down the stairs and into the family room where they were sitting. She always came running when her father came home. Michelle wondered if she had some kind of a daddy-detector located somewhere in her brain.

"Hello, Daddy. Did you bring me something to eat?"

Michelle and David separated to make room between them on the couch for their daughter. David patted the vacant spot, and Sasha dashed to sit in it. Sometimes Michelle felt invisible to her daughter once her father was around, but she blinked the thought out of her mind. There was plenty of love to go around.

Two weeks had passed since Dana mentioned Freddie was writing a letter to her. *How long does it take to write a letter?* Michelle thought. After all, Freddie was recovering from a near death experience, plus he resided in jail. Still, she was as curious, as a nosy neighbor as to what was in this letter.

Early the next morning after David had already left for work, Michelle lay in bed enjoying the peace and quiet. Her eyes sprang open and she screamed when she felt the room begin to shake. A terrified shout came from Sasha's room prompting Michelle to call out, "Jesus, help!"

The shaking stopped and Michelle stiffly climbed out of bed. She needed to get to her daughter. "Sasha!" she screamed. "Sasha, baby."

Before Michelle could get to her bedroom door, her daughter ran into her room like the house was on fire. What just happened? Michelle slipped on her slippers and a robe and grabbed Sasha's hand. They ran down the stairs and out the front door, holding hands the entire time. Outside, they saw other neighbors walking around in a daze.

They walked to the edge of the yard and looked down the street. Cheryl was standing in her yard too. She held up her hand and motioned for Michelle and Sasha to join her. When they reached her yard, Cheryl eyes grew large and said, "Did you feel that earthquake? It nearly scared me to death."

Michelle looked at her friend with raised eyebrows. The city has never experience an earthquake before; at least none that she could remember. "An earthquake?" she finally said. Michelle shook her head in disbelief and held Sasha's hand even tighter.

When all of the other neighbors began dispersing and going back into their homes, Michelle did the same, keeping her daughter close to her as they made their way back.

"Mommy is the earthquake over?" asked Sasha before they stepped into their house.

Michelle squeezed her hand and nodded her head. The telephone rang as they entered the house, and Michelle's mother was on the other line.

"Honey, did you feel that earthquake? Are you and Sasha okay?" Bethany asked.

Michelle reassured her that they were fine and spoke with her for an additional ten minutes before ending their call. The phone rang again immediately

"Michelle, are you and Sasha all right?" This time it was David checking up on her and his family. Before she could respond, he spoke again. "Our office building shook, and everyone was rushing down the stairs to get out of the building. Baby, are you and Sasha all right?" he asked again.

Michelle reassured him that his family was intact. And after their brief conversation ended, she and Sasha ran upstairs to get dress so that they could go and spend some time at Cheryl's house. They were dressed and about to leave the house, when the phone rang for the third time.

"Michelle, are you and Sasha okay?" Katrina sounded concerned.

"Yes, we're fine," Michelle assured her best friend. "What about you? How are you doing?"

Katrina informed Michelle that she had survived the earthquake unscathed too. Michelle was glad to hear that Katrina and her unborn child were safe. She was in her fourth month now, and her belly seemed to be growing daily. They talked for five more minutes before Michelle excused herself and hung up the phone. Michelle and Sasha walked from their house hand in hand.

Cheryl treated her company to muffins and juice as they sat around her kitchen table. "That earthquake sure scared a lot of people," she said before biting into a banana nut muffin. As soon as she swallowed, she added, "Dana's visiting with Freddie at D.C. jail, as usual."

Michelle nodded. The news certainly didn't surprise her. Dana seemed to spend more hours at the jail than she did at home.

Cheryl rose from her seat. "I'm going to check on the children."

Sasha sat in a chair in the middle devouring an apple cinnamon muffin. Michelle gave her a stern look, and she slowed down her eating. "I want to see the little children," said Sasha with a mouthful of muffin.

Michelle handed her daughter a napkin and she wiped her mouth then cleaned up the crumbs on the table. When she'd finished cleaning up after herself, Michelle escorted Sasha to the area where the children were.

It would be another hour before Dana finally joined them at the house after visiting the inmate who was now her husband. She saw Michelle in the room and walked to her with the use of her cane. "Me and Freddie were talking across the table when the floor shook. That earthquake scared him more than it did me."

Michelle looked at her not knowing how to respond. All she could contribute to the conversation was a faint smile.

Dana sat next to Michelle on the couch, opened her pocketbook, and pulled out a white envelope that she handed to Michelle. "Here," she said. "Freddie told me to give you this."

Michelle palmed the envelope and looked at it suspiciously. Dana rose gingerly from the couch and walked over to pick up her baby from the crib. She carried him to the kitchen, half limping and half walking. Michelle watched her until she disappeared, and then she looked for somewhere where she could be alone to read the letter. An earthquake and a letter from Freddie—all in one day. She hoped she wouldn't faint or anything.

Michelle looked at Cheryl, and then rose from her chair." I got to go; I'll talk to you soon."

Sasha wasn't ready to go home; she was having fun playing with the children. But Michelle clutched her hand anyway and pulled her along.

When they arrived at their house, David was standing near the front door. He looked at them and said, "I just needed to come home and check on my family. I love you all so much."

Those words from him sent Michelle running into his arms with the letter still tucked in her pocket. Sasha soon joined them for a family group hug. David sat with Sasha in the family room while Michelle read the letter from Freddie in her bedroom.

Hello, Michelle. I know you think it's strange to get a letter from me, but I had to write. I want to apologize to you for everything. I've changed. Honest to God. God changed me. I thought I was going to die. I thought my life had come to an end for real. I cried out to God because I didn't have anywhere else to go. I begged Him to give me a second chance. I wanted to be with my kids and stuff. I really didn't think God would listen to me, but He did. I honestly can say God loves me, and I'm trying to love Him back.

Michelle paused for a moment to digest all she had read, and then started reading again. *When you and your friend, Katrina came into the nightclub, you were two silly women. I'm sorry to be so blunt, but you two were silly. You got to be wise to come into a place like that or somebody will take you for all you're worth. Did you know that that old club is a church now? Those people from that church came to the jail to pray for me. Back in the day when you, me, Katrina, and Leo left the club for my place, I handed you a drink and soon you were out like a light. I secretly slipped a pill into your drink. I'm sorry, I'm sorry. God knows I am. We both know what happened next. The next morning, I kicked you out and called you nasty names. I confess, and I'm truly sorry for all the pain I caused you. I hope one day you can forgive.*

In the letter Freddie also talked about how Dana had forgiven him for shooting her in the leg. He referred to Dana as a gift from God. He said that his wife was like the woman in Proverbs 31. Michelle sat on the bed holding the letter in her hand and staring at it as if it were a television screen.

She couldn't get out of bed, but it was a delightful can't get out of bed. She smiled, and then pulled the covers over her head full of thoughts; good, joyous, godly, thoughts.

"Michelle, are you coming down?" called her husband from downstairs.

"Yes, I'm coming," she called back. But she savored five more minutes of bliss before removing the covers and hopping out of bed. She returned the letter to its envelope and placed it in a drawer in her nightstand. "I'm coming" she yelled on her way down the stairs. She entered the family room with a big grin on her face.

"Mommy's happy," said Sasha as she hugged her mother.

David looked at her, and the big grin made him curious. "Wanna let me in on your secret?"

Michelle nodded. "I'll let you read it later." And she kept her word.

That night after dinner, David read Freddie's letter once in the kitchen, and then he re-read it in their bedroom. He placed the letter back in its envelope, and then handed it to Michelle. "I would have broken his neck if I had known," said David, "but he did repent and beg for forgiveness. That's a tough one." He sat on the bed next to his wife and drew her in for a warm embrace.

"I'm not mad at Freddie anymore," said Michelle. "I just feel so much love around me, and Lord knows I appreciate it." She thought while snuggling with her husband that she had to let Katrina read the letter. The letter had wiped the dirty slate in her life clean.

David played hooky from work the next day and spent the entire day home with her. The following morning, the family walked to Peace Diner for breakfast. Sasha was ecstatic to have pancakes for breakfast. After they'd eaten, David went to work, but in the evening the family went to Union Station and bought Sasha some books from the bookstore. It was the summer and her parents wanted her to do some reading during the season. The park was the next stop on the Davidson's agenda. Michelle and David sat on the bench as Sasha played on the toys. Michelle reached into her bag and pulled out a disposable camera.

"When did you get that?" said David staring at the camera.

Without answering, she pointed the camera at him and took his picture. David was a good sport and began making goofy faces and posing in silly positions while the camera kept clicking away.

"My turn." Michelle handed him the camera and began a series of poses for him to snap. She pointed to Sasha. "We need pictures of our daughter," she suddenly said.

They walked to the sliding board, and David snapped a picture before Sasha landed on the bottom.

"Take another picture, Daddy," the child said with a wide grin.

Her father obliged and began snapping pictures of their daughter posing on the toys. They didn't leave until all the film had been used. They held hands as they were leaving the park. Dinner was eaten at a booth at Peace Diner, and prayers capped off the night.

The next morning, Michelle was at the diner again; this time with Katrina. With school being out, David had taken Sasha to work with him today. She was going to help her daddy in his office. "How are you feeling?" Michelle asked her pregnant best friend.

Katrina giggled. "Michelle, I'm not ill."

"I have something for you to see," Michelle told her, "but I don't want to get you too emotional, okay?"

Katrina stared at her friend and poked out her lip. Michelle reached into her pocketbook and pulled out the letter from Freddie and handed it to her. Katrina raised an eyebrow and took the letter out of the envelope and began reading. Michelle studied Katrina's face as she read the letter.

"Wow," said Katrina, not taking her eyes off the letter.

Michelle took a sip of her root beer soda, and then reached for her cheeseburger and took a bite. She took a second bite before placing it on the dish and chewing slowly while she waited for Katrina to finish reading the letter. Gospel music streamed from the restaurant's speakers, and Michelle began humming along.

"Oh wow," said Katrina with a gasp, still concentrating on the letter.

Michelle ate the last of her sandwich and was ready for dessert. She scooted out of the booth and walked to the front counter. When she walked back, she was carrying a bowl of black walnut ice cream.

Katrina looked up at her spooning the dessert into her mouth and shook her head. "Michelle, stop making a pig of yourself."

Michelle put her spoon down and stared at her friend, waiting to hear her thoughts about the letter.

"I can't believe this letter," Katrina finally said. Tears began to well in her eyes. "Freddie came clean about everything."

Michelle hadn't meant to upset her pregnant friend. She reached for a napkin and handed it to Katrina.

"It's okay, Michelle," Katrina assured her. "These are happy tears.

Chapter 21

"I'm still scared from that earthquake," confessed Michelle on the phone to Katrina. "When the floor shifts beneath you, that gets you thinking all kinds of stuff."

The earthquake that had hit Washington, D.C. was 5.8 to 6.0 on the Richter scale. It had been the talk of many residents in the days that followed.

Katrina returned, "I know. Last night, I had a dream we had another earthquake." Her voice was barely above a whisper when she added, "But God is good all the time. Hallelujah."

Michelle nodded in agreement with her best friend, but her mind was on more than just the earthquake. First Lady Jenkins had suggested that Michelle take a full day to pray for her marriage and her family. She thought that was a marvelous idea,

"You got any plans for tomorrow?" asked Katrina.

Michelle smiled. "Yeah, I'll be praying for my family all day tomorrow."

Katrina agreed that it was a wonderful concept, and said she would be doing likewise before hanging up the phone.

Michelle kept her word. The next day, she didn't go outside her house for anything. She didn't even walk outside to visit Cheryl down the street. That day was dedicated to prayer and meditation. She prayed for her marriage and her family all day, and felt good about doing so.

The following day, she slipped on a jogging suit and decided to give Cheryl a hand with the four children. Cheryl opened her door at the sound of Michelle's knocking, and together they walked deeper into the house.

"What's up?" Michelle asked her. "How are things going?"

Cheryl nodded her head and smiled, showing a mouthful of teeth. Michelle couldn't understand how she could be happy being left with the burden of taking care of someone else children most of the time. She followed Cheryl into the family room where the children were playing. Michelle was surprised to see that Dana was actually there holding the baby and not gone somewhere to visit Freddie. Michelle waved to her and Dana waved back.

Cheryl took the four-year-old child by the hand and walked into the kitchen with Michelle on her heels. They took a seat at the kitchen table with Cheryl holding the child on her lap. She flashed a huge toothy grin and fanned her hand in front of her face.

Michelle's eyes stopped on the ring on Cheryl's finger. "Wait. What?" she said through a gasp as she eyed the ring. "Yeah, me and Paul jumped the broom, last night you know, we eloped." Michelle knew Cheryl was planning a wedding, but she never expected anything like this from reliable Cheryl.

Cheryl broke out into a giggle. "I know you're shocked. I'm the one who got married, and I'm still shocked." Cheryl stroked the cheek of the child she was holding, and then kissed the little girl on the forehead. "She'll be living with me and Paul for a while," she said, cuddling with the child on her lap.

Michelle was confused. "Does that mean Dana and her other children will have to move out?"

Cheryl nodded her head up and down and went on to inform her that Dana and her children would be leaving in a month. "Sister Precious and Brother Ed want to help Dana out with her children," Cheryl told her as she reached across the table and popped the lid off a container of cookies and offered them around.

The little girl immediately reached for one and brought it to her mouth. There were only a few cookies in that container. Cheryl told Michelle there were more in the refrigerator and asked if she would get them for her. Michelle rose from her seat and retrieved the cookies from the frig and placed them on the table. The little girl reached for another one, and the conversation continued.

Michelle knew Cheryl wouldn't put Dana and her kids out on the street. The plan was for Dana to rent the basement of Precious and Ed's house. Dana was still walking with a cane, but she had obtained employment at a licensed daycare center. They placed her as the assistant in a room with three-year olds. Children that age didn't require a lot of picking up or carrying, so it was a position that Dana could manage without difficulty. This also made it convenient to take her children to work with her. It looked like everything had been taken in to consideration for the wellbeing of all concerned.

Michelle processed all of the information as she sat on her bed that night in her bedroom. The next morning, she woke up and slid out of bed and dropped to her knees. She planned to pray for everyone she knew and loved this morning. Sasha was at work with her father again. She was definitely a daddy's girl. Michelle closed her eyes and prayed out loud, calling out the names of the people in her life. It would be an hour before she'd get up, get showered, and get dressed before going down to breakfast.

* * * * * * *

"I like coming to work with you," said Sasha to her father.

He smiled and raised his hand to give her a gentle high- five. He then grabbed her hand and walked to the window so that they could look out at the world together. "Where do you want to go for lunch?" he asked her, already knowing what she would say.

"Peace Diner, where we always eat our food."

David nodded. . They always ate at the church owned diner. They supported the church because it was doing great things in the community. "Did your mother say she'd be praying for everyone today?"

Sasha nodded, and he led her to the center of the room. They got on their knees, held hands, and prayed for the people they cared about.

* * * * * * *

Michelle knelt on a rug on the kitchen floor and prayed for the second time today. This time her prayer was focused on her child. She prayed for Sasha and her wellbeing, thanking God for giving her the child and asking for wisdom to guide and instruct her daughter in a way that is pleasing to Him.

The phone rang and Michelle rose from her knees to answer it. It was Cheryl on the line. "What are you doing today?"

Michelle answered, "Praying. I got to go." She hung up the phone. She was in a spiritual praying mode and didn't want to break that feeling. Michelle lowered herself to the floor and continued praying.

* * * * * * *

On this day, Michelle walked into Cheryl's house wearing chocolate Capri pants and a ruffled blouse. The loud music could be heard before she crossed the threshold. "David and Sasha will be over shortly" she told her neighbor.

Cheryl nodded in understanding and began walking through her house to the back patio for her Fourth of July cookout. Michelle smiled when she reached the patio and waved to her best friend. Katrina was sitting on a lawn chair, and her husband was sitting by her side. Cheryl's new husband, Paul was manning the grill. Katrina was now five months pregnant and showing more than ever. Michelle walked over and talked with her and her husband for a while.

So far, Kayla was the only child at the cookout. Dana and her children no longer lived with Cheryl. A knock on the door sent Cheryl walking through the house to answer it. A few minutes later, David and Sasha made an appearance on the back patio. The girl smiled at her mother then dashed across the patio to play with Kayla.

David placed an arm around Michelle's shoulder, and she patted his hand. They joined Katrina and her husband, who were sitting and eating ribs and coleslaw. Michelle reached down and placed a hand on her friend's expanding belly and smiled.

Twenty minutes later, Nicola arrived with Davita, but without her husband. Michelle hated to admit it, but Davita looked more like David than Sasha did. The girl joined Sasha and Kayla in play.

Nicola walked over to join Michelle and David. "How's everyone doing?" she asked.

"We're doing, fine." David answered for the both of them.

"My husband had a previous engagement," Nicola explained, "but I decided to come anyway and bring Davita."

David smiled and excused himself to go join his two daughters. Michelle never saw David as playful as when he was with his daughters.

"I love watching David with his girls," said Nicola as if she were reading Michelle's mind.

Michelle nodded her head in agreement. She really didn't want to have a one on one conversation with the former girlfriend of her husband; especially not one about the child he'd with her. She searched for a way to change the subject. "Let's go see what Katrina's up to."

Nicola nodded and followed Michelle to Katrina's chair. They sat in the empty chairs that were near her. Cheryl brought plates of food to them, and they immediately dug in.

"We Fall Down" by Donnie McClurkin was booming throughout the patio.

"I love that song," said Michelle before forking coleslaw into her mouth. Nicola had her eyes closed swaying from side to side to the music. Michelle looked toward the house and saw Cheryl talking on her cell phone. She walked toward Michelle's chair and handed it to her. "Who is this?" she wanted to know.

"It's Freddie," Cheryl told her. "He's calling collect from jail."

Michelle shuttered a little before bringing the phone to her ear. "Hello?"

"Hello, Michelle," returned Freddie. "Did you get my letter?" He had to know the answer to his own question, but she answered anyway.

"Yeah. It like blew me away; the content and all."

He didn't speak for a second, and then he went on to explain to her that he was now a Christian and wanted to come clean. He apologized to her again about all he had put her through. Michelle was glad that Freddie had given his life to the Lord, but she still felt uncomfortable talking to him. She was glad when he asked her to put Cheryl back on the phone.

After giving the phone back to Cheryl, Michelle's eyes met Katrina's and they exchange a glance. Michelle resumed eating her barbeque spare ribs and coleslaw. As the event came to a close an hour later, and the hostess gave everyone goodie bags to take home. David, Michelle, and Sasha said their goodbyes and walked from the celebration and up the street to their own house.

They crashed on the couch in the family room and kicked off their shoes. Michelle closed her eyes and replayed in her mind the conversation she had with Freddie. The Hope and Faith Center, the former nightclub, was having a bazaar to raise money for their prison outreach ministry. Michelle read the information in *The Washington/Baltimore Afro American* newspaper; her family subscribed to the paper. She wanted to go to the bazaar and decided to call Katrina to see if she felt up to the trip. Katrina agreed to go with her to Saturday's bazaar.

Michelle scooted down from the stool in the kitchen, walked to the refrigerator, and pulled out a snack. With Sasha going to work with her dad most days and the aftercare program closed for the summer, she was bored and restless and needed something to do with her spare time.

On Saturday, Michelle and Katrina rode that morning to the church in Temple Hills Maryland, right across the Washington, D.C. line. Katrina was the driver; Michelle didn't drive.

"Keep the dream alive, don't let it die. And never give up on you . . ." Yolanda Adams was singing on the radio, and Michelle and Katrina were backing her up. They moved to the music as they sang.

After about twenty minutes of driving, Michelle pointed to the bazaar." There it is."

Katrina slowed down before entering the parking lot. When they walked inside the church, they saw tables of clothes, pottery, and food. First they checked out the food table, having been captured by the sight of the nuts and fruit. They each purchased an assortment of fruits and nuts for their family. Michelle was trying to lay off all the sweets that she and her family had been consuming. She was afraid they all might turn into human sugar cubes.

Michelle felt a tap on her shoulder and spun around to see Dana and Cheryl. "What are y'all doing here?"

Dana informed them that this was her new church. The people had come to jail to pray for and with Freddie on a weekly basis. He suggested that she attend this church, and he'd join her there once he got released from jail.

Cheryl smiled. "I just came with her," she said pointing to Dana.

Dana leaned on her cane. "The pastor here is a great man of God."

"We were actually about to leave," Cheryl said. "Sister Precious and Brother Ed are babysitting the children for Dana, and we need to get on back."

Michelle nodded and she and Katrina gave them hugs before they departed from the church. Katrina wanted a bottle of juice, and they walked to the table together. A man stood nearby watching them, and as they got closer, Michelle recognized the familiar face. "Hi. Pastor Wynn, right?" She reached out and accepted his handshake.

"Yes, I thought I recognized you ladies," he replied.

"The vibes in this place are totally different, now that it's a church," said Katrina.

Pastor Wynn smiled. They talked to him for a long while about the transformation of the church. He was an easy person to talk to. He was a spiritual man. They shop at the bazaar for an additional twenty minutes, and then left. On the ride home, they spoke about the conversation they'd had with the pastor. He'd told them, that he had been saved for ten years and been an associate pastor for three. The church's prison ministry visited penitentiaries on a weekly basis. The pastor had handed each of them a business card and had asked them to keep in touch.

"Pastor Wynn seems to be a man after God's own heart," said Michelle as they rode down the street. "If I weren't already at a God-loving church, I'd join his."

Katrina nodded in agreement, and then asked, "What's wrong?" when she heard Michelle release a long sigh.

Michelle looked at her friend. "I need to find something productive to do with my time."

"Why don't you start writing songs again?" Katrina suggested, keeping her eyes on the road.

Michelle looked over at her friend and smiled. She used to love to write song lyrics. "Yeah, I almost forgot about that," she said. Michelle used to write poems too. She smiled at Katrina again. That was why she was her best friend.

"Keep the dream alive, don't let it die . . ." they sang on the drive home along with Yolanda Adams.

"Mama, can we go the park?" asked Sasha as Michelle walked through the door of her house.

Michelle bent down to hug her daughter and after releasing her, looked up and saw her husband standing near the stairs.

"I'll go if Dad agrees to go with us." Michelle smiled. She would make her husband the heavy and not her.

David laughed out loud when Sasha looked at him with pleading eyes. Then he said, "Okay, but only if we go to the diner first. I'm as hungry as a rattlesnake."

Michelle held up the bag of fruit she bought at the church bazaar. David walked toward her sniffing the bag, and Sasha eyes lit up like a Christmas tree. Michelle dodged both of them and scurried into the kitchen with her family on her heels. She placed the fruit on the kitchen table and they each ate a banana before walking out of the kitchen and out the front door; her family followed close behind. She was glad that her family had responded to fruit in such a positive way.

When they entered Peace Diner, they walked to a booth and slid inside. David picked up a menu from the table. It was just a habit; his menu was rarely opened. He always ordered the same thing: meatloaf, mash potatoes, and green beans.

Michelle sat looking around the diner, and she spotted the first lady sitting two booths behind them. "David, I'll be right back. Order me whatever you get." She slid from the booth and waved as she approached Mary Jenkins, because first lady was sharing a booth with another woman from the church.

"Excuse me, First Lady, but I'd like to speak to you when you get some time." Michelle prepared herself to walk back to her booth, but the woman sitting there stopped her.

"Wait. We're done with our conversation, and I'm about to go." The woman slid out of the booth, waved, and walked away.

Michelle eyed the first lady as if asking for permission to sit.

"Have a seat, Michelle," she offered.

"Thank you. I'll make this quick," Michelle promised. "I'd like to join the music ministry at the church. I write poetry and gospel lyrics."

The first lady looked at her and asked, "Do you also sing?"

Michelle giggled because she couldn't carry a tune. "No. If I did, birds and planes would no longer fly in Washington, D.C."

The first lady chuckled. "Sure, we'd love you to join the music ministry."

Michelle smiled, and as she excused herself to leave, the first lady asked if she needed more marital counseling. Michelle nodded her head up and down. "Yes," she said. Then she slid from the booth and rejoined her family

Michelle sat in church on Sunday morning with her family on one side of her and Katrina on the other. She decided not to ask her friend to go anywhere else with her until after her baby was born. Katrina was five months pregnant and Michelle wanted her friend to have a healthy and happy baby. She would miss hanging out with her for a while, but her health and that of her unborn child was more important.

Michelle was extremely happy about getting involved with the music ministry at the church. The timing was perfect. It would keep her occupied enough where she wouldn't feel the need to do too much going anyway.

Pastor Jenkins walked to the podium carrying his Bible. "Good morning this glorious day, saints."

The congregation returned his greeting, and they stood in preparation of receiving what the Lord had for them.

Nicola approached Michelle and her family after church. "Do you all have a minute?" she asked.

What she wanted was simple: Sasha and Davita to spend more time together. David loved the idea, and Michelle didn't object to the two half-sisters spending more time together either. But when Nicola offered to take both Sasha and Davita to the park today, Michelle froze for a moment. She had no problem with the child, but she still couldn't get herself to totally trust the mama. David did not have a problem with Nicola's offer. The look on his face told Michelle that it was up to her.

"Sure; I guess that will be all right" said Michelle reluctantly.

Nicola's seventy-five year old husband joined them and kissed her on the lips. Michelle really did like the elder, but why did he kiss Nicola on the lips in church? Nicola returned his kiss, and he blushed. David gave his approval for Sasha to spend the evening with Davita and Nicola. The woman told Sasha to wave to her parents as she left the church with her family.

Something about Sasha spending time with Nicola distressed Michelle, but David seemed as pleased as punch. Precious and Ed walked over to their pew to talk.

"That woman really bothers me," said Precious as she watched Nicola leave the church.

Michelle couldn't agree more, but decided not to say it in David's presence. Just a simple nod of her head had him looking at her with anger in his eyes.

"Nice seeing you," David said in a dry tone to Precious, and then he turned to Ed and said, "Can I talk to you outside for a minute?"

The women watched the men walked toward the door. Precious waited until they had walked out before she spoke again.

"I guess I should apologize for my comment about Nicola," she said. "But that thirty-five-year-old woman married my seventy-five-year-old father."

Michelle had the same low opinion of Nicola, and she noticed how upset David got when she nodded in agreement with Precious. "Well, no need to apologize to me," said Michelle through a laugh, and Precious laughed too.

David's reaction made Michelle wonder if he still had feelings for Nicola. After all, they had a child together.

"I hear you want to join the music ministry," said Precious, changing the subject. "That's my department. Give me a call."

Michelle hugged her before going outside to join her husband. She and David walked side by side toward their house. As they walked, Michelle kept wondering why David reacted so strongly when Nicola was thought or spoke of in a negative manner. At that moment, David looked at her and stopped on the sidewalk. Michelle stopped as well.

"Michelle, you're the only woman I love," he said.

She shuttered for a second. Was this man reading her mind? Michelle opened her mouth to speak, but nothing came out. And when David began walking again, she did the same. David reached for her hand and clutched it, and she squeezed his hand in return. She was the only woman that he loved, and she smiled as they walked home hand in hand.

Chapter 22

On Monday evening, Michelle got around to calling Precious. "Would you please thank you husband for investigating Freddie? I never got a chance to thank him."

Precious promised that she would, and then went on to tell Michelle all about the music ministry at the church. Michelle listened patiently as she was told her how her God-given talent as a lyricist could fit into the music ministry. Precious explained that they performed original and traditional gospel songs. She needed Michelle to bring over some of her songs so she could take a look at them.

Precious said she had a niece who was a gifted singer, and she was always looking for original songs too. Michelle knew her niece, Bree; she had heard the young woman sing before. What a talent! Precious said her niece was putting together an album of original songs, and they were meeting every Saturday at her house until it was completed.

"Why don't you bring some songs over on Saturday," suggested Precious.

Michelle was so happy and excited she thought she would bust with delight. Talking about her passion for songwriting brought out a zeal she hadn't experienced in a long while.

"When can we meet?" asked Sister Precious.

Michelle wanted to tell her they could do it in twenty minutes, but she knew that wouldn't happen, so she just said, "Anytime."

"Let's wait until Saturday when we can have the whole day. How about my place Saturday at ten in the morning?"

That sounded like a winner to Michelle. She needed the time to write some new songs and to gather the songs she had already written.

Michelle arrived at Precious's house at ten as agreed, on Saturday morning

"Come on in." Precious moved aside for Michelle to enter the house. "Have you eaten breakfast?"

Michelle nodded her head yes. So, they went right to work. She followed the woman to the family room. Bree was already at the house, eating breakfast in the kitchen.

"I hope it stays quiet," Precious said. "Dana and the children are still asleep in the basement."

Michelle had almost forgotten that Dana was renting the basement in Ed and Precious's house. "Oh, it should be all right," Michelle assured her.

Just then Bree walked into the room and she hugged Michelle. "I didn't know you wrote songs," she said. "I'm looking for songs for my album."

Michelle nodded and pulled out the songs that she had written for Bree to review. She planned to get her songs copyrighted the first chance she got. The three of them sat around the table in the family room. Precious looked at a few of Michelle's songs, and Bree looked at some as well.

Precious began nodding her head and smiling. "These are good."

Bree added, "Girl, you can write you some songs."

Michelle smiled at their appreciation of her talent. "Give God the glory," she said. "He gave me the talent."

Bree smiled at her response, and then said she'd like to get some musicians together with the songs and see what happened.

Michelle nodded; she thought it was a wonderful idea.

"Where are you going?" The voice came from behind them, and they all turned around. A little child walked into the room followed by a woman.

"I'm sorry I didn't mean for her to disturb you all," said Dana before grabbing the little girl's hand and pulling her away.

Precious walked to them and kissed the little girl on the forehead. "It's no problem, sweetie."

Dana smiled and walked her daughter out of the room, and Michelle and Bree resumed their talk of music. Michelle felt vibrant and alive when talking about music.

"Michelle, can I see that second song again?" asked Precious.

Michelle handed her the sheet of paper. She was having the time of her life. Time passed entirely too fast. Before she knew it, it was time to go. "When can we get together again?"

Sister Precious looked at Bree and said, "Uh, same time next Saturday morning."

Michelle nodded and waved before walking to the front door. Sister Precious and Bree followed behind her.

"Michelle?" It was Precious's voice.

Michelle turned around and saw both women standing with their arms stretched out. She walked back and hugged them both before leaving. David and Sasha were waiting for her outside in the car.

"How did it go?" asked David as soon as she climbed in.

"Mommy," said Sasha from the backseat.

Michelle turned around, leaned against the seat and gave Sasha a kiss on the forehead. She turned back around and looked at her husband. "It went great. We plan to meet back here next Saturday."

David nodded and continued driving. "Your parents' called; they miss you." David went on to explain to Michelle that her parents had said that they hadn't seen her for a while. He said her father threatened to park himself on their doorstep if she didn't visit soon.

Michelle knew that wasn't an empty threat; her father would actually do it. She looked over at her husband. "Do we have time for a quick visit now?"

"Sure," he answered without giving it a second thought. He liked his parents-in-law very much.

Forty minutes later, they were sitting around her parents' kitchen table eating the cupcakes that Michelle brought over as a peace offering.

"Mm, these cupcakes are so good," said Joe while chewing the treat.

Michelle agreed with her dad; they were delicious. But she didn't tell him how much the cupcakes cost. As frugal as he was, her father would hit the roof. She knew her father had a huge sweet tooth, but this would be the last sweet treat she planned to purchase for him.

"We got to get together more often" said Bethany.

"Yes we do ma'am," said David eyeing his wife like it was all her fault.

"Can Sasha spend the night?" asked Michelle's father. "Girl gonna be a grown woman before I get to see her again."

"Sure," said David, "but not tonight; she has church in the morning."

Michelle's parents exchanged glances, and then her dad came up with a bright idea of his own.

"Let us take our granddaughter to our church tomorrow." He placed his hand on the child's shoulder.

David looked at Michelle, and she nodded her head as if to say it would be okay. Sasha was smiling as she held a cup of juice in her hand. David and Michelle kissed their daughter on the cheek and hugged Bethany and Joe before leaving the house.

When they arrived home, Nicola was on their doorstep with Davita. "Where is Sasha?" she asked as they approached her.

"She's spending the night with her grandparents," David told her, and then he invited Nicola and Davita into the house.

Michelle's eyes darted to her husband. Why did he have to invite her inside? She walked inside when David unlocked the door, and whether she wanted to or not, Michelle knew she had to be a helpful hostess. "Can I get anyone a snack or something to drink?"

Nicola nodded. "I'll take whatever you have."

Michelle wished the woman would just leave her house, but her fondness for the child would make it bearable. Michelle walked into the kitchen to get food for the woman while David, Davita, and Nicola headed for the family room to take a seat. Michelle entered the family room with a tray of food fifteen minutes later.

David sat on the couch next to his daughter, and Nicola sat on the other side of him. In Michelle's opinion, they were laughing, talking, and behaving like a family. As much as she tried to fight it, she still got a little jealous whenever Nicola was around David. Michelle put the tray on the coffee table and got everyone's attention. They all were having such a good time; they practically ignored her.

"Help yourself," she said, pointing to the tray. "I'll be back in a few minutes." With that she walked out the room and up to her bedroom where she plopped on the bed. That woman always rubbed her the wrong way. David seemed to love Nicola's phoniness. Why did so many men seem to be blind to stuff like that? She didn't know and probably would never understand it.

Michelle kicked her shoes off and lay down on top of the covers. Ten minutes later she got up and stretched before walking back down the stairs and entered the family room. She blinked her eyes twice, not believing what she'd just seen. She walked farther into the room and got in Nicola's face. "What do you think you're doing?

Nicola shrugged her shoulders and acted like she didn't understand what Michelle was talking about.

"What is it, honey?" asked David.

Michelle stared her husband down. "What do you mean, *what is it*? I saw Nicola kiss you." Her hands were planted firmly on her hips.

"Is that all?" Nicola asked. "I only kissed him on the cheek because he gave our daughter a twenty dollar bill."

Michelle's mood lightened. "I guess I overreacted," she said. But that didn't change the fact that she still wanted that woman out of her house. She felt like a fool for leaving David with Nicola, in the first place. Michelle knew she wasn't the kind of woman to spy on her husband. Michelle's thinking was that if a man is going to cheat, he going to cheat. It was as simple as that.

Nicola clutched her daughter's hand. "I think we'd better be going. Thanks for the food." Having said that, Nicola and Davita headed for the door.

When they had gone, David gave her a kiss on the cheek, "You're the only woman I love, other than my mother; okay?"

They walked to church on Sunday, talking as they went along. Michelle was half smiling when they reached the building and went

169

inside. She smiled when they sat down beside her best friend. Michelle looked at Katrina and smiled. "How are you doing? You don't have long now." It was the month of August, and Katrina was six months pregnant.

"I'm doing okay. How are you?"

Michelle thought about the question for a moment and said, "We can talk, later."

Katrina nodded, and they sat waiting for morning service to begin. Pastor Jenkins walked to the podium carrying his Bible.

That evening, Michelle sat on her bed talking on the telephone to Katrina. "I saw that woman kiss David on the cheek. Is that too much or what?" Michelle waited for her friend to respond to the news.

"Well, it was only on the cheek, but I wouldn't want her to kiss my husband either," returned Katrina.

"Why am I so jealous of that woman?" Michelle heard herself say into the phone.

She heard Katrina sigh through the phone. She didn't want to stress out her pregnant friend with her problems. She'd have to find a way to deal with Nicola, since it was obvious that she wasn't going anywhere. David seemed to like having the woman around; he seemed a little flattered or something. He thought the kiss on the cheek wasn't a big deal, and Katrina sort of agreed with him. Michelle decided to change the subject, but in her heart she knew the woman was making a play for David.

"Michelle, are you still there?" asked Katrina.

"Sorry," Michelle said. "Do you and Frank want a boy or girl?"

Katrina informed her that her husband wanted a boy this time and so did she. After the call ended, Michelle's thoughts again wandered to Nicola. The woman was thirty-five and had married a seventy-five-year-old man. Did she marry the man as a ploy to get David back? Michelle didn't know, and only time would tell. She knew who she should talk to about the Nicola problem though, and she reached for the phone on the nightstand beside the bed.

Monday at noon, Michelle sat in Peace Diner having lunch with the first lady. "Why am I so jealous of Nicola?" she asked before taking a sip of her root beer soda.

The first lady looked at her and patted her hand. "We need to find out whether the reasons for these feelings are real or imaginary."

Michelle nodded her head, and for the next hour, they sat discussing the situation while eating. Michelle gained insight into the situation from the first lady of Peace Baptist Church. She was rational and reasonable.

"Go with your gut feeling and not your imagination," she said. Before sliding out of the booth, she added, "Call anytime if you need to talk about anything, okay?" Then she hugged Michelle and walked out the diner.

Michelle almost wanted to cry, because her gut feeling was telling her Nicola was after her husband. She finished her meal and left the diner. On Saturday morning, she was back at Precious's house with her and her niece, Bree.

"I want to buy this song of yours," said Bree, holding the sheet in her hand.

Michelle smiled and bounced up from her chair. She walked over to where the woman was standing. "Thank you, Bree. And thank you, Lord," she added with raised hands. Michelle couldn't be happier that someone was buying a gospel song she had written.

She broke into a type of Holy Ghost dance. Precious and Bree laughed, and then Precious turned on the radio which was set on the gospel music station. The music permeated the room, and Michelle continued her praise dance with the women joining in. The music was loud and seemed to bounce off the walls of the room.

They heard someone enter the room, and when they looked around he had joined in celebratory dance. Ed took the hand of his wife and swung her around and around. This dancing went on for another twenty minutes, leaving everyone exhausted but still happy. Ed reached into his pocket and pulled out his handkerchief to wipe the sweat off his face. Michelle sat on the couch wiping her forehead with a paper towel. Precious and Bree were in the kitchen getting refreshments.

"Well how are you, Brother Ed?" Michelle said, now using the paper towel as a fan.

"I'm good. I've been to jail to see Freddie," he revealed. "The man has changed. He acts like a Christian now."

Michelle nodded. "Yeah, it seems that way." She was sincerely pleased that the man had turned his life around.

Ed told her that it was going to be hard for Freddie to find a job once he got out of jail. He said he might help the man get work. Precious and Bree walked back into the room carrying a tray of food and beverages. They sat chatting and dining on the cold cut sandwiches and punch. Gospel music was still playing on the radio.

Michelle was smiling and felt all tingly inside. She had sold her first song, and she was doing what she loved; writing songs. She knew songwriting was a fickle business, sometimes songs sold, and other times they didn't. She probably couldn't make a living from it, but nonetheless she knew she couldn't give it up either. She took a bite out of her sandwich and chewed it slowly.

When Bree paid her for the song, she planned to photocopy the check and frame it. Michelle chuckled inside to herself because her dreams were coming true. Precious, Ed, and Bree sat at the counter chatting. The counter top was too small for another person to sit there, so Michelle sat in a nearby chair.

Ed bounced down from the stool and walked to Michelle. "I'm thinking about going into business for myself. I might be able to employ Freddie one day, when he gets out of jail."

Michelle stopped chewing and nodded. Brother Ed waved to her before walking out of the room. Minutes later, Dana appeared limping and carrying her smallest child followed by her four-year-old.

"Oh, I'm sorry. I thought everyone had left," she said.

Precious smiled at her and took the baby out of her arms. "It's okay; have a seat. We were winding down anyway."

Once Dana was seated, Precious handed the baby back to her before taking the empty tray and trash back to the kitchen. Bree helped her, and they walked out of the room together. Dana sat on the couch holding her baby and sitting next to her oldest. She looked up at Michelle. "Was

Freddie blackmailing you?"

Michelle stared at the woman with her mouth opened. She closed her mouth and opened it again "Yeah. Did he tell you?"

Dana shook her head. "No. I just overheard a conversation he had with Leo awhile back. I'm sorry about Freddie blackmailing you."

Michelle smiled and nodded at the woman. She wondered if Leo had any remorse at all that he'd blackmailed Katrina. She hadn't gotten any letter of apology for what he'd put her through.

Dana explained that Freddie was a different person now. He was a god fearing Christian. She told Michelle that she had forgiven Freddie for shooting her. She was now his wife and didn't want to look back. She told Michelle she only wanted to look ahead; the past was the past, and she couldn't change it. Dana also told Michelle that she was from Philadelphia, but wanted to make Washington, D.C. her permanent place of residence. She said her mother wasn't speaking to her because she'd married Freddie. So D.C. would be her home, and she'd wait until Freddie was released from jail and they could become a real family.

Michelle was speechless; she just listened as the woman talked on and on. She pondered all that Dana had said, and a long stream of air released from her jaws.

Dana looked at Michelle and smiled. "Maybe we can take all the children to the park sometimes." She paused, and then said, "How about it?"

Was the woman asking for a play date with her four children and Sasha?

Dana picked up a piece of paper and a pen from the table in front of her and began writing. When she finished writing, she held the paper in front of her. "This is my cell phone number; you can call me anytime."

Michelle walked over to retrieve the paper. She looked at it briefly before folding it up and placing it in her pocket. All of a sudden, the inside of the house seemed to be smothering her. Michelle decided to wait for David and Sasha outside, and she waved to the woman before leaving the room. Before walking out of the house, she stopped by the kitchen to hug Precious and Bree.

She spotted the car approaching. David was driving slow and stopped in front of the house. She dashed into the car and closed the door. They were heading home. When they arrived at their address, Nicola and Davita were on their doorstep yet again. Michelle lingered behind trying to calm herself down. She watched from the car as Davita jumped up and ran to her father. Sasha smiled, glad to see her half-sister, and Nicola was smiling as well. Heck, everyone was smiling except for Michelle.

After a moment to gather herself, Michelle got out of the car. Using quick steps, she walked into the yard displaying the most plastic, phony smile that she could muster. "Hi, everyone." She waved, pulled out her keys, and went into the house alone.

Once in the family room, she peeked out the window at everyone. Nicola would have to stop just dropping by without calling first. David was smiling as he lifted each of his daughters in the air. Nicola was all up in his face beaming, as if he was her dream husband. *Did she just touch him on the shoulder?* Michelle saw them walking toward the door, and she got out of the window and walked quickly into the kitchen.

"Can I take the girls to the park?" she heard Nicola say as they entered the house.

"It looks like rain," David replied. "Instead of going to the park, just let the girls play in the family room."

Michelle covered her ears with her hands. That meant Nicola would be here for a while. Fifteen minutes later, Michelle made an appearance in the family room with a plastic smile plastered on her face. She walked into the room and over to the table where Sasha and Davita were coloring in coloring books. She took a seat and began coloring in the Bible themed coloring book alongside the girls. She was actually quite fond of Davita; the girl's mother was the problem.

She took a glance over at David. Nicola was all up in his face gabbing. She saw Michelle looking at her and gave her a wave and smile before picking up a magazine.

"How you like your summer vacation?" Michelle asked Davita.

"Fine. I like coming over your house playing with Sasha," the girl returned.

Michelle smiled at her. "And we like having you." She sat and colored with Sasha and Davita for ten more minutes before excusing herself and walking out of the room.

Nicola was still sitting on the couch reading a magazine, and David was sitting in a chair reading the sports section from *The Washington Post*. When Nicola knew Michelle was gone, she looked around the room, stood, and stretched. The girls were still coloring in the corner of the room. David looked up from his paper, and when their eyes met, Nicola held out her index finger and motion for him to come to her. He put down the paper and walked to where she was standing.

"My marriage isn't working out, quite like I thought."

David looked at her and raised an eyebrow.

Nicola continued. "Maybe I never got over you, "she said in a soft tone, and then waited for a reply.

He smiled lightly, but said nothing. Nicola walked to the corner of the room where the girls were coloring and joined them. She smiled as she began coloring. David was her first and only love. Maybe one day they could reunite. *Stranger things have happened*, she thought and then giggled.

Michelle made a second appearance into the family room. "Would anyone like some snacks or refreshments?" she said, still being the reluctant hostess.

"I would," said Sasha. And then Davita joined in.

Michelle grinned at them. "Okay," she said, "then follow me to the kitchen."

When they were gone, Nicola eyed David. "Would you mind carrying Davita's toys to my car?" She pointed to a box in the corner of the room.

"Sure," he said walking over to pick up the box.

Nicola held the front door opened for him, and when they reached her car, he put the box in the backseat. When he turned around, she kissed him on the lips before she sat in the driver's seat.

David stared at her for a moment, and then he turned and walked back to his house.

Nicola smiled. This was only step one in the quest of getting him back. She knew he wouldn't tell his wife, because he liked the flattery and attention he wasn't getting from Michelle. Nicola got out of the car and closed the door before strolling back into the house. When she walked back into the family room, there was a tray of snacks on the table. She made herself a plate and went to sit with the girls.

Nicola saw Michelle put her arms around David as they sat on the couch, and she felt a twinge of jealousy. She thought to herself, *Michelle you're not woman enough to keep him*, and that thought made her giggle. David caught Nicola's eye and stared at her and this made her feel victorious. She stood and gathered her daughter before bidding them goodbye.

Nicola and Davita arrived home, and she was greeted by her husband. "Hey, beautiful; I really missed you."

She wasn't even thinking about him or trying to think about him, for that matter. She did care for her husband, but love? No way. "I need to put Davita to bed and stuff." She took the child by the hand and walked upstairs.

"I'll be waiting for you, honey," he said.

Nicola didn't even want to think about it or him. She only wanted to think about David, her first and only love. If she took enough time, maybe her seventy-five-year-old husband would be sleep when she returned. That was wishful thinking on her part. But Nicola was correct about one thing; David never mentioned to Michelle that she had kissed him on the lips.

Chapter 23

Michelle didn't know how it happened, but she somehow ended up at the park with Sasha, Dana, and Dana's four children. The woman had called her and suggested that they all go to the park together, and Michelle couldn't think of an excuse for not going.

Dana's two smaller children were strapped into a double baby stroller, and the older two were playing on toys with Sasha. The thought wouldn't leave Michelle's mind. How could Dana marry a man who shot her in the leg, went to jail for shooting her, and then decided to marry her while he was still in jail serving time for shooting her. Dana said he'd asked for her forgiveness, and she forgave him. Michelle could understand forgiving him, but marrying him? She couldn't wrap her mind around that one.

Michelle looked at the woman sitting next to her on the park bench. In fact, Michelle stared at the woman in disbelief.

"What is it?" said Dana after she caught Michelle staring. And then, as if she were a professional mind reader, she said, "Oh, I know. You want to know why I married Freddie after all he put me through."

Michelle didn't even try to deny it. Instead, she nodded her head.

Dana shrugged her shoulders. "I could always see something special in him." She raised her hand to stop Michelle's oncoming interruption. "Hear me out. He was acting real trifling, but I knew that wasn't who he really was." Dana went on to explain that Freddie was high on something when he shot her in the leg. She admitted that sometimes she felt like a fool for marrying him. Her mother thought she was a fool too.

She told Michelle that she'd grown up in the church, and she went six days a week as a child in Philadelphia. When she turned eighteen, she had stopped going because she wanted to live her own life on her terms. Dana told her there was a lady that lived on her block when she was growing up who wore really tight clothes, make up, and the latest hairdos. She'd modeled herself after that woman, wanting to be exactly like her. She'd patterned herself after that woman instead of her God-fearing mother. She admitted now that she had made a big mistake.

Michelle sat on the bench and thought about all that Dana had said.

She now thought better of the woman than before they had arrived at the park.

David was sitting in the kitchen of their home when the phone rang. "Hello?"

"Hello, David; it's Nicola. And how are you doing with your handsome self. I'm just joking," she quickly added. But words had already been said, and it was impossible to take them back.

"I'm okay, Nicola. How's my daughter?"

For dramatic effect, Nicola waited a few seconds before responding. "*Our* daughter is doing just fine and misses her daddy, as usual."

David sighed before he spoke. "Davita has an invitation to come over anytime she pleases."

Nicola wanted Davita, David, and her to be one big happy family, but she had to play her cards right. "David, I apologize for kissing you on the lips. I don't know what came over me." She was smiling on the inside as she waited for a response from him. She waited and waited for him to respond, and guessed that the lengthy delay was a good sign, but couldn't be sure. His hesitation wasn't due to his lack of privacy; that she knew for sure. She had seen Michelle and Sasha leave the house as she watched discretely from four houses down in her car.

When David finally spoke, he said, "You don't need to apologize."

Nicola nearly jumped for joy; that comment made her day. She planned to continue complimenting him and making over him until she won him back. She was married to another man and no one would suspect she was chasing after David. "Ooh, you are so sweet," she cooed into the phone. She ended he call soon after. She didn't want to chance Michelle and Sasha coming home and catching him talking to her.

"Nicola, where are you, honey?" she heard her husband call to her.

Go away, old man, she thought to herself and started giggling uncontrollably.

Michelle and Sasha walked into their house minutes later and went into the kitchen, where David was sitting at the kitchen table. Michelle put her arms around him, and he didn't respond. She removed her hand from his shoulder and grabbed Sasha's hand and walked out the kitchen and up the stairs, thinking all the time, *What's wrong with David?* "Sasha, go get a book so we can read it together."

While the girl ran to her room to get a book, Michelle kicked her shoes off in her bedroom and waited for her daughter's return. Their story time lasted for about half an hour, then Sasha and Michelle went to the girl's bedroom where they knelt beside Sasha's bed and prayed before saying goodnight sealed with a kiss.

The next morning, Michelle debated whether to resume her aftercare business for the coming school year. She considered running the idea by Katrina to get her opinion on the matter. She wanted to devote the majority of her time to songwriting, but knew she needed a regular, stable income as well.

The house was quiet and felt empty when Sasha was gone. She had been going to work with her dad for pretty much the entire summer. Michelle got out of bed and prepared to shower before going into the kitchen. After breakfast, she returned to her bedroom and sat on her bed for two uninterrupted hours writing songs. Writing songs after breakfast had become a part of her morning schedule.

Michelle looked around the bedroom, and her eyes stopped on the framed photocopy of the check she earned for writing the song for Bree. She rose from the bed and slipped into a pair of jeans and a blue top. She needed to go to the bank and deposit the real check. Michelle felt good about herself; her songwriting session today had been fruitful.

Opening the drawer of her nightstand, she pulled out her wallet and stuffed it in her pants pocket. Michelle scurried down the stairs and out the door. She was locking her front door when she heard someone call her name and turned around to see her neighbor.

Cheryl waved at her and Michelle walked out to greet her. "I'm going to Safeway," she said. "Where you off to?"

Michelle informed her that she was on her way to the bank. The bank and Safeway were near each other, so the two women decided to go together.

"The diner sells my cookies now," said Cheryl, practically giggling. "Now I'm trying to get Safeway to carry my cookies as well."

Michelle congratulated her, and then shared her own good news. "I sold my first song. That's why I'm on my way to the bank."

Cheryl looked at her and smiled, then patted her on the shoulder. "That's awesome!"

Michelle continued, "I'll need some cookies from you when my aftercare program resumes."

"Just say when," Cheryl told her. She was happy to get the business.

They reached their destination. Safeway was across the street from the bank. "I'll go to the bank first, then I can meet you at Safeway," said Michelle.

"Sounds like a plan to me," return Cheryl before crossing the street to go to the grocery store.

Michelle entered Safeway fifteen minutes later and grabbed a basket. As she shopped, she looked for Cheryl along the way.

"Michelle." She heard someone call her name and turned around to see Mary Jenkins.

Michelle walked over to where she was standing and gave her a hug. "Anytime I want to see the first lady, I need to come to Safeway," said Michelle with a chuckle.

"First ladies and their families have to eat too." Mary laughed along with her.

They chatted for a few minutes before parting ways and going down different aisles. Michelle walked to the meat department; she had a taste for liverwurst. She placed the package in her basket and kept shopping, keeping an eye out for Cheryl. The need to get some fruit for Sasha to snack on had her walking toward the produce section. She was pulling a plastic bag from the roll when Cheryl caught up with her.

"Yes! Thank you, Jesus!" she exclaimed. "Safeway has agreed to carry my cookies; at least for a while."

Michelle placed the plastic bag of oranges in her basket and gave Cheryl a small hug for the success of her cookies. It was nice to see that both of their career dreams were coming true. They left the grocery store twenty minutes later heading for home.

Michelle grinned from ear to ear as she sat at Precious's house on Saturday morning. She came alive when it came to talking about gospel music and writing songs.

"I already recorded two songs for my upcoming album," said Bree to Michelle. "Your song and one that I wrote."

Michelle couldn't wait to hear the recorded version of her song. The anticipation had her squirming in her chair.

"I'll bring it next time I come," Bree promised.

Michelle wished she'd brought it today, but she knew she was being overly anxious. She picked up a tablet from the table and continued writing lyrics. Her tablet was already half full.

Sister Precious pulled her chair closer to Michelle and said interrupted her creative flow. "I'm sorry; I need to talk to you, when you get time."

Michelle closed her tablet and placed it on the table. "What's up?"

Precious appeared to be deep in thought. Michelle had an idea about what might be bothering the woman. It was probably the same thing that was bothering her.

"Is this about Nicola?" Michelle offered.

Sister Precious nodded and said, "I hate that woman is using my father. She don't love him."

Michelle nodded. "What did she do, this time?"

"She's spending all of my father's money, and he doesn't seem to mind one bit."

Michelle knew that Precious's father was well off and that Nicola probably wasn't spending *all* his money. Still, the woman did have expensive taste. Michelle knew firsthand what a pain Nicola could be; that was for sure. She reached over to console Precious. Nicola could be an unrelenting headache.

* * * * * * *

Nicola knew Michelle's schedule because she spied on her constantly. She was infatuated with David; it was more like an obsession. Nicola knocked on the front door of their house holding her daughter's hand and smiling.

David opened the door and moved aside so that they could enter. Sasha was in the kitchen eating breakfast, and David scooped up Davita and swung her around.

"Whew, Daddy," said the girl.

He kissed her on the forehead before putting her down. "Why don't you go join Sasha in the kitchen." he said, and then watched her disappear around the corner.

"Where is Michelle?" asked Nicola, playing dumb.

"She's over at Sister Precious and Brother Ed's house."

"Oh so that means, we're all alone, *handsome*," she said giggling. "You knew I was only kidding when I called you that, right?" She'd really meant every word she'd said, and David looked at her as if he knew it.

He walked into the family room and took a seat. "I'm married, but I never forgot the times we had, together."

Nicola sat beside him and placed her hand over his and left it there. David stared ahead and didn't pull away. Nicola looked at him with more compliments to give. "Remember when we were boyfriend and girlfriend, and we went to the carnival?" When David nodded, she continued. "You won me a teddy bear, and I still have it."

She told David how precious the stuffed animal was to her, and then she kissed him on the lips before getting up and going into the kitchen to check on the girls. Nicola took a seat at the kitchen table between the two girls and said, "Your daddy is the best father in the world." Then she hugged both of them.

She knew David would be going to pick up his wife in a couple of hours, and she was making the most of her time at the house. Michelle needed to know that she was reclaiming her first love. Her plan was to give Michelle subtle hints of her goal.

Nicola made up a story about needing to talk to Precious about something. That won her and Davita a ride with David and Sasha to pick up Michelle. She wanted Michelle to see how things would look in the future with her and David together. When they arrived at the house, David beeped his horn, and Michelle came immediately outside.

Michelle spotted Nicola sitting next to David, and her eyes grew large as two golf balls. Nicola smiled, when she got the reaction she was seeking, and then she waved goodbye to David and Sasha. She held her daughter's hand as they walked to the porch where Michelle was standing and watching.

"Hi, Michelle. David was sweet enough to give us a ride." She smiled and walked her daughter past Michelle and into the house.

Michelle was as mad with David as she was with Nicola. Did he really like this woman or not? Michelle didn't know or care at this point. She walked to the car and climbed inside. She turned to the backseat and gently squeezed Sasha's shoulder.

"Mommy!" the girl squalled through a laugh.

Michelle turned back around in her seat and looked straight ahead. She didn't have anything nice to say to David.

He looked at his wife and then away. He seemed clueless as to why she was so angry with him.

One day, Michelle knew she would have it out with Nicola. It was only a matter of time, she thought to herself riding down the street. That night before bed, Michelle prayed for her marriage and prayed that she wouldn't harm Nicola.

The next morning the phone rang, and it was her best friend. She had missed talking to Katrina, and was glad that she'd called from her cell phone before her work shift began.

"Hi, Michelle. I'm at work now, but I'd love to meet for lunch today."

Michelle smiled at the offer. She promised to meet Katrina in the cafeteria of the building where she worked. And at noon, they were sitting together eating lunch.

"How are you feeling?" asked Michelle, before biting into her sandwich.

"Not bad," said Katrina reaching for a glass of cranberry juice and taking a sip.

Michelle sighed. "I wish I could say the same, but Nicola is getting to me. I know she's chasing David. I don't have much proof, but it something I feel in my gut."

Katrina nodded before taking a bite of her chicken salad sandwich. There had to be something to what Michelle was saying; she knew her friend wasn't one to jump to crazy conclusions.

Michelle forked some coleslaw into her mouth and chewed before changing the subject. "How long are you going to continue working?"

Katrina took a moment to swallow the food that was in her mouth. "I plan to work up until my due date, if possible."

Michelle wasn't surprised by the answer. It was just like Katrina to work until her doctor told her not to. She looked at the clock on the wall. It was almost time for her friend to get back to work. Michelle wiped her mouth with a napkin and rose from her chair, "I'm going to be going, now. Can you make it back upstairs okay?"

Katrina nodded and Michelle waved before leaving the cafeteria. She smiled to herself because it felt good chatting with Katrina like they used to do. The brief girlfriend time had lifted her spirits, and Michelle felt creative all of a sudden. She planned to go home and complete some songs she had been working on that morning.

When David and Sasha got home that evening from his job, Michelle could say she'd had a very productive songwriting day. It was two weeks away from the beginning of the new school year, and it was almost time for Michelle to crank up her aftercare program again.

Sasha needed to spend a week with her grandparents before school started or Michelle's parents would pay her a visit; a very unpleasant one. She didn't want to get her parents riled up. Sasha would definitely be visiting them soon. When she picked up the telephone to call her parents, Michelle discovered that it would be even sooner than she'd thought. Her father said he'd be there to get his granddaughter the next day.

"Sasha" Michelle called walking out of her bedroom into the hallway after ending the call with her father.

The girl came running to her. "Yes, Mommy."

Michelle took her daughter's hand in hers, and they walked down the stairs to the family room together. They took a seat on the couch, and Michelle placed her arm around Sasha and cuddled with her. When she told her that she would be visiting her grandparents for a week, Sasha responded in a positive way because she loved her grandparents.

"What would you like to do today, baby?" asked Michelle. "Just you and me."

Sasha looked up as if she needed advice from God. "I want to go to the park and eat a sloppy joe sandwich," replied her daughter.

Michelle released Sasha from the tight embrace and moved to grant her wishes. She stood in the doorway of the room. "David, Sasha and I are going out; we'll be back in a while," she called.

Michelle heard him say, "Okay," and then she took Sasha's hand once again, and they walked out of the family room and out of the house.

The next evening, the house seemed quiet with Sasha gone. Michelle heard a key in the door and turned to see David walking into the house holding something in his hand. He walked into the family room where she was seated on the couch and joined her. She looked down at his hand. "What are those?"

"These are tickets to a fundraiser for Councilman Polk's re-election," he said waving the tickets in front of her face. Do you want to go?"

"I'd love to." She said it like her husband had asked her out on a date.

The thought was exciting. They could get all dressed up and spend some time together. Michelle threw her arms around David and planted a kiss on his lips. They stayed that way for a while; their marriage hadn't felt that good in a long time.

The tickets for the event were not cheap by any means, but Councilman Polk was one of a few politicians they could believe in. He voted for summer jobs for youth and affordable housing; things that she and David believed in. The event would take place in five days, and she had to get ready. She hoped she could persuade Cheryl, Katrina, and their husbands to also attend. She walked out of the family room and up the stairs she had plans to make.

In a spur of the moment decision, Michelle galloped down the stairs and peeked into the family room to tell David she was going to visit Cheryl. She walked out the front door and down the street to her neighbor's house.

* * * * * * *

The phone rang at the Davidsons' house.

"Hello?" said David.

"Hello," cooed Nicola. "I was wondering if you might want to visit with Davita." She knew he would never turn down a visit with his daughter. Her elderly husband was out of town on a trip with some brothers from the church. Davita was gone too. She was spending a few days visiting with her aunt, but David didn't need to know any of that. Nicola smiled to herself. "Come over in about an hour, hon. . ." She'd almost called him honey, but caught herself. She got off the phone and prepared to get gorgeous for David. This could be the turning point in their relationship she told herself, singing softly.

Michelle walked back into her house forty minutes after she'd left, and her husband was about to head out. "Where are you going?' she asked him.

He told her he was going to visit Davita. Then he gave her a hug and walked toward the door

"Wait," said Michelle just as he was about to reach for the doorknob. He turned around to look at her.

Nicola had showered, perfumed herself, and had on a flattering multi-colored sundress. He would be here soon, and she was looking her best. She checked her watch. *Not much longer now*, she thought to herself. Nicola counted the seconds as her watched ticked away.

She walked to the window and pulled the curtain back and she saw a car approaching her home. The car slowed down and turned into her driveway, and her eyes opened wide. It was David's car! She pushed the curtain back in place at the window and walked to the front door waiting his knock. When it came a minute later, she flung open the door and stared with an opened mouth.

"David, sent me to get his daughter," said Michelle.

Nicola didn't say a word because she couldn't speak. Her lips felt like they were frozen shut.

"Helloooo," Michelle said with a slice of attitude. "I said David sent me to pick up his daughter."

Nicola shook her head, then shrugged her shoulders. "Uhm, she's not here. She's with her aunt right now."

Michelle stared at the woman. It was just what she thought. She hadn't imagined anything. This woman was after her husband.

"I meant to call David and tell him Davita was with her aunt," Nicola lied.

Michelle said nothing. She stared the woman down for a few more seconds before turning and leaving, She smiled walking back to the car because she had defeated Nicola . . . this time.

The next day, Dana called to have another play date with their kids Michelle accepted her invitation, and they arrived at the park with what looked like a boatload of children who headed straight for the toys. Michelle and Dana sat on the bench with her two littlest ones in a double stroller.

"Is your leg bothering you?" asked Michelle, noticing her rubbing it with her hand.

"Sometimes, but I can take it." The shooting had left Dana with a permanent limp when she walked. She went into her tote bag and pulled out an envelope of pictures and stared at them before handing them to Michelle one by one. They were pictures of Dana, Freddie, and their children that were taken during family day at the jail.

Michelle studied each photo as it was handed to her. In the pictures, Freddie smiled as if he had been voted father of the year or something.

Dana interrupted her thoughts. "The children look just like Freddie, and I like that fact."

Michelle handed each picture back to her, and then excused herself

187

and walked to where Sasha and the children were playing on the toys. Michelle had to admit that Dana was pretty good company. She had thought the woman must be insane to marry a man that shot her, so she certainly thought she was too dumb to hold an enlightening conversation. She was wrong.

Michelle watched Sasha at the top of the sliding board suddenly slide down to the bottom where she stood. Dana's three- and four-year-old soon followed suit. Michelle kind of liked this outing with Dana and her children and even agreed on another play date in the near future. Who would have thought she be buddy-buddy with Freddie's wife. When they were done, she returned Sasha to her grandparents' house before she made it home.

The Davidsons ate most of their meals at Peace Diner. David felt like Michelle did enough work caring for their daughter; he didn't want her slaving away in the kitchen. They had the means to afford the reasonably priced meals at the church's eatery, so unless Michelle just wanted to cook, he had no problem eating out. As they sat in a booth at the diner, David placed his hand gently on top of hers and Michelle's whole face sparkled like a fine diamond.

She noticed that lately he'd been much sweeter to her than usual. He looked for opportunities to reach out to her. When they crossed paths in the house, he would give her a kiss for no reason at all. He was putting spark back into a marriage whose pilot light she thought had burnt out.

The waitress came by, and they placed their order. This woman was more than a waitress to them; she was a member of Peace Baptist Church and knew them by name. "Is Sasha gone away for the summer?" asked the woman.

Michelle nodded. "Staying with her grandparents."

The waitress smiled, took their order, and walked away.

David was looking at Michelle like he was in a trance. Michelle blushed; she didn't mind him staring one little bit.

Chapter 24

Michelle and Cheryl sat in the beauty parlor in chairs across from one another, getting their hair done for the political fundraiser event. They had already gone shopping, and their gowns now hung in their respective closets. Ditto on the fingernails and toes; they were now shiny and well groomed.

"I haven't gotten the full treatment in a long time," confessed Michelle. Cheryl looked at her and nodded her head in agreement.

The beautician turned Michelle's chair to the side and continued working on her hair. She felt almost like a princess preparing to go to the ball with her prince, David. She usually did her own hair. Most of the time, she didn't have the patience to wait at a beauty parlor. But since she was attending a special event, she decided to wait it out this time.

That evening, Michelle sashayed in three-inch heels into the ballroom of The Washington Hilton Hotel, along with David, Cheryl, and her husband, Paul. They took a seat at the round table draped with a white tablecloth. Michelle wore a lavender colored gown, and her hair was in a French roll with cascading curls framing her face.

The room quickly filled up and Councilman Polk took the floor to make a brief speech. Everyone was glad of that because everyone knew how long politicians could jabber on. He thanked everyone for coming out in support of his campaign, and he spoke about the good people of the ward he represented. Councilman Polk was a candidate that they believed in. The attendees applauded at the end of his speech, and he waved before walking into an adjacent room.

Michelle looked at her tablemates and smiled as they all sat in the elegant ballroom. When the music played, the people at her table rose and hit the dance floor. Michelle stood on the dance floor in David's arms swaying gently to the music. Cheryl and Paul were directly behind them slowly dancing as well. Michelle and David stayed on the floor for the second song and afterward, he led her back to the table holding her hand.

Cheryl and her husband were already seated as David pulled back Michelle's chair, so she could have a seat. Cheryl pulled a pocket camera from her purse and motioned for Michelle and David to pose. They obeyed and she snapped the camera once, and then twice. She then handed Michelle the camera so she could return the favor, and snap pictures of her and her husband.

"Say cheese," said Michelle before she clicked the camera. They were creating memories that she would never forget. She handed the camera back to Cheryl, and when she placed her hand on the table, David quickly placed his on top of hers and she looked into his eyes and almost giggling in delight.

The food served at the event was very little, and the appetites of the attendees weren't satisfied, but food wasn't everything. They were having a great time, and that meant much more to them.

It was the end of August, and school had begun in Washington, D.C. So had Michelle's aftercare program. She smiled at the children and their parents leaving her house at the end of her first day of service. When all the other children were gone, Michelle sat next to Sasha on the couch in the family room with her arm around her daughter tickling her shoulder, and then her tummy. Sasha was giggling and squirming all around the couch as Michelle laughed out loud.

The week came to a rapid close, and on Sunday, Michelle sat at church focused on the illuminated cross near the pulpit, all the while thinking that God was the light that guided her path along the way.

Things were still magnificent at home with David. She looked at her husband on the pew beside her and beamed with joy.

"Good morning, saints," said Pastor Jenkins from the pulpit. "I pray and hope that this day finds you in good spirits and health. Please take out your Bible."

After church service ended, Michelle hugged her pregnant friend. "How are you feeling?"

Katrina smiled and touched her belly. "I'm fine; just sort of fat," she said with a laugh.

Michelle had missed hanging out with her friend, but this was the stage when Katrina needed the most rest. She gave her a hug and waved before walking out the church. David and Sasha waited for her outside on the sidewalk, and she joined them for their walk home.

The next Saturday morning found Michelle at Precious's house working on her songwriting and listening to Bree's vocals. Other than going to church, music and songwriting gave her the biggest thrill. Bree's album was about half done, and the woman was now singing the song that Michelle had written. Michelle thought she would faint from joy, when she heard her words come to life. She applauded loudly, and when Bree finished singing, she took a small bow.

"That was fantastic!" Precious clapped her hands and beamed with delight. "Does anyone want something to eat?" she asked after calming down. When Michelle and Bree nodded in the affirmative, she said, "Okay, I'll be right back."

"Wait," called Bree. "I'll help you."

When the two women walked out of the room, Michelle reached for her tablet and a pen to continue writing songs. She had only been writing for a few moments when she began to feel like she was being watched. She turned around and looked up to see Ed.

"I hope I didn't disturb you," he said. He walked to where she was sitting and took a seat next to her.

Michelle decided to take a break and placed her pen and tablet down on the table. "How are you?" she asked him.

He nodded his head up and down. "I'm doing fine. I'd like to talk to you about Freddie." Michelle stiffened her shoulders. "Oh, it's good news about him," he quickly added having seen her reaction.

Ed went on to tell her that he'd been visiting Freddie on a regular basis at the jail and that he has gotten himself together through Jesus. He told her that Freddie prayed and read the Bible on a regular basis. Freddie likened himself to Paul in the Bible and informed Ed that Paul had become his role model.

"Really?" Michelle heard herself say. As he continued to describe the new Freddie, she was convinced that he was telling the truth about the man.

Ed informed Michelle that it was definite. He was going into business for himself. Working on the force as a police detective had lost some of its luster for him, and he was opening a private detective agency. Michelle congratulated the detective as his wife and niece entered the

191

room. Precious and Bree carried a tray of sandwiches and a pitcher of punch. They sat it all on a small table near the entrance, and Ed rose and walked over to the table to help himself.

Michelle smiled. She would love to continue her conversation with Ed about Freddie; maybe next Saturday. For now, though; she wanted something to eat. Besides, Ed had already left the room with his plate in hand. She recalled the detective once telling her that Freddie was interested in law enforcement. The thought made her laugh aloud. Precious and Bree turned to look at her with raised brows, wondering what was so funny. Michelle smiled at them, fixed a plate, and sit down to dine.

She picked up her club sandwich with the chewy hard roll and filled her empty belly. Michelle knew she would be thinking about her conversation with Ed for the rest of the day. "The sandwich was tasty," she told to Precious.

Michelle looked at her watch. David would be coming to get her shortly, but she wanted to holler at Precious's basement guest before going home. "Is Dana downstairs?"

When Precious nodded yes, Michelle asked her permission to go visit with the woman and it was granted. Michelle knocked on the basement door and called out to her before entering.

"Come on down," called Dana. Michelle walked down the stairs and Dana limped over to greet her. "This is a pleasant surprise," said the woman, and she and Michelle took a seat.

Dana had done a great job decorating the place. As they sat and chatted, Dana told Michelle that Ed has been like a mentor to Freddie and that she greatly appreciated all that he and Precious had done for her and her children.

Michelle listened to what the woman had to say and nodded at the appropriate time. She knew the woman probably wanted to talk to an adult; talking to children all day might drive a person insane. They were indeed gifts from God, but talking to more adults could work wonders for a mother's mental health.

Three of Dana's four children were napping, and the baby was the only one awake in his crib playing with a toy. The baby began to cry, and

Dana attempted to get up out of the chair, but Michelle lowered her hand to indicate she would take care of everything. Dana smiled and Michelle walked to the crib and scooped the child out and into her arms. She walked back to her chair and sat the baby on her lap, cooing to him while rocked him.

"I remember when Sasha was this little," Michelle remarked. "They get big fast." A beeping horn outside alerted Michelle that visiting hours were over. She rose with the baby in her arms and carried him to Dana. "I got to go; David's here." She waved goodbye and walked up the basement steps.

Later that evening, as Michelle and her family sat in Peace Diner eating their meal, thoughts of Freddie roamed through her mind. What did Dana say; that Brother Ed was some type of mentor to Freddie? Michelle honestly believed the man had changed, and when he got out of jail he would be a decent husband to Dana and a good father to the children.

Michelle believed that the changes wouldn't happen overnight though. Ed would help him get a job once released from jail. Freddie's future didn't look that bad; hopefully he wouldn't screw it up this time.

"Mommy, did you hear me?" asked Sasha sitting across from her in the booth.

"Hmm." Michelle saw crab cake on the plate in front of her. She had been so deep in thought about the Freddie issue that she hadn't even heard David ordered it for her. She looked over at David, and he was staring at her. "Thanks, honey; I loved crab cakes." She cleared her mind of everything because she wanted to be mentally there for her family. Sasha forked a piece of crab cake into her mouth, and Michelle did the exact same thing.

On Monday morning, Michelle was at Cheryl's, taste testing cookies

"How do you like these?" asked Cheryl, pointing to the oatmeal-raisin cookies that were still warm on the cookie sheet.

Michelle reached for one and took a bite. "Ooh, these are good and chewy; just like I like them."

Cheryl smiled as she stood at the kitchen counter with her hands in dough. Michelle sat at the table and reached for a peanut butter cookie from another cookie sheet on the table. She was enjoying her job as a taste tester. She turned in her seat and gave Cheryl the thumbs-up sign because she sure could bake some cookies. Cheryl took a small bow at the waist and laughed out loud.

The phone rang and Cheryl looked around with dough on her hands. "Can you get that?"

Michelle rose from her chair and walked to the phone on the wall. "Hello?"

It was Freddie calling collect from jail. The operator wanted to know if she would accepted the charges. "Cheryl, it's Freddie." Michelle held the phone in the air.

Cheryl asked Michelle to accept the charges while she stacked the dough in a bowl and cleaned her hands.

Freddie came on the line before Cheryl could get to the phone. "Cheryl?" he asked.

"No, this is Michelle," she answered.

"Oh. How are you?" he asked.

"I'm fine," Michelle told him. "How are you doing?

"God is good" was his answer to Michelle's question; nothing more.

Cheryl dried her hand on the dish towel and walked toward Michelle. Michelle told Freddie goodbye and handed her the phone and took a seat back at the kitchen table. Cheryl and Freddie talked for about fifteen minutes before she said goodbye and hung up the phone.

"My cousin is getting a lot better," Cheryl announced. "All he wants to talk about is the Lord."

Michelle smiled before reaching for a sugar cookie, biting into it, and giving a report on how delicious it tasted. As she prepared to leave, Cheryl rewarded her for her service by giving her a baker's dozen of molasses cookies. Michelle thanked her and walked out of the house heading for home.

The next day, Michelle knelt with her aftercare charges in the family room to pray individually and collectively. When they were done praying, it was time for a snack, and they all walked into the kitchen.

194

They made graham crackers sandwiched between applesauce with whip cream on the top.

Michelle smiled as she watched her five charges delight in their snack. It was Katrina's daughter turn to bless the snack today. Michelle prayed daily for the children in her aftercare program. While they ate, Michelle glanced out the window. Maybe she would take the children outside. The weather was warm, and the sky was clear.

Turning to the children she asked, "Would anyone like to go outside after snack?"

The offer delighted the children and they sounded like a chorus of agreeable voices. When they were done eating, the kids gathered in her backyard where there were toys and they remained there playing until their parents arrived.

After she'd given the last parent and child a hug as they left, Michelle and Sasha began straightening up the family room. It was a fairly easy task because she'd trained her charges to pick up after themselves. When they were done, Sasha picked up her backpack and went up to her bedroom to do her homework. Michelle had told her daughter that she could finish it later, but Sasha wanted to do it now. Michelle kissed her on the forehead and hugged her before the girl left the room.

Finally able to relax, Michelle was seated on the couch in the family room with her feet propped on the ottoman when David walked through the door. He placed his briefcase on the coffee table and sat down to cuddle with Michelle on the couch. Things continued going well with them.

The phone rang and David went to the kitchen to answer it. Michelle sat looking around the room, but a curious feeling swept over her like a swiftly moving hurricane. She rose from the couch and walked into the kitchen staring at David on the phone.

He took the receiver from his mouth and covered it with his hand. "It's Nicola," he said before returning to the conversation.

Michelle smiled and walked out of the kitchen and up the stairs to their bedroom. She sat on the bed and gently lifted the phone and listened quietly.

"I care for my husband, but I'll always love you, David," said Nicola over the phone.

Michelle bit her tongue and almost said something, but caught herself.

"That's not right, Nicola," returned David. "Michelle is the only woman I love."

Michelle smiled a million smiles in that one moment. But did he say that because he knew she was on the extension? She decided he had said it because he actually meant it.

"I'm sorry, David; I didn't mean to disrespect Michelle, but it's hard for me to control my heart."

Michelle was debating whether to speak at this point or not. She had heard enough. The woman wasn't ever going to stop making a play for her husband. Michelle slowly and gently hung up the telephone. Nicola was a threat to her marriage and would do anything to reach her sick minded goal. She would roll all this information around in her head and think of a way to defeat Nicola. Michelle walked out of her bedroom and down the stairs entering the family room. She was looking out of the window when David joined her.

She turned around looked at him before rushing into his arms. "I love you, David," she said nestled in his arms.

He didn't know where all of this was coming from, so he just went with the flow. David led her to the couch where they sat snuggling with one another.

The next morning, she sat at a booth in Peace Diner with First Lady Jenkins.

"You should be happy with the way your husband handled the situation," was her reply when Michelle told her what transpired in the telephone conversation with David and Nicola the previous day.

Michelle nodded her head in agreement, but she couldn't understand why she still felt so insecure after the telephone incident?

"I know what happened may leave you feeling unsettled or whatnot." The first lady smiled and patted her on the hand.

Michelle nodded again. She knew the first lady was right about her relationship with David. He had only goo-goo eyes for her alone, yet there was a nagging little voice in her head playing tricks with her mind. She and the first lady prayed together before parting ways.

"Call anytime," were the departing words of her pastor's wife.

Time spent with the first lady was always a breath of fresh spiritual air. Michelle finished the remains of her breakfast and paid her bill. As she stepped outside the diner she saw Nicola and her husband about to enter the place.

"Oh, Michelle. How wonderful it is to see you," said Nicola walking closer to Michelle with her arms opened for a hug.

Michelle extended her palm toward the woman to ward off a hug. "Nice to see you Nicola and Elder," she said with a stiff controlled voice, and walked swiftly away thinking how much she disliked the woman. The steam from that brief encounter propelled her all the way home with steam to spare. She walked into her house and up to her bedroom. Suddenly a smile crossed her lips. She knew she had David's heart and figured that should be enough, at least for now. In her bedroom she turned to the gospel station, kicked off her shoes, and rejoiced to the gospel music while sliding across the brown carpet.

As church service was winding down on Sunday evening, Pastor Wynn from The Hope and Faith Center spoke to the congregation at Peace Baptist Church. "We have a vibrant prison ministry at our church, and your leader, Pastor Jenkins, asked me to start one here."

Sounds of agreement vibrated throughout the church.

"We go out weekly to minister to the inmates at the local jail. If any of you would like to join us, sign this roster," he said holding up the sheet of paper in his hand.

Michelle and Katrina exchanged glanced and then turned and listened attentively to the visiting pastor. Michelle couldn't decide whether she wanted to be involved with the prison ministry or not. She looked at her husband sitting near her on the pew. David was nodding his head to what the pastor was saying.

"I'll leave the sign-up sheet with your pastor. I look forward to you joining me in this much-needed ministry." When Pastor Wynn backed away from the podium everyone applauded him. "God bless you all," he concluded before walking away from the podium.

"That prison ministry sounds interesting," whispered Katrina.

David tapped Michelle on the shoulder. "I think I might be interested in something like that."

Michelle nodded in agreement. She wouldn't mind helping to rescue lost souls with the ministry herself.

"Michelle."

Someone called her name as she and her family was about to head toward the exit doors. It was Ed. He and Precious began walking in Michelle's direction, and when they reached her, Ed spoke. "I'm signing up for the prison ministry. I've already been going to the jail to see Freddie anyway."

"I might sign up as well," said Michelle.

"Yeah," David chimed in. "I'm interested in joining the prison ministry too." He was looking down the aisle of the church to where the sign-up sheet was located.

They said their goodbyes and stopped to put their names on the roster before leaving the church. The prison ministry was the topic of discussion on their walk to eat dinner. Peace Diner was closed on Sunday, so they would have to dine elsewhere today.

September in Washington, D.C. was pretty warm, and it caught the Davidson family at the park on a Monday evening. Sasha was on the sliding board while Michelle and David sat side by side on a park bench. Michelle eyed a couple entering the park with a young girl, and she did a double take and stared. It was Nicola, Elder Peterson, and Davita and they were walking toward their bench.

When the girl spotted David, she started running, shouting, "Daddy!" over and over.

David rose from the bench to greet his daughter. Davita leaped in the air as she neared her father, and he caught her in mid-air and swung her around while she squeaked.

"Great to see you all," said a fake, phony sounding Nicola when she and her elderly husband reached the bench.

Davita left the adults and ran over to play with Sasha on the toys. Nicola and her husband sat on a bench next to Michelle and David. Michelle silently prayed that they would go home soon. Nicola suddenly turned and planted a lingering kiss on his lips, and Michelle turned away from them.

Nicola rose from the bench and smoothed out her clothes like she'd even been sitting long enough for them to wrinkle. "Nice seeing the two of you, but me and my dynamite husband have got to go." She called Davita to join them, and then they all said goodbye and left the park.

Michelle looked at David. His eyes were locked on Davita and Elder Peterson walking away with their arms linked. He looked upset by the display of affection Nicola lavished on her husband. Was the woman trying to make David jealous or something? And was she succeeding? She and David both knew it was all an act, and that Nicola didn't really love her husband.

When they entered their house, David was quiet and visibly upset. He swiftly walked upstairs to their bedroom and closed the door. Had Nicola gotten to him? Did he still have feelings for that woman? Michelle hated her own insecurities, but what was she to think when he kept acting this way when it came to his ex? Michelle took Sasha's hand and they walked into the kitchen. David acted like he needed his space, and she was going to give it to him.

Sasha sat at the kitchen table eating a snack. "Mommy, my sister's birthday is in September, and she's going to have a party," said Sasha. "Can I go to her birthday party?" When Michelle didn't respond right away, the child added, "Please Mommy, can I go?"

Michelle hadn't been told anything about a birthday party. David had never mentioned it. She smiled at her daughter, but didn't reply to her question. Instead, she changed the subject. "How would you like some peanut butter cookies? Ms. Cheryl made them." Michelle rose from her chair and went into the refrigerator and pulled out the cookies. She and Sasha sat at the kitchen table eating the treats.

"These are good," Sasha said with her mouth full. The girl acted like she was trying to swallow the cookie whole.

Michelle took her hand. "Take your time and chew."

The phone rang and Michelle rose to answer it, but it only rang once. At first, she figured that whoever had dialed their number had realized they'd dialed wrong and hung up. But just as she was about to return to her seat, she began to wonder if maybe David had answered it from upstairs. The curiosity was killing her. "Sasha, could you take your cookies in the family room? I'll be there shortly."

As soon as the child was gone, Michelle gently reached for the phone and quietly listened to Nicola's voice on the other end.

"Our daughter's birthday is coming up, and I'm throwing her a party. Can Sasha come?

"Yeah, I guess that should be okay," said David. "I love that my two daughters are spending time together."

Nicola's response was, "Oh, David; I love you. The party is going to be great."

Michelle listened carefully, and eyes rolled up toward the ceiling. She couldn't remember the last time anyone had annoyed her more than the new Mrs. Peterson.

"Plus, I get to see you," added Nicola.

David didn't say anything for a few seconds, and then he spoke. "The way you treated your husband at the park; you acted like you were in love with him."

Michelle was upset with David; he sounded like a jealous boyfriend. She tightened her lips to keep the angry words from coming out.

"David, you know what a good actress I am," she replied through a giggle. "Plus, you only have eyes for Michelle, right?"

The conversation they were having was getting on Michelle's nerves. She gently placed the phone on the hook and took a seat at the kitchen table to ponder what she just heard. "It really doesn't matter does it" spoke David "My wife is the only woman I love" Michelle had hung up the phone before he spoke those words.

Chapter 25

On September 7th, they were at a birthday party at Nicola's house. The place was huge and elegantly decorated; chandeliers hung from the ceiling in the main room. They followed Nicola out to the back deck of the house where the party was taking place. Orange, blue, red, and white balloons were tethered to the fence. Nicola reached down and hugged Sasha. Michelle wanted to clean her daughter with disinfectant. The woman walked back into her house, leaving the Davidson family alone.

Elder Peterson walked onto the back deck and over to the family. "Sure is a nice day for a party," he said.

Michelle smiled. She liked the elder; she just felt sorry for him. He'd married an evil witch and didn't even know it. "Yes it is," she returned.

Nicola returned to the back deck and stood beside her husband. "Here you are," she said with a prescription bottle in one hand and a glass of water in the other. "You forgot to take your medication this morning." She handed him a pill and the glass.

The elder sat down in a nearby chair and took his pill, washing it down with several swallows of water. Nicola stood over him like a mother giving instructions to a child. She patted him on the shoulder after he finished and waved to the others before walking back into the house.

"She takes such good care of me," said Elder Peterson from his chair.

Michelle and David turned around when they heard footsteps coming their way. Precious and Ed were walking toward them.

"Hi, everyone," said Precious waving. Ed smiled and nodded his greeting.

"Glad you all could make it," her father said.

Precious walked the short distance to where he was siting and said in a low voice, "Daddy, did you take your medication this morning? Dr. Owen told me to remind you because sometimes you forget."

Elder Peterson nodded his head. "My lovely bride brought the pill out to me," he bragged.

It was easy to see that Precious couldn't stand the woman that her father had married. Knowing that Nicola had married him for his money and not love seemed to make her blood boil. She patted her father on the shoulder and walked back over to chat with Michelle and her family. David pulled out his camera and took some pictures when he saw his two daughters running around the large deck.

Nicola walked onto the back deck and over to her husband. "Honey, I think you need to go upstairs and lie down."

"I am a little tired," he replied. Then he got up from his chair, hugged everyone, and went inside.

Nicola joined Davita and Sasha in their child's play. In total, there were about fifteen children at the birthday party. Michelle and Precious stood together watching the woman's interaction with the girls.

Precious spoke in a low voice to Michelle. "I can't even stand her a little bit."

Michelle nodded in agreement. The woman had made several plays for her husband, so she was feeling what Precious had just said.

Precious hugged Michelle and placed Davita's gift on the table. "I only came by because my father asked me to. The only positive in coming was that I'd get a chance to see him. And now that Daddy's gone to take a nap and I can't see him anyway; I'm leaving." She meant every word because she immediately found Ed and the two of them left.

David was still taking pictures of his daughters, and Nicola jumped between the two girls, posing and grinning like she was the happiest woman in the world. Michelle shook her head. It was a pathetic scene.

* * * * * * *

Michelle really missed hanging out with Katrina. Her best friend was now seven months pregnant, so Michelle had practically stopped calling and being around her for fear of stressing her out and distressing her unborn baby. She decided to go visit her friend, but she would only stay a little while. "Sasha, are you ready to go?" she called out to her daughter from downstairs.

Sasha ran out of her bedroom and down the stairs. "I'm ready to go, Mommy."

Michelle took her by the hand and they walked out of the front door, together.

"Girl, I'm so glad to see you," said Katrina as she welcomed Michelle and Sasha into her house. She patted Sasha on the shoulder as she passed by her. Katrina led them into her kitchen and asked Sasha if she wanted to go upstairs and play with her daughter. Sasha joyfully ran out the kitchen and up the stairs to Kayla's room.

Michelle and Katrina sat across from one another around the kitchen table. Michelle poked out her bottom lip and sucked her teeth.

"What's the matter with you?" asked Katrina staring at her.

Michelle didn't mean to be so obvious about the way she was feeling. "It's that conniving Nicola. She keeps bothering me."

Katrina nodded and took her friend's hand. "How does David feel about Nicola's behavior?"

Michelle had already pondered that same thing to herself many times. She had mixed feelings about the question. David obviously knew Nicola had a thing for him. She secretly heard the woman tell him that over the phone. He had put the woman in her place that time, but still . . . "Sometimes I think David is flattered by all the attention she gives him."

Katrina stared at her for a second. "You know what that means; you got to step up your game, girl."

Michelle began to laugh. "I don't know how to throw flattery around like Nicola," she said. "I might come off sounding like a phony."

Katrina wagged her finger in Michelle's direction. "I'm just saying; step up your game, okay?"

Michelle smiled. "Enough about that. Let's talk about your unborn baby."

And that's exactly what they did over sandwiches and glasses of apple juice. Katrina didn't know whether her unborn baby was a boy or girl; she and Frank wanted to be surprised. She was still working, and the latter stage of her pregnancy wasn't nearly as bad as the earlier stages when she threw up on a daily basis. Katrina secretly wanted another girl but her husband clearly wanted a boy; a Frank Jr. The nursery was all set up; decorated in with neutral colors. Michelle was planning on throwing Katrina a surprise baby shower, but somehow she felt that Katrina knew that.

"Do you think you and David will have any more children?"

The question threw Michelle for a loop. She'd never thought about it, and she and David had never discussed it. "Another child?" She mulled over the thought. "I don't know; maybe."

Katrina rubbed her belly. "Well, can you at least commit to being the godparents of mine?"

Michelle beamed with delight at the sound of her friend's question. Michelle and David were already the godparents of Kayla.

Katrina informed her that after the baby was born, she planned to take some time off from her job. "If the baby is a girl, her middle name will be Michelle."

Michelle gave Katrina a big hug before picking up half of her club sandwich from the plate and taking a bite.

"Why don't you call anymore," asked Katrina.

Michelle swallowed her food before speaking. "With all the stuff that's going on with Nicola, I don't want to stress you out."

Katrina informed Michelle that her calls didn't stress her out. She said they did just the opposite.

That made Michelle smile. She would start calling her friend again and just keep the conversation light.

* * * * * * *

The lights were dimmed in the large room, and the music was blasting. And it wasn't gospel music either. Michelle and Katrina sat at a table sipping beer and staring at all the people on the dance floor.

"Would you two ladies like to dance?" asked a man and his buddy standing in front of their table. "I'm Freddie and this is my boy, Leo, and we think that the dance floor is calling out for the four of us to make a scene."

Michelle and Katrina exchanged glances. The men looked perfectly harmless, so they smiled and rose from their seats to fulfill the men's request. Freddie was a moderately tall man, and he was dressed in a casual neat fashion. Michelle accompanied him to the floor and they danced to two up-tempo songs. From her place on the dance floor, she could see that Katrina was dancing with Leo.

After dancing to two upbeat songs, they were sweating. Michelle fanned herself with her hand. "I'll sit the next one out."

Her dance partner walked back to her table with her. As they sat, she saw Katrina and her partner heading for the table as well. They always stayed together when they went to the club.

"How long have you been coming here?" asked the man sitting next to Michelle.

"Uh, I guess for few months now," she said.

Freddie looked her over. "Can I buy you a drink?"

Michelle nodded yes. The man motioned for a waitress and she soon walked over to their table and took their orders. .

"Do you have a man?" Freddie asked Michelle. When she said she didn't, he smiled and started off talking about politics in the city. Michelle joined in giving her opinion about the elected officials. Katrina and Leo also joined in the conversation Then, Michelle and Freddie broke into their own conversation, and so did Katrina and Leo.

"Would you like to dance some more?" asked Freddie.

The song was a slow one, and she hesitated before accepting his offer. Michelle rose tugging at her short skirt. Freddie reached for her hand and led her to the dance floor. He behaved like a gentleman, not getting too close to her. She noticed Katrina and her date were once again dancing nearby. Freddie took her hand and led her back to the table once the song had ended. They talked more about politics, about food, and a host of other topics as well.

It was almost two o'clock in the morning, closing time for the nightclub. "I never had such a great time at the club; not to mention the great conversation," said Freddie. "Can we take you ladies to breakfast?"

Katrina had heard and made friendly eye contact with Michelle. Her look said that she wanted to go to breakfast with them.

"Okay," said Michelle.

Michelle suddenly screamed and turned over in her bed. She was having a nightmare, reliving the night she and Katrina had met Freddie and Leo. Thank God that David had already left for work.

Saturday morning found Michelle at Precious's house going over songs and lyrics. The song she sold to Bree had been recorded and was now playing as they sat in the family room. Michelle had heard the recording before, but each time she was amazed that she had actually written the words. The song came to an end, and she sat staring into space.

"That's a nice song you wrote," said Precious smiling. "It really ministers to my soul."

Michelle's small smile grew wide. "Thank you. That means so very much too me; it really does."

After the Saturday music session was over, Michelle decided to go to the basement and visit with Dana. "Would it be all right if I go downstairs?" she asked Precious.

The woman walked over and hugged her. "Sure; see you next Saturday."

Michelle rose from her seat and walked out of the room. She knocked on the basement door and waited for a reply. Dana opened the door moved to the side to allow Michelle to enter. As they walked into the space, Michelle noticed that Dana's limp was a little less pronounced than it had been.

"I haven't seen you in a while," Dana said as they each sat down. "I'm glad you stopped by."

Michelle smiled at her. The two younger children were asleep in their bed and crib. The three- and four-year-old were sitting at a table coloring.

"I love to hear the music down here when you come over on Saturday morning," Dana remarked. "I like the way your church is teaming up with my church for the prison ministry too." She went on to tell Michelle that Freddie had told her that the prison ministry had made a huge difference in his spiritual walk.

It had slipped Michelle's mind that she and David had signed up to participate in the prison ministry. They hadn't made a single visit. She planned to change that immediately. "When is the next time they're going to the jail?"

"Next Saturday," answered Dana.

Michelle heard a car horn beep, and she knew David was outside. She rose from her chair and hugged Dana. "Call me," she told her. "David and I want to go to the next prison visit."

As soon as she was securely in the car, she reminded her husband of their obligation. "David, the next prison visit is on this coming Saturday, and we need to go," she said after buckling her seat belt.

David nodded and pulled into traffic heading for Peace Diner for a meal.

Michelle hadn't thought too much about Freddie lately, except that awful nightmare. The talk of visiting the jail brought thoughts flooding through her mind like the waters of The Potomac River.

The Davidson family sat in the diner eating their meals. Michelle couldn't understand why her husband always ordered the same thing. Personally, she liked to try different foods. Today she decided to order the same meal as her husband: meatloaf, green beans, and mashed potatoes.

Sasha was eating a hamburger and baked tater-tots. Michelle knew it was just a meal, but she treasured times like this with her family. They say children grow up overnight, and she knew she would wake up one day and Sasha would be a woman; then it would just be David and her. As fast as time was racing by, she knew exactly what would happen. Sasha would be a teenager, and then an adult before she knew it.

On Monday morning, Michelle stepped out of her house to visit with Cheryl.

Her neighbor informed her that she needed a cookie taste tester, and Michelle agreed to help her.

Michelle walked to the house, and knocked on the door.

Cheryl opened the door with a welcoming smile. "Come on in; glad to see you."

Michelle entered the house and Cheryl led her to the kitchen where she had a seat around the table. She took warm cookies off a cookie sheet and placed them on a dish, and placed the dish on the table in front of her guest.

Michelle reached for a molasses cookie, bit into the cookie and closed her eyes because it was so good.

Michelle raised the cookie in the air. "Cheryl, these molasses cookies are good; they taste like ginger. I'm going to buy some of these for my aftercare program and some for desert for my family. The next one to try was a sugar cookie, and it would be followed by a shortbread cookie. Michelle looked over at Cheryl and smiled, while chewing the tasty cookie.

The following day, Michelle delivered Kayla home from her aftercare because Katrina had asked her to. Michelle didn't have a problem doing something for her best friend.

Ten minutes after Michelle left the house, her phone rang and David answered it. "Hello?"

"Hello, David; it's Nicola." The woman sat in the front room of her house talking on the phone with her feet elevated on the ottoman cushion.

Her husband walked through the front door. He waved to her before heading into the kitchen of the large house where he took a seat at the table. He remembered what his daughter had said about Nicola; that she'd married him for his money and didn't love him. Elder Peterson remembered how the words had stabbed him like a murderous knife. He wasn't as dumb as his daughter thought. He knew Nicola didn't love him, and that was okay with him, as long as she stayed with him.

All of a sudden, he got suspicious and wanted to know who Nicola was talking to on the phone. He didn't care if she loved him or not, as long as she didn't disrespect him in front of others. He rose from his chair and carefully picked up the telephone and placed his hand over the mouth piece.

"David, your birthday is coming soon," his wife was saying. "I could never forget the birthday of the man I love."

Her husband listened and grimaced. He had heard enough of this conversation and carefully hung up the phone. He walked back to the table, took a seat, and placed his head on the table. Nicola had just disrespected him in his own house. It took him twenty minutes to compose himself, and when he did, he walked out of the house without a word.

"Nicola, I could never return your love," said David in response to Nicola's statement.

"Well, you can't blame a girl for trying." She laughed, but she was dead serious. "I'm interested in going to the jail for prison ministry. I'll see you and Michelle there," she added before hanging up the phone.

She rose from the chair to locate her husband. He'd walked past her but didn't mention where he was headed. She walked out of the front room into the kitchen, but he wasn't there. *Where could he be?* Nicola walked out of the kitchen to the stairs. Her husband was nowhere in sight.

Elder Peterson slipped back in just as quietly as he'd slipped out. He kept the promise he'd made to himself while he was away and kept his distance from her. He needed to avoid her until he could control his anger.

Nicola found him in his home office. When she walked in, he stared at her for a moment, and then he turned away. She gave him a peculiar look and then said, "I'm going to bed now; don't work too hard."

Elder Peterson owned lots of property in Washington, D.C. He picked up an ink pen from his desk and threw it at the closed door. That woman had hurt him so deeply and badly.

Nicola turned over in her bed. She reached her hand toward her husband's side and opened her eyes when she felt the emptiness beside her. He was apparently still working. The clock on the nightstand said it was five o'clock in the morning.

She sat up, got out of bed, and walked to his home office. Nicola tapped on the door and called his name, but there was no answer. She knocked again before gently nudging the door open. She looked around the room and screamed. Her husband lay faced down on the floor. Nicola ran over to him and shook him a few times. No response. She ran to his desk and picked up the phone and called the ambulance.

The phone rang at The Davidsons' house. They both sat up wondering what time it was. Michelle looked at the clock on the nightstand; it was 5:30 in the morning. They both looked frightened. Early morning calls were infamous for being bad news.

Michelle answered the phone, since she was the closest. "Hello?"

"Hello, Michelle; it's Precious." Sobbing sounds came between her words. "I'm sorry for calling so early but Nicola gave my father a heart attack."

"What?" Michelle said through a gasp.

"What's wrong?" David wanted to know.

Precious was crying louder now. "I'm at the hospital," she said.

Michelle covered the mouthpiece with her hand and quickly informed David what had happened. He buried his face in his hands.

"Are you at Washington Hospital Center?" Michelle asked Precious.

"Yes," she said between sobs.

"I'll be there in forty minutes," said Michelle before slamming the receiver down on the phone. David started getting up too, but she stopped him. "You stay here with Sasha; I'll catch a cab," she said hurrying to get ready.

Chapter 26

The funeral for Elder Peterson was held at Peace Baptist Church a week after he died from the heart attack he'd suffered. His body lay in a casket at the front of the church. Michelle and David rose from the pew and walked to the front to view the body. Elder Peterson laid there looking peaceful, as if he were sleeping and not dead. Michelle and David stood carefully viewing the remains for a few minutes before they walked away.

Nicola was sitting in the first row with her head down wearing a black dress and black hat with a veil covering her face. Michelle and David walked over to her and gave her a hug.

David reached for her hand and held it. "If you need anything, don't hesitate to call."

Michelle nodded to confirm what he had said.

Nicola squeezed David's hand and said, "Thank you. Thank you both very much," releasing his hand.

Michelle's eyes searched the room for Precious, who was on the front row in another section of the church. She and David walked to where she sat. Precious was a crumbled mess resting in her husband's arms.

Michelle tapped her on the shoulder before reaching for her hand and holding it in hers. "We love you, Sister Precious. Please call if you need anything." She released the woman's hand and patted Brother Ed on the shoulder.

David spoke quietly to the couple, before he and Michelle returned to their seats. Today was Friday and they still planned to minister to the inmates at the jail tomorrow. Nicola said she knew her husband wouldn't want them to cancel their plans to minister to the inmates.

It was kind of like goodbye Elder Peterson and hello Freddie. On Saturday morning, they all climbed unto a van heading for D.C. jail. They were following the van ahead of them, driven by Pastor Wynn and the members of The Hope and Faith Center Church. Michelle stretched out her legs in the van that carried nine church members. She knew Freddie had changed and was now, a Christian man, and she hoped she could look at him without being haunted by the past. She said a silent prayer and felt better. David saw her eyes closed and knew she was praying and he copied that action.

Afterward, he clutched her hand and gave it a small squeeze. She looked at him and smiled as he asked, "Are you a little nervous about seeing Freddie?"

She thought about it for a second, and had to answer honestly. "A little bit, but I believe that he has changed for the better."

Twenty minutes later the two vans pulled in front of the jail. Everyone got out of the vans and walked together to the jail. After passing through security and obtaining entrance, Michelle looked around. She shivered slightly at the thought of being in a jail.

They were all ushered into an opened space and saw the inmates all seated and the security guards standing nearby. In an instant, Michelle's fears practically disappeared.

"Thank God, you came. I can't believe you're here," said Freddie standing and walking over to her.

Michelle couldn't believe she was there either. She couldn't believe she would be sharing the word of God with Freddie. "I'm glad I came too," she replied. "If I can help save one soul from hell, it will be worth it."

Freddie smiled at her, and his smile was big and bright, beaming like a golden sun. Michelle returned a smaller smile before looking away. The man that she'd nearly hated just a few months ago now sat close to her exchanging pleasant words and smiles with her. Who would have thought that was possible? She sure didn't see it coming, but God knew they would be near and nice to one another one day.

"I'd like to say I'm sorry again," said Freddie. "Will you please forgive me?"

The small smile Michelle had earlier grew larger and she nodded her head yes to his question. David sat on the side of Michelle and took in the entire conversation. Pastor Jenkins stood at the front of the room ready to preach and teach from the Bible, and the inmates looked eager to hear the Word and attentive expressions were displayed on their face.

Pastor Jenkins preached the sermon that had stirred up his congregation many Sundays ago. "I wish I could Moonwalk, I know you might be saying. I'd like to retrace my steps, go back in the past, and change something," said the pastor.

Replies of, "Oh, yeah Lord" and "Amen" came back from the church members and inmates in the room.

The pastor preached the entire sermon, and as he closed, the inmates clapped and shouted giving praises to the Lord. Pastor Jenkins rocked the house. The gospel choir followed with some contemporary gospel music and the inmates swayed to the music and seemed lost in love. The evening ended with prayers. The two combined churches stayed at the jail for two hour and left the jail a better place than they found it.

Michelle was surprised, that she couldn't wait to return next week. Tears ran down her face and she wasn't even a crier. On Monday morning, the church weekend visit to the jail still played and replayed in her mind; especially her time with Freddie. She slid out of bed to go wake up Sasha for school. David had already left for work. She thought if she put a little pep in her step, she'd have time to take her daughter to breakfast at Peace Diner. Her mouth watered as she thought about the breakfast menu.

David sat at his desk at work and relaxed before the work day started officially. The phone rang and he reached to pick it up, since his secretary hadn't arrived yet. "Hello. David Davidson; may I help you?"

He heard a laugh on the other end of the phone, and then a voice that said, "Hello, David Davidson. It's me, Nicola." When his response was delayed, she said, "David are you, there?"

"I'm sorry, Nicola; yes, I'm here. Do you need anything?"

Nicola giggled inwardly to herself as she prepared for her dramatic scene. She needed David to be her husband forever and ever. "I'm still grieving the death of my beloved husband and sometimes . . ." She began sniffling and then she started sobbing and speaking through her tears. "Sometimes I need someone to talk to, to eat lunch with." She then blew her nose loudly into the phone.

"We could go to lunch," David told her. "Do you want to go to Peace

Diner?"

Nicola didn't want to go to the church owned diner. She wanted to chat and eat lunch with him alone. "Could you come to my house around noon? I really don't feel like leaving the house."

David thought about it for a moment. He knew Nicola still carried a torch for him, but he'd told her at her husband's funeral, that he would be there for her anytime. Michelle had heard him say those words to her. "Sure," he replied. "I'll be there at noon, and Nicola, please take care of yourself. Our daughter needs you."

Nicola stifled the laugh in her throat that was begging to come up. "Thanks David. I'll see you at noon," she said before hanging up the phone. She slid to the floor on the plush carpet and rolled across it in glee. She loved David more than Michelle did, more than Michelle ever could. The trick was to get David to realize it.

* * * * * * *

Michelle rose from her seat at the kitchen table to answer a ringing phone. "Hello?"

"Hello, Michelle; how are you doing?" asked the first lady.

Michelle smiled at the sound of her voice. "I'm doing great."

The first lady went on to tell Michelle that she was concerned about Nicola and her mental wellbeing after the death of her husband.

"Yes, I'd like to aid her also," said Michelle.

The first lady paused before replying. "I thought a group of us from church could take her to lunch."

Michelle nodded her head up and down. "I'd like to be involved with something like that. Count me in." Michelle and Mary Jenkins chatted for fifteen few more minutes before hanging up the phone.

Walking back to her chair, Michelle thought that she would like helping Nicola get through the grieving process, because she must have liked her husband a little bit, right?

David walked through the door of Nicola's house at noon. She was beaming from ear to ear as he walked passed her and entered the house. She closed the door behind him and motioned with her index finger for him to follow her into the kitchen. They walked from the foyer and down the long hardwood hall into the spacious kitchen. She walked to a small table in the corner of the room, and they took a seat around the table.

David looked around at the spacious kitchen; it looked three times the size of his. He placed his hand on the table, and Nicola placed hers on top of his. David didn't move his hand.

"I'm glad that you came. Seeing you breathed life into me." Nicola smiled up at David.

He gently lifted her hand off of his. "I told you I would be there for you."

She rose from her chair and kissed him on the cheek. "I'll go get lunch," she said before walking from the table.

David squirmed in his chair. He felt a little uncomfortable being alone with Nicola in her house, but he had promised her he would be there for her. Nicola returned minutes later carrying a tray of food. She placed the roast beef sandwiches and coleslaw on the table along with a pitcher of tea before returning to her seat.

David examined the food and his mouth began to water. He looked at Nicola and smiled. "Let me say the blessing over the food," he said reaching for her hand. After praying, he wiggled his hand free from hers. He picked up his roast beef sandwich with horseradish and took a bite and moaned as he chewed. "This is so delicious, Nicola."

She knew he would love it; she had remembered his favorite foods. What was that old saying? *The way to a man's heart is through his stomach.* She knew all of David's favorites. He loved meatloaf, green beans, mashed potatoes, and roast beef. His favorite dessert was chocolate cake with chocolate icing, and that was just what would be served to him next.

Nicola picked up her sandwich and took a bite while looking at David with puppy dog eyes. He was such a wonderful man "Can we do this on a regular basis? It'll keep my mind off my deceased husband."

When David nodded and took another bite of his roast beef sandwich, Nicola's heart almost pounded out of her chest. She and David

215

had had a daughter together, and they were a real family; not Michelle, David, and Sasha. When she brought out the chocolate cake, David's eyes looked upward, as if he was thanking God for the heavenly treat. Nicola beamed at him. She would do anything to bring a smile to his face. She was making the man she loved happy.

"You don't have to tell Michelle about lunch if you don't want to," said Nicola to David, and he nodded and picked up his fork and dug into the chocolate cake. She couldn't stop grinning. David was the best man in the world.

David glanced at the clock on the wall; he had to go. He finished his cake in record time, wiped his mouth with a napkin, and rose from his seat. "I got to get back to work," he told her. "Thanks for the lunch and call if you need anything." He began walking out the kitchen, when Nicola caught up with him and hugged him before kissing him on the lips.

David moved away from her and continued walking to the front door with Nicola on his heels. When he reached for the door knob she put her hand on his and he turned around to face her.

"I shouldn't have done that," she said. "Please forgive me."

David nodded.

"Can we continue to have lunch together?" she asked.

David shook his head up and down again.

Satisfied, Nicola took a step toward him and gave him a sideways hug. "I'll call you. I'll call you at your office, okay?"

David nodded his head for the third time, and then he was out the door, leaving Nicola with a huge smile glued on her face.

On Friday evening, the women all sat around the table at Peace Diner. They were there to show love and support for Nicola. The first lady sat next to Nicola and Michelle sat on the other side of the woman. Cheryl and Dana sat across the table from them.

"I appreciate all the love y'all are showing me, and I'll never, ever forget it," Nicola said.

The first lady patted her on the hand. "As followers of Christ, we're supposed to support one another as we go through the trials of life."

Nicola caught a glimpse of a woman reading the paper in front of her with a picture of the First Lady of the United States on the cover. "I love the way that woman dresses," Nicola suddenly blurted.

The women looked curiously at Nicola, not knowing who or what she was referring to.

"I'm talking about Michelle Obama," clarified Nicola.

Mary Jenkins nodded. "Yeah, she's the real first lady."

Michelle couldn't believe Nicola only admired Mrs. Obama for her fashion choices. This lady was an ivy-league educated lawyer. "Do you also admire her great achievements?" asked Michelle.

"Of course I do," Nicole stated, "but I love the way the woman hooks up her fashions. I try to wear clothes similar to hers." Then she touched her straight hair. "And I try to wear my hair like she wears hers."

The women at the table laughed.

"I like her fashions as well, but I also respect her for her many achievements," chimed in Cheryl.

Dana nodded. "I couldn't have put it any better."

Nicola looked at Michelle. "You have the same name as First Lady Obama, and your daughter's name is Sasha just like hers."

Michelle smiled and nodded. "Plus, both of us live in Washington, D.C." She laughed, and everyone joined in.

"You ladies are like the sisters I never had," said Nicola

Everyone smiled at her for the kind words she had just said.

"Excuse me," said Michelle rising from her seat to go to the rest room.

"Wait for me," said Dana as she got up slowly to follow Michelle. Once inside the restroom, Dana turned and faced Michelle. "Do you know Nicola is really fond of David?" she asked.

Her words seemed to come out of nowhere, and they had Michelle standing ramrod straight as she thought about that for a moment. She knew that Nicola liked her husband and had made a play for him in the past. But her husband had just died, and surely she wouldn't be pursuing David at this time. She didn't believe that Nicola was in love with her husband, but still. Michelle looked at Dana, "I know she likes David, but her husband just passed away."

Dana looked at her with widened eyes. "All I'm saying is just keep your eyes open, okay?" and with those words Dana walked out of the restroom without ever going into one of the stalls.

Michelle, still in thought, made her way to the bathroom stall and went inside. When she returned to the table, Nicola was holding the newspaper with the picture of Michelle Obama on the front. Michelle could barely look at Nicola after what Dana had said to her. And she had almost forgotten about Precious. The deceased was her father, and she actually loved him, unlike Nicola. They should be consoling Precious instead of that phony-baloney Nicola.

Michelle still met at Precious's house on Saturday mornings to write songs and talk music, but she hadn't talk to the woman about how she was feeling after the loss of her father. She planned to change that on this upcoming Saturday morning. Michelle looked at the clock on the restaurant wall and suddenly she couldn't wait for this evening with Nicola to be over.

Chapter 27

Saturday morning found Michelle at the park with Sasha, Dana, and all her kids. Precious wouldn't be home until the afternoon, so Dana had suggested a morning at the park with the children. The children were all playing on the toys, except Dana's youngest two, who were strapped in the double stroller alongside the bench where she and Michelle sat.

The September weather remained warm and sunny in the city. Dana turned on the bench to face Michelle. "You wouldn't believe the wonderful phone call I got last night."

Michelle's ears perked up.

"Nicola did the sweetest thing for me."

Michelle frowned. She didn't want to hear from another Nicola fan. Dana had been a good friend to her; she hoped that wouldn't end now. Just the other day, she'd told her that Nicola was after David.

"Nicola offered me and my kids a house of our own," Dana announced gleefully. She informed Michelle that Nicola said that she could pay rent according to her income, and she also offered Dana a job taking care of Davita.

Michelle thought to herself that Nicola just kept on winning. It didn't seem fair.

Dana looked at her. "Don't worry, Michelle; I'll keep on being your friend."

Michelle smiled, and then laughed before hugging the woman. "I'm going to check on the children," she said rising from the bench and walking over to the toys.

At noon, they left the park for Precious's house. Dana and the kids wouldn't be living in her basement for much longer. Nicola had offered Dana a house that she could afford. Michelle sighed; she couldn't wait to start their gospel music session. Her spirit needed some uplifting.

"Are you going to jail for the ministry next week," asked Dana as they all walked to the house.

Michelle nodded. She had planned on going this week and allowed it to slip her mind. "I'll be there," she said as they waited on the curb for the light to change. It blinked green and they stepped off the curb and into the street; Dana rolling the stroller, and Michelle guiding the children across the street.

Dana was smiling when they reached the sidewalk. "I can't believe me and the children have a house of our own." Dana went on to explain that she appreciated all that Precious and Ed had done for her, but there was nothing like having her own place.

Michelle was glad that good things were finally happening for Dana. When they reached Precious's house, she and Bree were sitting on the front porch waiting for them.

"Glad to see you all," said Precious and they all joined her on the front porch for a while.

Dana turned to face her. "I'm moving out," she said. "Nicola has offered me and my children a house for a bargain."

Precious stared at the woman. She really liked Dana and her children, but the mention of Nicola's name tied her stomach in knots. She still felt Nicola was somehow responsible for the death of her father.

When Dana rose from the porch to take her children in the house, Michelle rose as well. "I'll help you in with the children," she said offering Precious a smile before taking the steps into the house.

Once inside, Michelle helped Dana and the children down the basement steps, followed by Sasha. She wondered why her daughter was being so quiet. Michelle visited with Dana for half an hour before walking toward the basement steps with her daughter.

"Mommy, can I stay down here and play?" asked Sasha.

Michelle nodded yes and she mounted the stairs to go to her songwriting and music session. She went into the family room where Precious and Bree were already seated at the table. She bent down and hugged Precious. "I want to be there for you," she told her. "Call me day or night if you need anything."

"Isn't that sweet?" said Bree rising from her seat. "I'll let you ladies talk; I'll be in the kitchen," she said before walking out of the room.

Michelle took a chair next to Precious who had begun softly

weeping. "It's okay to cry," she told her.

"You don't know how much your words mean to me," Precious said. "Everyone at the church seems to only be there for Nicola. My husband has been my main source of support."

Michelle patted her gently on the arm and listened sympathetically as the woman continued to speak.

"Nicola never loved my father." Precious went on to tell Michelle how Nicola had charmed her father into marrying her, and now after his death she had everything he owned. Elder Peterson left Nicola five houses, a life insurance policy, and a big, fat bank account. "If she had loved my father," Precious said, "I wouldn't mind her getting all his wealth."

Michelle sat next to her letting her vent; she just nodded sympathetically to the woman.

Precious wiped her eyes with a tissue and rose from her chair. "I'm going to let you and Bree get busy with your songs," she said before walking toward the door.

"Wait," said Michelle. "Let's have lunch at the diner sometimes; call me when you're available."

Michelle was glad to have helped a friend. An hour later, she and Sasha left the house and climbed into the car to join David.

* * * * * * *

"I'm glad we could meet," said Michelle before forking coleslaw into her mouth as she and Precious shared a booth at Peace Diner on Monday evening.

Sister Precious smiled and nodded while still chewing her food.

Michelle continued. "What do you all plan to do with your basement once Dana and the children move out?"

Precious looked upward for a few seconds. "We're not really sure. Ed wants to make it a rec room."

Michelle nodded, picked up her sandwich, and took a bite.

"Katrina doesn't have long until the baby is born," said Precious.

Michelle agreed. About the only time she saw her best friend these days was at church. She looked across the table at Precious. "I need to go visit her. Do you want to come?"

Precious said that she did, and at seven that evening, Michelle and Precious were sitting across from Katrina in her kitchen chatting away.

"I'm glad that you all came over; I don't get out much these days," said Katrina.

Michelle smiled at her best friend and reached for a walnut piece on the dish in front of her.

"I hope you're getting by," said Katrina to Precious.

The woman gave a faint smile and patted Katrina on the hand. "I holding on with the help of the Lord, my husband, and good friends like the two of you."

Later that night after Michelle had prayed with Sasha, the phone rang in the kitchen of her house. Michelle looked at the clock on the wall. It was ten o'clock. "Hello?"

Dana was on the other end of the line." "Michelle, I hope I'm not calling too late. I'm having a house warming party for my new house and wondered if you could make it"

Michelle smiled and twisted the phone cord around her index finger. "Sure."

The next Saturday she skipped her songwriting session and went with other church members to D.C. jail to help minister to the inmates.

"Let us all bow our heads in prayer," said Pastor Jenkins standing in front of the room. "Father, we come to you with thanksgiving in our hearts, and we know that if it were not for you, we wouldn't be here today."

As the prayer continued, wailing sounds could be heard throughout the room and volley of "Amens" went up. The combined choirs of Peace Baptist Church and The Hope and Faith Center followed Pastor Jenkins with up-tempo praise songs. The room shook from the praise action in the place, including the roaring vocal sounds. Everyone in the crowd seemed to be clapping their hands and stomping their feet.

Michelle had a few minutes to exchange Bible verses with Freddie before they parted ways. A tear ran from her eye when she saw what the Lord had done with Freddie, and she let the tear fall to her chin without wiping it away. They assembled outside by the church van to leave the jail, still singing praise songs to the Lord.

Sunday morning in the Davidsons' household meant church, and sure enough Michelle, David and Sasha sat in the pew listening to a solo singer perform. Bree was singing "God Is Not Sleeping," by Mavis Staples.

"If you've got a dream, hold on, hold on. God is not sleep." The woman sung like an angel. Eyes were closed, and the congregation swayed to the music. When she was done, the congregation jumped to their feet clapping loud and long.

Monday evening found Michelle and her aftercare charges at the library. Cheryl had volunteered to help her with the children.

"I plan to take them to the library twice a week," informed Michelle. "Then we can have some cookies and juice when we get home."

Cheryl liked that idea. "Yeah, I'm the cookie lady; I do all the baking."

Michelle rose from her seat at the table and walked over to where two of the children she brought to the library were reading books. Cheryl looked around the library and went to read with a few of the other kids. Michelle had read somewhere that reading was the only proven way to increase test scores. So she planned to keep the five children in her charge at the library on a regular basis. Some of the children didn't have library cards, and she planned to discuss that matter with their parents.

"Mrs. Davidson, I like this book about witches and wizards."

Michelle looked at the little girl standing in front of her holding the book in her hand. *Why were people writing books about witches and wizards for children to read?* she thought to herself. "Can I take a look at that book?" asked Michelle. The girl handed it to her, and Michelle looked at the cover and flipped through the pages of the book, shaking her head. She didn't want the girl to read the book and gently told her so. The girl walked away with her lip poked out because she wanted to read it.

Michelle returned the book to its place on the shelf. The other books in that section were books about vampires, goblins, and other unholy creatures. She shuttered before walking away. They stayed at the library for an hour before lining up to check out books and head for her house.

On Monday morning, Michelle sat at the diner with Precious eating breakfast. She had made good on her word to spend quality time with a friend and lend an ear as well.

"I appreciate you being there for me during this trying period," said Precious. She forked some hash brown potatoes into her mouth and swayed a little to the gospel music that was playing softly throughout the diner. She seemed happy until she glanced at the door of the diner. In that moment, her eyes grew large and sad.

Michelle noticed her shocked expression and turned to see who had just entered the eatery. Yikes! Nicola of all people had come in and upset Precious's Monday morning.

"God please forgive me for what I'm thinking about that woman," Precious mumbled.

Michelle eyes met Precious's and filled with sympathy and understanding. Nicola wasn't her favorite person either; not even close.

"Ladies, how are things going with you all?" Nicola asked as she approached their table.

"We're doing fine." Michelle answered quickly before Precious gave her a piece of her mind. "And how are you doing?" Sister Precious placed her hand on her water glass, and it happened so quick, that Michelle didn't see it coming. Nicola now stood in front of their table soaking wet. Precious had just tossed a glass of ice water all over her. Nicola turned her head to the side to look at Precious and turned away, before heading to the restroom to dry off.

Michelle wanted to give Precious a high five, but didn't. The huge smile on her face clearly said she approved though. Precious just stared ahead and said, "Maybe I shouldn't have done that."

Michelle disagreed and wanted to quickly change the conversation before Precious started to feel too guilty. As far as Michelle was concerned, the cold water was good for Nicola. She surely needed to cool off. "Are you going to Dana's housewarming party?" asked Michelle.

"I haven't made up my mind yet," was Precious's reply.

Michelle understood her hesitation. They both knew that Nicola would be there too, and neither one of them looked forward to spending any more time with her than they had to. But Michelle had planned on going just to show support for Dana. She wanted to lighten the mood. Bree had bought another song from her, and both songs would be on the woman's upcoming album. "I can't wait for Bree's album to come out with my songs on it," Michelle said.

Precious looked at her and smiled for the first time since seeing her nemeses walk into the diner. "You deserve it," she said. "God has blessed you with incredible talent."

They stayed seated in the booth for five more minutes, before hugging and leaving for their respective homes. When Michelle walked through her front door, the telephone rang and she scrambled to answer it. "Hello?" she said, partly out of breath

"Hey, Michelle."

She recognized that voice; it was her best friend in all the world and they made plans to meet for lunch at Katrina's place of employment At noon Michelle and Katrina sat in the cafeteria of her job, talking about everything under the sun.

"Girl, get out of here! Bree bought another one of your songs?" Michelle laughed at her best friend's remarks and patted her on the hand. "You're going to be rich," finished up Katrina. She could talk to Katrina about any and everything without reservation. "I'm going to Dana's housewarming party; Frank is coming with me."

Michelle nodded and was glad to hear the information. Katrina bit into her turkey burger and frowned. Michelle noticed that her friend was trying to eat healthy during her pregnancy and the turkey burger looked extremely dry. Michelle bit into her tuna fish sandwich on toast. She stopped chewing, when she saw Katrina staring at her. "What?"

Katrina shook her head. "Can I have a few of your fries? I've been craving them." With Michelle's permission she reached across the table and plucked up three fries and ate them one by one.

They hugged after lunch and Katrina went back to work, and Michelle left the building with a smile on her face. Heck, she had forgotten to tell Katrina about the water tossing incident.

Chapter 28

"Can you have lunch with me tomorrow at my house?" Nicola asked the question as soon as David's secretary had patched her through to his line.

David thought about it for a second. "Sure; how about tomorrow at noon?"

Nicola quickly agreed and floated off the phone in euphoria. The next day, David rang her door bell promptly at noon, and she ushered him into her house, kissing him on the cheek and giving him a long, tight hug before he pulled away. "Let's go," she said walking into the kitchen with David following close behind. She reached for his hand and held it as she led him to the kitchen.

"My husband's death still hurts," she said as they arrived at the kitchen table and took a seat. She hadn't let go of his hand, and David had to wiggle his hand free from hers. She sat across from him, staring into his eyes. He turned away because he felt embarrassed. "I'm sorry, I didn't mean to stare, but I never tire of seeing your face."

He blushed and turned away again. On the plate in front of him, Nicola removed the lid displaying meatloaf, green beans, and mashed potatoes. All of his favorites. Throughout the meal, her eyes gazed at David lovingly.

"Can I be honest with you?" she asked as he cut into his meatloaf. "I keep having this reoccurring dream that we are married, and we're a happy family with our daughter, Davita." She paused for a second "I hope dreams come true."

David put his fork down and stared her straight in the eyes. "That will never happen. I love my wife." When she didn't respond immediately, he picked the fork back up and continued with his meal.

After a brief pause, Nicola smiled and shook her head. "I can't let my dreams die, silly."

David knew Nicola was hitting on him, but he could control the situation in an innocent way. He thought she was probably just lonely with the recent death of her husband and was just seeking attention.

"I hope we can continue to have these lunches at my house," she said.

He nodded and turned back to his plate of food. Before David left the house, Nicola put her arms around him and held on tight before he finally pulled away. She kissed him on the lips before he turned, and a wave of guilt swept over him like a gigantic ocean.

"Nicola, don't do that again." He could actually see a vision of his wife in his mind's eye as he spoke. "I shouldn't and you shouldn't be disrespecting my wife like that. Michelle is the only woman I love."

Visibly disappointed, Nicola frowned. It was clear she wanted to say something, but David's eyes dared her to voice one unkind word about his wife. She swallowed hard, took one step backward, slammed her door shut, and stomped back in the kitchen.

There would be no more lunches at Nicola's for David Davidson. It was a decision he made before even getting back in his car. One mistake was enough. David wouldn't repeat it. He was going to concentrate on his marriage as was required of him as a Christian man. He would make it up to Michelle if it was the last thing he did in life.

* * * * * * *

 Michelle lay across her bed putting the finishing touches on some gospel lyrics she had been working on. She closed the spiral tablet, sat up on the bed and placed her writings on the nightstand. She rose from the bed and stretched a bit; this had been a difficult songwriting experience.

Walking out of the bedroom, she headed downstairs to the kitchen. It was lunchtime and she was hungry. She was sitting at the table chomping on a turkey and cheese sandwich she'd prepared when she heard a knock on the door. "Who is it?" she asked when she reached the front door.

"David."

Michelle stood with a puzzled look on her face. It was definitely her husband's voice, but why was he knocking? She knew he had his door key with him. Shrugging off her mounting questions, she opened the door and there David stood, staring into her eyes.

He slowly walked into the house and closed the door behind him, all the while keeping eye contact with her. Michelle had never seen him like that before. She wasn't even sure what to think.

Stepping closer, David gently put his arms around her in a tight embrace. "I love you," he said in a tone that was barely above a whisper.

He was acting some kind of strange, Michelle thought. "David are you all right?"

He pulled away and reached for her hand, leading her to sofa in the family room. Once they were seated, he placed his arm around her shoulder. "I'm sorry," he said.

Michelle couldn't quite think straight. David had come home in the middle of the day apologizing. There could be only one reason for his behavior. She looked her husband dead in the eyes and asked, "Are you having an affair?"

David appeared taken back for a moment. "No," he replied. "At least, not like you mean, but—"

"No, but you are emotionally attached to Nicola. I know it and you know it as well."

David nodded his head in agreement. "Yes, I was. But not anymore. I'm sorry, I was so wrong."

"We need to put boundaries on her," demanded Michelle, "and we need to do it now."

He nodded his head energetically. "We'll box her in. She won't be able to move left or right, said David.

Michelle smiled. That sounded perfect to her ears, and her smile grew larger.

"Are you up for a second honeymoon with me, Michelle?" he asked.

She looked at him, and suddenly her mouth became extremely dry. Michelle rose from the couch. "I need to get some water."

David rose too. "Need a ride?" He lifted Michelle off her feet and in to his arms and began carrying her into the kitchen.

Michelle was shocked and happy at the same time. Maybe her marriage was finally heading in the right direction.

* * * * * * *

The Davidson family arrived at Dana's housewarming party on Saturday evening, after the prison ministry at the jail. The gospel music was playing loudly, but not blasting. When they entered the house, the first person they saw was Nicola.

She walked over and gave them all a small hug. "Sasha, Davita is out on the back deck with Kayla," she told the child. Sasha smiled and went to join them outside.

Michelle was glad to hear that Katrina's daughter was there. That meant the mother was there as well. Michelle's eyes searched the room.

"Are you looking for Katrina?" asked Nicola. "She's out back with the kids."

Michelle nodded before walking out to join Katrina on the back deck. When she exited the room Nicola smiled at David and stared into his eyes. All she got in return from him was a blank stare. Her number one goal—to become his wife and live happily ever after—had disappeared right before her eyes.

Dana came to the entrance of the room and saw Nicola looking lovingly at David. *Michelle better watch out for that one*, she thought walking into the room and over to where they were standing. "David, I'm glad you and your family could come," she said, giving him a little pat on the back. "You, Michelle, and Sasha make such a beautiful family." she said that part with special emphasis so that Nicola would know that she need to back off of David.

Nicola looked at her and rolled her eyes, but Dana continued, "Where is your lovely wife, Michelle?"

"She's on the back deck with the children; I'll go join my very, very lovely wife" he said, nodding to them and walking out the room.

When David was gone, Nicola stared at Dana, narrowing her eyes. Dana smiled and went to join the others outside. Nicola stood alone thinking, *I can't trust that woman after all I've done for her.* David soon returned to the room with Michelle, and gathered his wife in his arms in a tight embrace. Nicola stared at the happy couple and then looked away; David had sent her a silent but clear message.

Everyone was back inside now and seated in the decorated center room; streamers and balloons hung from the ceiling. The volume of the music had been turned down, but it was still audible as they sat around the room chatting. David, Michelle, and Sasha sat together on the couch. Nicola looked at them together and almost cried from envy. In her twisted mind, David belonged with her and their daughter.

Nicola walked over to Dana, who was standing near David and his family "I got to go," she said. "Thanks for inviting me." She waved before walking to the door and walking out. The thought of seeing David with his happy family was too much for Nicola to bear.

The phone rang in the house and Dana answered it. "Yes, I'll accept the charges." A moment later, she said, "Yeah, yeah; the party is going great, honey. Yes, she's here. Okay." Dana pulled the phone from her ear and called for Michelle. She held the phone in the air and handed it to Michelle when she walked over.

"Hello?" Michelle waited for a response from Freddie.

"How are you?" he asked "I hope you're blessed." Freddie wanted to talk to her about the prophet, Paul from the Bible. Freddie said that he was his role model. He wanted to be just like him; go from persecuting God's people to protecting God's people.

Michelle listened as he did all the talking and thought how awesome God was. He had transformed Freddie from a selfish, greedy sinner to a warm and caring saint, and all she could say was, "Hallelujah. Glory be to God.

A week later, Michelle was thinking the very same thing as she and David lay together on the beach in the Bahamas. Their second honeymoon had begun.